C

Risen from the grave.

Something is out there,
getting closer,
moving in the darkness,
listening . . .

If Whispers Call

A young family is the target of a force from beyond the
grave. The Dark Tide intrudes on the already dangerous
and secretive city of Chicago, and the Hoffmann Institute's
newest investigation team comes face to face with a force
as impossible to believe as it is to destroy.

DARK·MATTER™

DARK●MATTER™

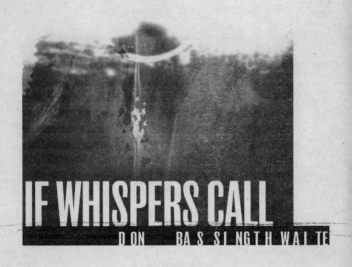

IF WHISPERS CALL

DON BASSINGTHWAITE

Wizards
OF THE COAST

IF WHISPERS CALL
Dark•Matter™

©2000 Wizards of the Coast, Inc.

Cover art by Ashley Wood
First Printing: December 2000
Library of Congress Catalog Card Number: 00-101967

9 8 7 6 5 4 3 2 1

UK ISBN: 0-7869-2018-1
US ISBN: 0-7869-1679-6
620-T21679

U.S., CANADA,
ASIA, PACIFIC, & LATIN AMERICA
Wizards of the Coast, Inc.
P.O. Box 707
Renton, WA 98057-0707
+1-800-324-6496

EUROPEAN HEADQUARTERS
Wizards of the Coast, Belgium
P.B. 2031
2600 Berchem
Belgium
+32-70-233277

Visit our web site at **www.wizards.com**

In Hollow Houses

Michael McCain retrieves a jar containing fragments of the brain of John F. Kennedy from a secret vault under the National Archives in Washington, D.C., moments before the building explodes.

Jeane Meara, an arson investigator for the Bureau of Alcohol, Tobacco, and Firearms, is sent to determine the cause of the explosion but finds her theories as unwelcome as they are impossible to believe.

Watching all this is the quiet form of Ngan Song Kun'-dren, an experienced agent of the shadowy Hoffmann Institute, a private organization founded to investigate and stop the rise of the Dark Tide.

McCain, Jeane, and Ngan are brought together when a bizarre creature begins to prey on the homeless population of the nation's capital. As they work to learn the startling truth of the thing below the streets of Washington, D.C., McCain discovers that he's a clone, Jeane is forced to leave the ATF, and Ngan is put in charge of the Hoffmann Institute's newest team of investigators.

All three are sent to Chicago and must learn to work together with hidden evils, secret agendas, and the forces of the Dark Tide around every corner.

For Ole

silence waiting

The autumn sun was bright and cheerful but cool, barely warming the late October air at all.

It was the sort of light that made Laurel Tavish dream of big piles of dry leaves and sprawling pumpkin patches. Never mind that she was quite certain that she had never in her life seen an actual pumpkin patch. The big corrugated cardboard bins at the grocery store that sprouted with watermelons in the summer and pumpkins around Halloween were pretty much the closest thing she could think of. My nostalgia, she decided, is constructed entirely out of television reruns and afterschool specials.

The baby inside her stirred and kicked hard. Laurel let out a little gasp. She stopped, hands on her swollen belly.

Will was at her side in a second. "Are you all right?" he asked. "It's not—?"

"No, it's not." She smiled at him. "It just kicked. We've got a soccer player in the making, love."

Will smiled back and leaned down to address her belly. "Or a football player. Who's Daddy's little punter? Huh? Who's Daddy's little punter?" Laurel couldn't help but laugh. Will looked up again and said, "Seriously, though—you're okay? You didn't have to come out this afternoon."

"Will, I'm pregnant, not an invalid. The walk is good for me." She shifted one hand to rub her hip and said, "Though I wouldn't want to walk too much farther without a break. Daddy's little punter is no lightweight."

Will leaned in and gave her a kiss before taking her other hand and leading her on down the gravel trail they followed through the woods. "Don't worry, princess," he said. "It shouldn't be far. The lady from the genealogical society said it was only a ten minute walk in from the road."

"She probably wasn't eight months pregnant when she walked it," Laurel grumbled, but she let him draw her on.

Television-induced nostalgia or not, it was a lovely day. They had driven out from Chicago and parked on a quiet street at the very western edge of the suburb of Midlothian, right where the urban sprawl gave way to the trees of the Rubio Woods forest preserve. Fortunately, the path that led into the woods was broad and reasonably level, no worse than walking down the sidewalk and a lot more pleasant.

Being with Will today meant a lot to Laurel. She wasn't sure how long his fascination with genealogy would last once the baby was born, but knowledge of its ancestors would be a lasting gift to their child. Today was special. Will had been able to trace his mother's family easily enough and his father's family even more easily. The Tavishes had left a small but not insignificant mark on Chicago for several generations. His paternal grandmother, however, had stumped him.

Johanna Tavish, née Harvey, had been something of a

puzzle until diligent research had ferreted her out. Johanna Harvey had been born in Midlothian, then an isolated community well outside of Chicago. Further research had finally located her family as well, buried in a long-closed cemetery that was now surrounded by Rubio Woods. In a way, Will was going home.

"There." Will gestured suddenly. "I see the fence."

His grip on her hand tightened, and his steps became quicker. Not too quick though. Laurel knew he was holding back because of her. She walked a little faster for him. Abruptly, they were there, peering through the rusted chainlink fence that surrounded Bachelor's Grove Cemetery.

For a second they were both silent, then Will said softly, "It's a dump."

It was. Of what must have been dozens of headstones and memorials erected from the cemetery's opening in 1864 to its closing in 1965, only a handful remained upright. All of the others had been knocked down. More than a few must have been carried away entirely. Even the ones that were still standing had suffered from time and vandalism. The grass and weeds had grown long over the summer and now lay matted on the ground, an irregular straw-colored carpet between the stones. The wind had piled fallen leaves in long drifts against the stones and the fence. The scattering of trees that had taken root in the cemetery had been stripped bare and stood over the graves like thin, dark carrion birds.

Laurel sighed and hugged her husband. "The genealogical society said it was in rough shape," she said.

"I know. I just didn't expect it to be quite so bad." Will hooked his fingers through the links of the fence and looked across the cemetery with disappointment on his face. "I don't know if there's even any point to going in."

"You've come this far. You might as well have a poke around."

The gate to the cemetery was locked, but next to it the fence had been cut and pulled back in a tangle of wire.

Laurel stepped through and said, "Come on. Have a little look. You might find something."

After a moment, Will followed her. "It's still a dump," he said.

"Just look at the stones, love."

He set off among the stones, glancing at the standing few, pausing a little longer to clear grass away from the ones that had fallen. Laurel watched him trace the weathered curves of a name carved into one of the stones. He looked up at her and smiled. "Robert Harvey, born 1928, died 1932."

"A cousin?" Laurel asked brightly.

Then the dates of Robert Harvey's life clicked in her mind and the levity in her voice sounded hollow. The boy had died at four years old. What had his mother felt as she saw her son laid in the ground? Laurel decided that if their baby was a boy, they would not name him Robert.

The child's death must not have struck Will the same way. He replied gamely, "Might have been. Nana was already married to Granddad and living in Chicago then, though." He moved on, spending a little longer at each stone now.

Laurel looked around for a place to sit. It had been a long walk in from the car, and her legs and hips were killing her. She eyed a large headstone that had fallen nearby but couldn't bring herself to sit on it. There was a log a little farther along. The bark that clung to it looked damp and crumbly, but at least it didn't mark a grave. Picking her way among the fallen stones in the thick grass, she went over to it and carefully lowered herself down. Getting off her feet was a relief. She watched Will wander from gravestone to gravestone for a moment, then let her gaze roam across the rest of the cemetery.

In spite of the neglect, Bachelor's Grove Cemetery was really rather peaceful. The bright sun banished any hint of darkness, and the cool air carried the comforting smell of damp earth and leaves. Down at one end of the cemetery, a pond—probably once a carefully tended ornamental lagoon, but now filled with leaves and a few reeds—escaped the fence to spill off into the woods. The trees thinned out on the other side of the water into little more than a screen. Laurel could see bright flashes and dark shapes as cars roared by on the Midlothian Turnpike beyond. The sound of their engines was a murmur in the background.

It was all ridiculously ordinary for what the woman at the genealogical society had told them was rumored to be the most haunted place in Chicago. Uh-huh. Laurel looked back to Will on the other side of the cemetery. He was watching her. She waved to him, and he lifted his arm to wave back.

And there was a sudden, very loud snap from the woods behind her. Laurel's heart jumped, and all she could think of were the stories the woman at the genealogical society had spun about ghosts. She twisted around, staring into the woods. There was nothing.

"Are you all right?" called Will.

Laurel laughed and waved to him again. "Just spooked."

He smiled. "Probably just a squirrel."

"I know." All the same, she suddenly didn't feel like sitting any longer. She stood up, stretching and turning as she did so that she got a good look at the entire cemetery. The sun was as bright as it had been moments before. The air still smelled of autumn, and the cars on the turnpike still rumbled. Silly, she told herself. She wandered across the cemetery to investigate the leaf-choked water of the lagoon.

Tucked down behind the broad trunk of a tree, Vanko Dimitriat gave his friend Boone a hard glare. Boone was crouched behind a thick bush nearby. Under his right foot were the broken pieces of a dry stick.

"Sorry, Van," Boone whispered.

"Knob," Dave grumbled. He and his girlfriend Tawny lay concealed behind a log.

"I had to move," Boone explained. "My knees hurt."

"Shut up," Van whispered. He peeked out from behind the tree.

On the other side of the fence, the man had gone back to looking at the gravestones in Bachelor's Grove Cemetery. The woman had gotten up and was walking down toward the lagoon. They weren't looking into the woods.

"They didn't see us," Van whispered.

Tawny poked her head up to take a look. "Damn," she said. "When are they going to leave? I'm laying in something wet."

Boone caught Van's eye. "Wouldn't be the first time," he mouthed silently. Van closed his eyes for a moment and gave his friend the finger.

He could already imagine Ma crapping bricks if they got caught in the cemetery. "A senior in high school!" she'd say. "You should know better. You're not too old to be grounded, you know!"

Of course, that was presuming the cops and forest preserve rangers who included the cemetery on their patrols didn't get them first. But then that risk was what made the trip out to Bachelor's Grove worth it. That and the guilty thrill of trying to conjure up one of the notorious ghosts.

Like they could put the cemetery off limits and figure everyone would just listen to that. Van grinned to himself. His backpack sat on the ground beside him. In it, jammed among homework and textbooks, were the things they would need tonight. A Ouija board, a big square of purple velvet, a few sticks of incense (carefully wrapped so that his entire backpack didn't end up smelling like cheap perfume), and an enormous, ugly quartz crystal that Tawny had bought yesterday at a garage sale for five bucks. Van had his doubts about the crystal, but Tawny was sure it would help.

Then again, it wasn't like they had gotten very far on their first try last week either. Under the light of a full moon they had sneaked out to the cemetery, joined hands, and called out to the dead . . . or at least that had been the plan. Van grimaced at the memory. It had actually been cloudy and cold, and Dave and Tawny had kept playing footsie with each other in the dark. In spite of all their appeals to the spirit world, the only thing that had happened all night was a big spider crawling up Boone's pant leg.

About the only part of the plan that had worked at all was stashing the séance gear near the cemetery during the day and recovering it at night. That way if the cops stopped them on the way to the cemetery after dark, they had nothing suspicious on them. They had decided to do the same thing tonight. Of course, they hadn't really considered what they would do if they ran into anyone at the cemetery during the day—the séance gear was just as incriminating before dark as after.

They had just reached the rusty fence when Dave had shushed them. The voices of people coming up the path behind them had been distinct. Cops? Rangers? Van had been the first one off the path, diving for the cover of the woods. Except that with the leaves fallen, the woods were very little cover at all. By the time the man and the pregnant woman had appeared on the path, it was too late to simply walk out and leave innocently. So they had stayed, waiting for the couple to finish their tour of the cemetery.

Who knew it would take so long? Van glanced around the tree again. The woman was beside the lagoon now. A thin mist hung over the cold water, condensation drawn out

7

of the sun-warmed air. The woman squatted down awkwardly, reaching out to trail her hand through the water.

She shrieked, a sound so loud and abrupt it made Van jump. She scrambled away from the lagoon.

"Laurel?" the man called as he came hurrying across the cemetery.

"Something grabbed my hand!" She was pale and shaking.

"Easy," the man said with a smile. He drew her into a hug. "It was probably just a frog or a leaf in the water."

"Frogs and leaves don't grab and hold on."

Van could feel his heart rate picking up. He tore his eyes away from the scene just long enough to glance over at Boone, Dave, and Tawny. They were all peering up from their hiding places, eyes wide. Everything was perfectly still and perfectly silent except for the man and the woman.

And the mist. When he looked back to the couple there was something different about the fog. It was thicker and heavier. It was growing, spilling across the surface of the water and wrapping around the thin stems of the reeds growing in it. It reached the bank. Long streamers wafted out into the cemetery, even though the air, Van realized, was absolutely, perfectly calm. A tendril of mist reached up to brush against the woman's belly.

She gasped and started, breaking her embrace with the man to brush away the mist as she might have brushed away a hornet or a wasp. "Will!"

The man grabbed her hand and held it. They saw the mist now, too. How could they not? It was a blanket across the ground, hiding their feet and continuing to spread through the cemetery. For a second, they stood stone still, then the man tugged the woman forward.

"Let's go," he said, and she didn't argue.

They headed for the cemetery gate. The hair on the back of Van's neck was standing. There was a knot in his stomach.

"Faster," Van whispered under his breath. "Faster. Get out of there."

Van knew he should be doing more, should be helping them. He didn't move, but the man and woman were moving more quickly now, hurrying through deep mist that rose to their knees and climbed higher with every step they took. They were fifty feet from the gates. Forty. The mist—thick fog now—was at their waists. Van didn't see which of them started first, but suddenly they were running, and the fog had risen to swallow them.

Van could see that quite clearly because the wall of fog came to a sharp end at the chain link fence around the cemetery. Not so much as a wisp slipped beyond it.

From inside the cemetery, there was a sudden gasp, cut short by an ugly thump.

"Laurel!" It was the man's voice, wracked with anguish.

Someone was breathing hard. Boone was swallowing air by the lungful. Van didn't turn to look. All he could do was stare into the cemetery and the mist.

There was movement inside Bachelor's Grove, near the gate, and the man staggered out of the fog, forcing his way through the hole in the fence. The woman was cradled in his arms. There was blood on her head. It smeared across her face and soaked into the man's shirt. The man glanced down at her once, then set off along the path at a lumbering run. His eyes were very, very wide, and there were tears on his face. He didn't look back.

Inside the cemetery, the fog swirled in turmoil, rushing along the fence like water boiling in a clear glass pot. It didn't reach after the man, didn't follow him at all.

Then, as suddenly as it had gathered, the fog began to disperse. The roiling movement subsided. The fog thinned, slowly drifting apart. Trees and gravestones in the cemetery reappeared, and the whisper of a breeze sent bits of the mist drifting through the fence. The eerie stillness was gone, too, leaving Van with a sharp awareness of sensation: the sound of Boone's breathing, the feel of rough tree bark under his own tensed fingers, the smell of the autumn woods. He moved for what felt like the first time in hours and looked over at his friends. Dave and Tawny were clutching at each other. Boone was shivering. Van realized that the rough bark under his fingers was actually under his fingernails as well. He had dug his fingers deep into the tree bark. He pulled his hands away from the tree. The movement broke the stillness of the moment. The others shifted as well. Van ran his tongue around inside his mouth, searching for a little moisture. When he finally got his mouth to open, his voice came out as a broken croak.

"I don't think I want to try anything tonight."

Slowly the others nodded agreement, then a quickening of the breeze blew a wisp of mist among them, and Dave yelped loudly. They broke, leaping out of their hiding places and sprinting for the path. Van snatched up his backpack. For a split second, something seemed to hold it. He ripped at it with frightened savagery—and the tree branch that tangled the straps broke so sharply he nearly staggered and fell.

A tree branch. He almost laughed at the sheer craziness of his fear. Almost, but not quite. He was still the first one back to the path.

The paramedics finished strapping the injured woman onto the gurney, lined the cart up with the rear of the ambulance, and pushed it inside. The spindly wheeled legs folded up underneath, and the locking mechanism snapped sharply, securing Laurel Tavish in place. Her eyes were closed, her skin pale and dull like the face of a wax dummy. The bandages that the paramedics had wrapped around her head were already soaking through.

God, I hate scalp wounds, Officer Anthony Jessop thought. There's always so much blood.

One of the paramedics nodded to him and said, "Ready."

She turned to the husband, Will Tavish, hovering in the background. Will's jacket was also soaked with blood. It smeared across one side of his chest, his shoulder, and his arm, the red broken by sharp lines where the cloth had creased under his wife's weight. A number of her long hairs were matted into the blood.

"Do you want to ride with her?" Jessop asked him.

Will Tavish nodded with the sharp, quick movements of a man who wanted something badly but had been afraid to ask, then gulped air and hesitated. "Our car . . ."

Jessop stepped forward. "Don't worry, Mr. Tavish," he said. "If you have an extra key, we'll drive it back to the station for you. You can come down and pick it up when you get a chance." He'd like to see one of the big city cops from Chicago make that offer.

Will nodded again and fumbled his keys out of his pocket. He struggled to release one from the ring until Jessop took it from him and slid the key off himself.

"Thank you," Will said, but his eyes were on his wife and the ambulance.

When Jessop handed the keys back, Will folded his hand around them so tightly that his knuckles went white. He climbed into the ambulance without another glance back. The paramedic slammed the doors shut behind him.

"Next stop: Presbyterian-St. Luke's Medical Center," she said, then gave a final nod to Jessop and went around and climbed into the ambulance herself. The driver gunned the motor, and the vehicle leaped away in a swirl of flashing lights. Jessop glanced down at the key in his hand. He slipped it into his pocket.

"Damn." James Greene, his young partner, stepped up beside him and said, "That's a kicker of an accident."

"Tell me about it." Jessop lifted his hat and scratched his head.

They had been on the scene outside Rubio Woods within minutes of 911 receiving Will Tavish's panicked phone call. Will had been sitting on the ground beside his car, cradling his wife. All they had managed to get out of him was that she'd fallen and hit her head. They used the arrival of the ambulance a short time later to take him aside and get a few more details. They had been running in Bachelor's Grove Cemetery, Laurel had tripped and slammed her head on a stone.

"Damn shame," Jessop sighed. "We'd better go in and have a look around."

Greene looked at him sharply. "You think it wasn't an accident?"

"Maybe. Best have a look to be sure though."

Jessop glanced at the sky. Where it had been clear and blue before, clouds were rapidly taking control. Big, dark clouds coming down out of the north, building over the trees of Rubio Woods. Almost like they were coming from the woods—and the old cemetery hidden there. He grimaced and headed for the path that led from the end of the street into the trees. Local ghost stories. He had spent too much time chasing kids and freaks out of Bachelor's Grove.

They were only about eighty feet into the woods when silence swept over them. It wasn't just the silence of a wild place disturbed by human presence but an abrupt, profound stillness. The suddenness of it made him pull up so sharp that Greene, following behind, ran into him.

"Hey," Greene complained, "keep it moving!"

Jessop paid him no attention. It was like being watched—and not watched. Like being stared not at but through, as though the watcher had its attention fixed on something far away and he just happened to be in the way.

Through the bare branches overheard, he could see the

looming clouds growing closer. The wind had picked up too, and it was cold. No, the wind wasn't colder. It was the temperature that had dropped, like a wave of cold passing over them. His insides twisted themselves into a knot. For a moment, he fought it, then looked back at Greene.

"Look like rain to you?" he asked.

Greene nodded. The younger cop's lips were pressed tight together, and his jaw was clenched. "Maybe. Maybe just a front coming through."

"We should get a camera. Take pictures of the scene in case it does rain."

"There isn't one in the cruiser. We'd have to go back to the station to get one."

Jessop shook his head. "Too bad. Better do that then." He turned around and headed back down the path, out of the woods. Quickly.

Do not muse at me, my most worthy friends;
I have a strange infirmity, which is nothing
To those that know me. Come, love and health to all;
Then I'll sit down. Give me some wine, fill full.
I drink to the general joy o'the whole table,
And to our dear friend Banquo, whom we miss;
Would he were here! To all and him we thirst,
And all to all.

—*Macbeth* (Act III, scene iv)

chapter
ONE

Working late tonight, Dr. Doyle?"

Dr. Shani Doyle smiled at the orderly in the corridor and eased the door to room 923 of Presbyterian-St. Luke's intensive care unit closed behind her.

"My shift's almost over, Jenny," Shani said. "Just looking in on Mrs. Tavish before I go."

"Anything new?"

"No change, I'm afraid." Shani shook her head and brought up her clipboard to make a few notes.

"Anything . . . unusual?"

Shani's pen froze on the paper, but she glanced up with clinical detachment. "Such as?" she asked lightly.

Jenny flushed a guilty red. "Uh . . . B-body temperature?" she stammered. "Heart rate? Anything the night shift should keep an eye on overnight . . . you know."

"I know." Shani turned her attention back to the clipboard and said, "Don't worry, Jenny. If anything comes up, I'll pass it on. Thanks."

"Uh . . . sure." Jenny shuffled nervously. Shani kept her eyes on the clipboard. Finally, the orderly added, "I'm going around and turning the lights in the halls down for the night. You want me to leave this one on for you?"

"Don't worry about it. I'll only be a minute." Eyes on the clipboard. Voice distant and dismissive.

"Oh. Okay. Good night, Dr. Doyle."

"Good night, Jenny."

Shani waited until the orderly's soft footsteps had receded down the corridor before closing her eyes for a moment, drawing a deep breath, and allowing herself to relax. When had one of the friendliest doctors in the hospital started getting so nervous around the staff? Bad question. She knew the answer to that.

She opened her eyes to stare at the top sheet on her clipboard. All of the standard notes on vital signs and physician observations were there. This information would go into Laurel Tavish's official charts, opened two weeks ago when the woman in room 923 had been rushed in from Midlothian, already deep in a coma. Shani put her initials at the bottom of the page and flipped to the last sheet on the clipboard. That paper would go no farther than a private file in her office.

"Anything unusual, Jenny?" Shani muttered to herself. "Hopefully not tonight."

Not long after Laurel's arrival at Presbyterian-St. Luke's, things had started happening in the intensive care unit. As far as Shani had been able to determine, the first to experience anything unusual was one of the nurses on duty the night after Laurel was brought in. The nurse had been walking down the hall outside Laurel's room when she looked up and found herself surrounded by a drifting mist.

Others had seen the same mist since then, always somewhere around Laurel's room, mostly at night, but sometimes during the day. It showed up, lingered for a short time, then vanished. There had been reports of a weird odor of wet dirt and dry leaves sometimes as well. And a couple of people on the night shift had seen a blue glow coming from under the door, as if a light was moving around in Laurel's room. Jenny had been one of the people who'd seen this light.

On her clipboard, Shani made a few quick notes. No mist tonight. No odor. No glow. No . . . Shani held her breath for a moment and listened. All she heard were the nighttime sounds of the hospital. No, she wrote on the clipboard, children.

Four nights ago, the patient in the room next to Laurel's had woken to the sound of children playing and laughing. He had blamed the noises on his medication, but two nurses on duty that night had also heard them. Last night, Shani had heard the sounds herself, the only reported phenomenon that she had experienced personally. The mist, the odor, the lights—somehow she suspected that if she did eventually experience them, they couldn't possibly be more eerie than the disembodied sound of happy children.

And yet eerie or not, she wanted to know more. She wanted to see the mist. She wanted to smell dirt and leaves and glimpse blue lights under the door of room 923. More importantly, she wanted to *understand* them, to figure it all out. The intellectual challenge made her heart race and her brain burn. The file in her office was slowly filling with notes documenting every incident that she could ferret out. Soon she would . . .

Intellectual challenge or not, the sudden dimming of the corridor lights made her jump, and it took her a minute to realize it was just Jenny turning down the lights. Just the lights—some investigator she was. How silly was that? She shook her head as she made a last few notes. How silly was this whole thing? What had she been thinking? It would all probably turn out to be nothing, just a series of coincidences strung together by imagination. Or maybe not. Either way, she wanted to know. She flipped the papers on the clipboard back down and headed for the elevators.

Her first step revealed that something was wrong. The air around her ankles and shins was cold, as if she had stepped into a draft. She glanced down.

Drifting mist surrounded her. As high as her knee, cool and clammy, it shrouded the corridor for a good fifteen feet on either side of her. There was no motion to it at all. When she took a step, the passage of her leg should have sent the mist swirling. It didn't. The mist—everything in fact—was very, very still. A shallow, tentative breath carried the taste of wet earth and dry leaves. Shani swallowed. She had wanted to experience the other phenomena that had been reported to her. Well, here they were.

She turned slowly back toward the door of room 923, a hollow feeling growing in her stomach. There was movement by the door, a lazy swirling as mist spilled out from under the door to feed the spreading cloud in the corridor. What must it be like inside the room? Shani stepped forward and reached for the doorknob—reached and gasped.

There was something in the mist, something as cold as the vapor, but dry and firm. It stroked across her calves and wrapped around her shins, tangling around her legs like a cat in the dark. Feet trapped, Shani swayed for a moment and almost fell. Clenching her teeth, she recovered her balance and thrust herself forward. She was going to open that door. Her hand closed around the cool, condensation-slick metal of the doorknob.

The touch in the mist was more than firm. For a moment, it was solid. Horribly solid. It wasn't just tangling her legs, it was tearing at them, pulling them out from under her while reaching up to shove back on her torso.

The force was irresistible. It tumbled her like a ball of

fluff and slammed her hard into the floor. Breath fled her lungs in one great, frightened gasp, and for a moment she couldn't breathe. Dark blobs of shadow swam across her vision, and she couldn't see, but she could hear footsteps come racing along the corridor, and Jenny was there. Jenny helped her up. Shani was blinking and wheezing.

"Are you all right?" the orderly asked.

Shani glanced around. The mist was gone. Vanished. Under the door of room 923, a blue glow winked once and faded away. Had Jenny seen it this time? Shani looked up at her, but the orderly's eyes were on her.

"Fine," Shani said. She managed a smile. "I tripped on my own feet. Long day, I guess."

"You're sure you're okay?"

"Absolutely."

The shock of the impact with the floor lingered. Shani felt nothing but a kind of stunned numbness as she went down to her office, revised her notes on the night, and slipped the sheet of paper into her secret file. The shock stayed with her on the drive home. It stayed with her as she climbed into bed. It stayed with her through restless sleep that saw her awake at dawn, watching the sun rise.

Her brain wasn't burning now. Her heart was racing, yes, but not from intellectual challenge. What had she been thinking? She was no investigator.

Fortunately, though, she knew people who were. At precisely nine o'clock she picked up the telephone, dialed a number, then waited nervously, fingers twisting the phone cord, until a voice on the other end of the line said brightly, "Hoffmann Institute."

Michael McCain drew a deep breath and brought the basketball up to his chest. He held it there for a moment.

Forty-seven feet away, the basket waited for his approach, mocking him under the cold, grey mid-November sky.

McCain snapped into action, dropping the ball down into a dribble and moving it up the court. At the twenty-two foot line, he broke into a crossover dribble and zigzagged in toward the basket. He imagined a defense spread out in front of him. Crossover left. Crossover right. For a moment he paused, confronted by another imaginary guard. A fast reverse dribble and he was past, going for the basket. He took two quick steps, planted his foot, and pushed off. His arm came up, pushing the ball toward the basket. Up. Up.

Too high. Too close. The ball ricocheted off the backboard and went spinning across the court. McCain bent over for a minute, hands on his knees, blowing hard, his breath making clouds in the cool air. The basket, towering overhead, continued its morning of silent mockery. McCain watched the ball roll on across the asphalt—until a foot came down on top of it.

"Yours?" A woman in her late thirties with long, straight, red-brown hair scooped the ball into the air with a flick of her toe and caught it. She passed it back to him, bouncing it off the pavement in a smooth motion.

McCain scrambled to catch it.

"Jeane," he panted, "aren't you supposed to be at the Institute today, doing something like . . . oh, I don't know—working?"

"I am working. I've been looking for you."

Jeane Meara walked onto the court so they could talk without shouting. McCain watched her approach. Only a few weeks ago, he had been a fresh young agent of the Hoffmann Institute in Washington, D.C. Jeane had been an even fresher recruit even though she was almost ten years older than him and a veteran of the Bureau of Alcohol, Tobacco, and Firearms. The Institute had a way of making even the most hardened veterans feel like rookies, at least for a little while.

That D.C. investigation had left Jeane with a disgraced dismissal from the ATF and him with more than a few uncomfortable revelations about his past. It had also, however, made them a team, and its resolution had earned them a transfer to Chicago. Them and the third member of their team.

McCain grimaced and said, "Ngan?"

Jeane stopped. "He sent me to collect you. He tried calling you, but there was no answer, either on your home line or your cell phone."

McCain sighed and began dribbling the ball. "I had a feeling you were going to say that. It *is* supposed to be my day off, you know."

"You shouldn't have stuck so close to home then. Nice place, by the way." She gestured around them.

The basketball court was located atop one of the warehouse-loft conversions that cluttered Chicago's River North district. McCain had taken to the area immediately on his arrival in Chicago. It had required some work with his connections to get his hands on the loft, but it had been worth the effort.

"The security guy at the door told me you were up here," Jeane added.

"How nice of him," McCain muttered under his breath. He turned around and aimed at the basket.

Jeane cleared her throat. "Ngan does seem kind of eager," she pointed out. "Something's up. He's meeting us at a hospital: Presbyterian-St. Luke's."

"I'm not finished with my workout." McCain jumped and shot. The ball bounced off the rim with a dull ring.

"Graceful," Jeane commented as he went after it. "How long are you going to be?"

McCain caught up to the ball and brought it back into a tightly controlled dribble. "I'm out here until I get twenty-one good shots."

One of Jeane's eyebrows rose slightly, and suddenly McCain was very conscious of the sweat that soaked his workout clothes.

"I'm not just shooting baskets," he said defensively.

"I saw. How many shots have you got to go?"

"Six," McCain lied smoothly. He could almost feel the basket smirking at him.

"All right." Jeane pulled off the fleece jacket she wore. "Just to get us out of here, I'll play you for them."

"What?"

McCain's hand faltered on the ball and it bounced over in Jeane's direction. She captured it easily.

"Based on those last two shots, if I have to wait for you to sink six more it's going to be an hour before you're even off the court. And this gives you a chance to practice against a real opponent." She paused, ball held at chest-level, then said, "Worried?"

McCain's eyes narrowed. Jeane was thirty-eight. He was barely thirty-one. She was wearing office shoes. He had sneakers. She was coming in cold. He had the advantage of being warmed up, and talking to her had given him a chance to catch his breath.

"No," he said and moved forward to block her.

Her feet betrayed a step to the left. He moved to intercept. Jeane crossed one leg over the other and swiftly broke right, driving past him and into a perfect layup. The ball barely even touched the hoop as it sank through. Jeane caught it underneath and tossed it to him.

"One," she said as he walked back out to the three-point line.

"Lucky," he said as he walked around the outside of the circle, dribbling slowly.

Jeane paced with him, arms spread. McCain executed a fast crossover and moved inside the line before she could block him again. She tried to reach around to steal the ball,

24

but McCain got free with a reverse dribble. Jeane was behind him. McCain found his balance, pushed off with his legs, and shot. The ball hit the backboard, connected with the rim, rolled around once . . . then slipped over on the far side.

Somehow Jeane was right there to tip it back in.

"Two," she called. "Remember to follow your shots in."

She threw the ball back to him.

"I'll do that." He faced her across the three-point line. "All right, Agent Meara, the gloves are off."

She beat him with four more baskets in a row. After the last basket, she threw the ball to him and asked, "Ready to go?" She'd barely even broken a sweat.

McCain sucked in a deep breath, trying to get his wind back. "Give me fifteen minutes to wash the egg off my face. This way."

He led her back to the stairwell that went down into the building. She glanced at him as they descended.

"You know, Fitz, you really suck at basketball."

The words echoed in the stairwell. He smiled. "Ah, now there's the Jeane Meara I've come to know. Always sweet, always tactful."

"I mean it." She looked him over and said, "You look like you'd be better at football."

"High school quarterback," he admitted. They reached his floor. He held the door open for her. His loft was just a little ways down the hall. "And my team won Yale intramurals five years running."

Jeane spread her hands. "So why play basketball now?"

"Because he didn't."

"Who?"

"Never mind."

McCain unlocked his apartment door and swung it wide. To some eyes, his loft might look sparsely furnished, stark and minimalist. He liked it that way. A sofa with clean straight lines, a few bookshelves, an entertainment stand with a miniature stereo system and a flat-screen TV. Simple black-and-white photographs complimented the room and the glass-panel warehouse windows.

Jeane pointed at one prominently displayed photograph in particular, a striking cityscape that had been his most recent purchase. "Dallas," she said. "Are you from there?"

"No."

"Ever been there?" she asked.

"Not as such," McCain said dryly. He headed for his bedroom and a hot shower. "Kitchen's through there. There's water in the fridge and glasses above the sink. Knock yourself out."

Presbyterian-St. Luke's Medical Center was a tall and sprawling white building just off the Eisenhower Expressway at the Ashland/Paulina exit, barely fifteen minutes away from River North and McCain's loft. Fifteen minutes, that is, once Jeane finally had McCain ready to go. It took him longer to dress and get ready than it ever took her. Then again, she favored simple, practical fashions. McCain had a predilection toward sharp, stylish suits, expensive ties, and careful grooming. It must have been the lawyer in him. At least he carried it off well.

She looked at him out of the corner of her eye and asked, "New haircut?"

"Yeah."

"Good." She stepped on the gas and moved smoothly into the exit lane, accelerating past a big moving van. "It makes you look less like a damn JFK clone."

McCain coughed suddenly, almost choking.

"You okay?" she asked.

He nodded, clearing his throat. "It's just your driving. What's the speed limit on this expressway again?"

Jeane smiled tightly. "Not high enough, junior." She sailed around the Ashland/Paulina ramp without slowing down.

Ngan was waiting for them in the hospital's crowded lobby. In spite of the busy masses of people Jeane didn't have any trouble spotting him.

Ngan Song Kun'dren was a small man, Tibetan by birth. He had to be close to seventy, though only his oddly blue eyes showed it. His face was leathery and creased, the roundness of it emphasized by a smoothly shaved scalp. In sharp contrast to McCain's stylish suits, Ngan habitually wore very simple, plain suits of navy or grey. He always seemed so calm and composed that it was almost eerie— Jeane had never known him to even raise his voice. He was so unassuming that it seemed he should just vanish into a crowd. In fact, just the opposite was true. People seemed to subconsciously avoid him, leaving little pockets of space around him. It was those pockets more than anything else that made him easy to find. If he wanted you to find him.

He saw them coming from across the lobby and gestured for them to meet him by the elevators. Easy for him, thought Jeane. The crowd was, naturally, thickest near the elevators, and while she and McCain were closer to them initially, Ngan still got there first. The crowd just melted away before him. He held the door of an elevator open so that McCain and Jeane could squeeze into the car after him.

"Hello again, Jeane," Ngan said. "Good morning, Michael."

"It was until you pulled me in." McCain turned to face the front of the elevator, putting his broad back to Jeane and Ngan. "There was a matter of a day off. I watched you sign the paper yourself."

Ngan sighed. "I have a lot of papers to sign now, Michael."

"Yes, well, I guess the promotion wasn't all just authority and hobnobbing, was it?" McCain looked back over his shoulder at them. "There's some real work involved."

Ouch. Jeane held her breath, waiting for a reaction. The

comment even earned darting glances from the strangers in the elevator with them. A pair of nurses exchanged knowing looks. They might not have known the whole story behind McCain's comment, but they didn't have to. Someone was bucking under a new boss. Jeane on the other hand did know the whole story.

With the team's transfer to Chicago, the higher-ups in the Hoffmann Institute had decided they needed a liaison, and Ngan had found himself saddled with the title of agent-in-charge. As far as she could see, the old man was the only logical choice—it wasn't like McCain or she were even potential candidates. They were inexperienced in institute operations. Ngan had been around for years. No contest.

And yet McCain never missed an opportunity to needle Ngan hard about his new responsibilities. Ngan never said anything, just rolled along in calm serenity. True to form, he didn't say anything now.

Jeane let her breath out in a puff and raised her eyes to the flickering numbers over the door. Moving from the ATF to the Hoffmann Institute hadn't been easy—quite aside from the weirdness of aliens and ancient spaceships buried under D.C. It was strange to be working for a civilian agency. In the ATF, McCain's attitude would have gotten him slapped down long ago.

She knew. That's what had happened to her.

The elevator car stopped on a floor of offices. Ngan led them down a long hall lined with honey-colored wood doors. There was a quiet hum in the background, the universal office noise of fluorescent lights, distant air circulation systems, and radios turned low behind closed doors. Very normal, very professional. Strangely soothing. Jeane knew that could be deceptive. She wondered why Ngan had brought them here. She had asked when he'd dispatched her to collect McCain. His answer had been as distant as he was: "Your first investigation in Chicago."

Very helpful. It was a relief when he finally knocked on one of the doors. The simple plastic name plate read **Dr. S. Doyle–Neurology**.

"Come in."

The doctor was already rising and coming around her desk by the time Ngan had the door open. She was a tall, attractive women with coffee-cream skin and long, luxurious black hair. Even in a lab coat, she had a sophisticated elegance about her.

"Mr. Kun'dren?" She had her hand out.

"Ngan, please, Dr. Doyle." He shook her hand. "My apologies. We were delayed."

Jeane noticed he didn't even hesitate in his explanation. No fuss, no blame. That was part of what made dealing with him both a pleasure and a frustration.

"My colleagues," Ngan continued, "Jeane Meara and Michael McCain."

Jeane offered her hand to the doctor, but McCain beat her to the punch, slipping between them with the speed and grace of a snake in an apple tree. "Fitz to my friends."

The doctor gave McCain's hand the briefest of squeezes. "My friends call me Shani, but I'll let you know when you can." She reached past him and said, "Ms. Meara."

"Jeane." She liked this woman already. As the doctor retreated behind her desk and gestured for them to take seats in the chairs arranged before it, Jeane flashed McCain a thumbs up.

"Stud," she whispered, brushing past him.

He growled at her. "My last prostate exam was warmer."

Ngan gave them both a look that made Jeane feel like a schoolgirl caught passing a note. Shani didn't seem to have noticed anything. She sat down at her desk, hands resting lightly on top. It struck Jeane that they were too still, as though she was trying very hard to keep herself from fidgeting.

Shani looked to Ngan and asked, "Where should I start? How much have you told them?"

"From the beginning, please," Ngan answered. "Michael and Jeane know nothing at all."

"Thanks." Jeane pulled out a notebook and pen. "I guess that means I have a lot of writing to do."

Ngan had taken the chair closest to the doctor's desk. He had to turn around to look at her and McCain. At least he had the decency to look a little embarrassed this time.

"A poor choice of words. What I meant, of course, was that I've told you nothing about this case. I wanted you to start with an open mind." He nodded to the doctor and said, "Perhaps the first thing you should know, however, is that Dr. Doyle is a trusted ally of the Hoffmann Institute and has been for several years. She called the office this morning on a matter of some urgency—thus my rush to recall you, Michael."

McCain didn't look impressed, but Ngan didn't wait for his approval. He turned back to Shani and said, "Please tell them exactly what you told me."

Shani took a deep breath, and her hands left the desktop to knot around each other. "First," she said, "I want you to know that I'm not the kind of person who's given to imagining things. I'm a doctor and a scientist. I read biographies and mysteries—I don't even like science fiction."

The first word Jeane wrote down on her notebook was "denial." She underlined it. The motion must have drawn Shani's attention to her, though, because when Jeane looked up again, the doctor was looking at her. Her eyes, Jeane noted, were hollow and afraid.

"Thirteen days ago," Shani continued, "I took on a new patient who had just arrived in our intensive care unit. Her name is Laurel Tavish. Her husband says that she tripped and hit her head very hard."

"Oh?" asked McCain. He was sitting back in his chair,

legs crossed and a skeptical expression on his face. "What does she have to say about it?"

Shani turned to McCain and said, "Nothing. Laurel Tavish is in a coma."

"That must have been some whack to the head."

"It was."

Jeane tapped her pen against her teeth. Against the wall behind the doctor was a fully loaded bookcase that included several books on head trauma. "It was definitely an accident?" Jeane asked.

"Definitely," Shani said, sitting back. Her hands unwound and came to rest on the arms of the chair. Jeane could hear confidence in Shani's voice now. The doctor knew what she was talking about. "I can see where you're going with this. The wound was consistent with a very hard fall—as were other bruises and scrapes on the patient's body. The police investigated. It was an accident. Not exactly routine, but mundane. I wouldn't have contacted the Institute if that's all there was."

"Then why did you call?" Jeane asked.

The doctor brought her hands up again, steepling her fingers and resting them against her chin. She took another deep breath and looked up at the ceiling, then began to speak. Jeane recognized the clinical detachment in her voice. She had used the same cadence herself many times in presenting evidence. She liked to think, however, that the evidence she had presented was a little more substantial than the events Shani described. Strange mists? Lights? A funny smell? As the doctor's recitation continued, Jeane glanced over at Ngan. He looked back at her with absolute neutrality. No help there. She kept writing, waiting for all of the insubstantial evidence to present itself.

When Shani finally finished, an uncomfortable silence fell in the room. The background hum of the office reasserted itself in Jeane's ears. McCain was frowning.

Ngan was watching both him and her, clearly waiting for some kind of response. Jeane looked down at her notebook and the list of occurrences that she had jotted down. There was a familiar pattern to the events.

"Dr. Doyle," Jeane asked bluntly. "Has the hospital been doing any work on the ventilation system in the last two weeks?"

The doctor gave a short laugh tinged with irony and said, "That's certainly what I've been trying to convince people of." She spread her arms wide. "It's all a coincidence. Just a fluke of some temporary ductwork. Except for the lights, of course—they're just reflections from lights outside the hospital. A helicopter. Lights bouncing off the building from traffic on 290. Spotlights from the United Center—the room faces in that direction."

Jeane looked at her carefully. "But you don't believe that yourself."

"Maybe I did once," Shani said, drawing her arms in again and folding them across her body, "but not after the attack last night."

"Then what do you think is creating these events?" Jeane asked.

Shani didn't answer, but an embarrassed flush crept across her face.

McCain leaned forward, looked at the doctor, and said sharply, "It's a ghost."

ghost?" asked Jeane incredulously.

McCain continued to look at Dr. Doyle as he said, "Vapors, odors, weird sounds, strange lights, unseen forces . . . Those are all elements of a classic haunting."

"You've got to be kidding."

"I don't mean that there's literally a real ghost," McCain scowled. "It's all in how the mind interprets events."

"You've still got to be kidding," Jeane persisted.

Ngan cleared his throat. That was enough of that, he thought. A team's strength was in its diversity but also in its coordination. It was time to stop the conflict before both agents lost their perspective. "An open mind," he reminded them both, "is an investigator's best tool."

Perhaps the advice was a mistake. Both Jeane and McCain immediately turned on him with expressions that demanded to know why he was taking the other's side.

Ngan sighed silently. He had been with the Institute for many, many years. He had done a lot of things in his time. Management was not one of them. What did he know about running a team? Some of the long-time managers with the Chicago branch of the Institute had tried giving him tips. R.A. Patterson, facility chief of personnel, had a tendency to bully agents into line. Lily Adler, field director of the Observation Division and an old friend of Ngan's, led by force of will—when Lily asked for obedience it was hard not to jump. Neither way was his way. He preferred to lead by example. Not that he had much time to set any kind of example anymore, unless it was the example of becoming buried in administrative paperwork.

Why, he thought, did they have to promote me?

Ngan looked to the doctor, hiding behind her desk as if it were some kind of shield. "Dr. Doyle," he said, "you've seen these events with your own eyes. What's your opinion?"

She shook her head. "My previous involvement with the Hoffmann Institute hasn't been extensive but it has been deep. I have a better idea than most people of what exists in the world, and I still don't know for sure what's going on here. It would be easy if all the things that have been happening were due to a ventilation problem, but I did check, and there haven't been any major changes to the hospital's ventilation system for more than six months." She turned back to Ngan. "What do you think?"

"Yes, Ngan," chimed in McCain, "what *do* you think?"

He refused to rise to McCain's persistent baiting.

The young man had a knack for taking advantage of the smallest misstep in a conversation, the slightest inconsistency in a story, and turning it to his advantage. Ngan had noticed even back in Washington that McCain did not like having secrets kept from him. Ngan did sincerely regret keeping secrets from him, but many of the secrets were for his—and Jeane's—own good. What they didn't know was less likely to harm them. What they didn't know made them better investigators. When the time came to know things, they would learn them, just as McCain had learned the biggest secret of his life in the basement of the National Archives.

"I think," Ngan said, "that maybe it's time for us to look at the scene ourselves. Maybe that will give us some idea of how to proceed."

And, he thought, a chance to actually work on the investigation. His promotion had tied him to his office for far too long, and he had the feeling he would be heading back there all too soon.

Ngan rose and said, "Dr. Doyle, if you would show us to the intensive care unit?"

They followed the doctor back up the long corridor of offices to the elevators. As they rode up to the ninth floor, she produced three guest badges for them. Ngan examined his before clipping it to his lapel. "Consultant" was emblazoned under a violently purple bar. It seemed as appropriate a term as any for a Hoffmann Institute team.

"What does the hospital administration believe we're consultants for?" McCain asked.

Dr. Doyle shrugged. "It doesn't really matter. We have all kinds of consultants visiting constantly: management, medical specialists, sales reps, technicians, physical plant. As long as you're accompanied by a hospital staff member, the badges should get you anywhere you need to go."

The elevator jerked and chimed and the doors opened on the ninth-floor nursing station. A dark red sign across the front of the desk read **Intensive Care Unit**. As if there could be any doubt.

There was a quiet to this floor that was different from the empty hall outside Dr. Doyle's office. The background hum was there of course, and there were even more people around, but everyone pitched their voices low, and they were all wearing soft-soled shoes or slippers. Worse, the air itself was thick with the smell Ngan had come to associate with American medical facilities, a stifling, unnatural, joy-less odor. This was not a place where he would want to come to die.

Dr. Doyle nodded to the nurses at the station and led them past it down one of the corridors. Ngan looked back. Were the nurses looking after them and whispering to themselves? The hospital administration might not know why Dr. Doyle had brought in these three consultants, but the nursing staff did. Fooling management was one thing. Fooling the working staff was quite another.

They turned a corner and stopped. Shani stuffed her hands into the pockets of her lab coat and announced, "This is it."

The corridor was quite plain. It was wide, the floor tiled in big squares of white flecked with grey, the walls painted a pale blue. A wide handrail was mounted on both walls. It was broken at regular intervals by deeply inset doors. A little way along the hall was an alcove that held a gurney. Another gurney was positioned just outside it. Beyond the alcove was a cross-corridor. Except for the spare gurney and a couple of chairs sitting outside doors, the hall was empty. Little plates beside the doors displayed the room numbers and held strips of paper printed with the names of the patients inside.

Shani pointed and said, "That one. Room 923."

There was nothing to distinguish the door from any of the others that led off of the corridor.

Jeane's pen was scratching in her notebook, and she was nodding to herself. "Any marks?" she asked with the detachment of a natural investigator.

"A bad-boy of a bruise on my elbow from the floor, but nothing from whatever I felt in the mist." She shot McCain a sharp glance. "And I can guess what you're thinking, Mr. McCain. I did feel something in the mist last night."

McCain blinked. "I'm not doubting that for a second."

"I am," Jeane said, then folded her pen into her notebook. "I don't know what you experienced, Dr. Doyle, but there has got to be an explanation besides—" she made a face— "a ghost."

"Jeane," the doctor answered, "if you can find a way to blame it all on the ventilation system, I will be a happy woman. For now though, can we take this discussion inside?"

Shani put her hand on the door and swung it wide.

Ngan wasn't sure what he had been expecting to see in the small room. He had seen comas before. In his time, he was sure he had seen all possible forms of unconsciousness, from the horrific trauma-shock of battlefield injuries to the flushed, hot stillness of fever, to the mindless silence of the victims of a creature he still had no name for. He had seen the indignities of invasive tubes, wires, and catheters. Somehow what was in this very ordinary hospital room made everything he had seen before seem distant, remote.

Laurel Tavish looked as though she had been laid out for a funeral, the stark white crispness of the hospital linens her shroud. Thin bits of tape held her eyes shut. A machine breathed for her, air pressure forcing her chest to move with unnatural, mechanical precision. Another machine fed her, a third excreted for her.

And it was all dominated by the huge, hard roundness of her belly. Dr. Doyle had neglected to mention that. Jeane looked away from the bed.

McCain just stopped. "Jesus Christ," he gasped. "She's pregnant."

"Very," Shani confirmed. "Normally she'd be giving birth at the end of the month." Shani slipped around to the far side of the bed. Behind her, the respirator hushed and sighed, Laurel Tavish's only voice. "We're waiting to see what will happen. We may have to perform a cesarean section and take the baby early, but in a situation like this there could be complications."

"Such as?" asked Ngan softly.

"Malnutrition, infection . . . We're not putting any drugs into her right now." She held her hands up like a balance. "If we wait too long, we endanger the baby. If we act too soon, the c-section might harm Laurel."

Ngan took a few more steps into the room, moving up to stand by the head of the bed. He looked down on Laurel Tavish. Laurel's face was pale under the wrappings of a head wound dressing. Ngan guessed that she was in her late twenties. She was young, though her haggard face and the dark circles of illness that lay under her eyes aged her badly. Two weeks ago, she might have been beautiful, looking forward to the birth of her child.

"Her first?" Ngan asked.

Shani nodded.

"Damn," said McCain. "What—"

He didn't get a chance to finish his sentence. The door opened, and a slender young man of thirty or so with a shock of sandy brown hair stepped through. For a moment he just stared at them as red swept across his face, then his voice sputtered into angry life.

"Wh-what is this? What the hell is going on?" His eyes sought out the doctor. "Dr. Doyle? Who are these people?"

If Jeane was a natural investigator, then McCain was a natural lawyer—or a natural con man. Before Ngan could even draw a new breath to challenge the intruder, McCain had stepped forward with his hand out. "Mr. Tavish?" he asked.

It had to be a guess, but it took the wind out of the young man's sails. Suddenly, he sounded more suspicious than angry. "Yes," he said but didn't take McCain's hand.

McCain pulled his hand back with ingenuous awkward-ness. "Sorry to intrude on you," he apologized. "I'm Robert Neil of Windy City Ventilation and Climate Control. My associates, Ms. Stand and Mr. Kwon. We're very sorry to hear about your wife, sir. I hope she's better very, very soon."

"Thank you." Mr. Tavish looked as if he wasn't sure what to think. "What are you doing in my wife's room?"

"The hospital has been having some ventilation prob-lems on this floor." Ngan noticed McCain managed to say that with a straight face. Jeane almost smiled. McCain kept right on without looking at either of them. "We need to check the vents in this room. I assure you, we are here under hospital supervision." He flashed his consultant's badge. "Dr. Doyle is watching over us."

Mr. Tavish blinked. "Oh. I guess that's all right, then." His anger had completely fallen now. "But do you think you could do your check another time? I came to spend some time with my wife."

"Absolutely. Good afternoon, Mr. Tavish." McCain ush-ered Mr. Tavish into the room, then waved the others to the door.

Dr. Doyle took his hand briefly as they passed and said, "I'm sorry we had to intrude, Will."

Mr. Tavish nodded. "I understand."

Outside the room, Ngan led them down the hall, around the corner to the cross-corridor he had seen before.

"Well done, Michael," Ngan said when he was confident they were out of earshot.

"It was," Shani added gratefully. "I could have been in serious trouble there."

"Thanks." McCain peered back around the corner for a moment, then turned back. There was a cunning gleam in his eye that only Ngan recognized. "Did you see his reaction when I guessed who he was? That's a nervous man in there."

"He's just been investigated by the cops," Jeane pointed out. "He might be having a bad reaction to strangers recognizing him."

"But the cops cleared him," McCain said. "Does he know anything about what's been going on here?"

Dr. Doyle shook her head.

McCain's eyes narrowed, and he looked at Ngan. "There's something more. I think someone should have a talk with him."

Ngan had a sense that it didn't matter whether he gave McCain approval or not. He was going to do it anyway, but it was a good idea. If Will Tavish was hiding something, McCain would find out. Ngan nodded.

McCain grinned and said, "Me and Mr. Tavish will be down in the coffee shop. Jeane, you might as well do your stuff in the room while we're out. Just come get me when you're done."

He disappeared around the corner. A moment later, there was the sound of a soft knock on a door.

"Wow," observed Shani. "Does he always work that fast?"

"Michael is brilliant when he has a plan," Ngan admitted.

And when he has a challenge, he added to himself. Put McCain in his element and he was unstoppable. Sometimes his plans ended up as stupid, dangerous stunts, but his execution was always flawless.

"He's smooth," Dr. Doyle said quietly.

Jeane gave her a hard look, then groaned. "You've got to be kidding."

"Jeane," cautioned Ngan, "I think Dr. Doyle can make her own decisions. Our job is the investigation. Whether it's the ventilation system that's responsible for these events or something less mundane, we need to figure it out." He thought of Shani's experience the night before and of the pale figure of Laurel Tavish and added, "Quickly."

McCain couldn't really remember when he had discovered his talent for interacting with people. As a child, maybe, but everyone trusts kids. High school? He hadn't really thought about it then either, though when he and his friends got into trouble, he was always the one who talked their way out of it. Yale? Certainly that was when he had realized how easy it was to convince strangers to take him into their confidence. Law school? Sure he was aware of it then, but with awareness also came the realization that he had always had the talent. He just couldn't remember when he had first consciously employed it. It was a circuitous path. He had learned quickly enough simply to accept the talent and everything he could do with it.

He knocked gently on the door of room 923, then opened it just enough to stick his head in. "Mr. Tavish?"

Will, sitting in a chair on the far side of his wife's bed, looked up. McCain didn't give him a chance to say anything.

"I wanted to apologize again—I'm really sorry we had to disturb your wife." He opened the door all the way and stepped into the room. "I know what it's like. My mom spent her last three months in a coma after the stroke."

Will gave him a thin smile and a nod that was really more of a weary sag. "Thanks . . ." He hesitated.

"Robert. Rob."

"I'm Will."

"Will. Listen," McCain shifted his weight nervously, backing up his words with body language "Do you want to go get a coffee? I mean, it might not seem like the right time, but I know it helps to talk. I've been there. When you came in—well, you looked like someone with a lot on his mind."

Will snorted. "That's an understatement." He shook his head. "Thanks for the offer, but I don't think I can."

Of course not. No one ever accepted an invitation on the first offer. "Come on, man," McCain pressed gently. "It'll do you good."

Will just looked away and shook his head. McCain kept his face relaxed, but inwardly he stifled a hiss of frustration. He was going to have to try another tack.

"You're not going to a support group, are you?" he asked bluntly.

That brought Will's head back up fast. A little too fast. Oh, yeah, somebody had a secret all right. McCain pressed his advantage. "You should give it a try. Just letting it all out really helps." Gently, gently, don't frighten him.

"I can't."

"Sure you can." He smiled at Will. "If it's facing a crowd that's worrying you, try it out with just one person first. Come down and have a coffee. I guarantee you'll feel better after."

Will glanced back down at Laurel. "I should stay with her. That's why I came over."

"Will," McCain said kindly, "you know she's not going to begrudge you a few minutes." He reached back and pulled the door open a bit. "Come on. I'm buying."

The chairs in the lobby coffee shop were hard and uncomfortable. And cold. The shop was separated from the lobby and the hospital's front door by enormous glass windows—glass walls really, Will supposed—but the outdoor chill still managed to pervade the room. Or maybe that was just him. It seemed so hard to tell lately.

Rob walked back from the serving counter, two coffees and two danishes carefully balanced in his hands. He dropped everything in the center of the table and shook his fingers in the air. "Hot." He nodded toward the danishes. "Cherry or cheese?"

"Neither." Will smiled, or at least tried to. Smiling was the polite thing to do, but he just didn't have the energy to put into it anymore. "I'm really not very hungry."

Rob shrugged. "Suit yourself." He took the cheese danish and ate it slowly, nursing both it and his latte. He looked at Will with bright, sharp eyes as he chewed.

Will tried to return that gaze but couldn't. Instead, he found himself looking everywhere but at Rob. He looked at the tabletop, down into the steaming murk of his coffee, and at Rob's coat slung over the back of a chair, then past Rob to the other people who populated the coffee shop. The place was fairly crowded, busy with life and energy as people came and went. Here and there among the tables though, there were people who sat alone—even if they happened to be sharing the table with someone else. They were quiet and withdrawn, dull somehow, waiting out something they knew would get worse before it got better.

They're me, he thought.

Almost.

He pushed the thought away, tried to push his despair away, too. This was stupid. Rob had taken the time to come back into the room, share his own experience with coma—and what did he do? Sit here staring off into space. If Rob was going to reach out, the least he could do was reach back. Rob was right. Talking to someone would help.

So what exactly are you going to talk about? Will asked himself. Are you going to tell him what happened in . . .

No! He wasn't going to give in. He wasn't going to lose his nerve. Will looked up and blurted out the first thing that came to his tongue. "Has anyone ever told you you look a lot like John F. Kennedy?"

That was intelligent. He snatched up his coffee and took a drink to cover his embarrassment. Rob just laughed. "More than once. I do a great Nixon impersonation, too."

Impersonations. An image welled up in his mind: Laurel with her hair dyed a rich, lustrous brown. She had done it just after they met. It made her look like Julia Roberts. God, how he wished he could have those simple days back. Just the thought of Laurel made him long for her. Made him want her. Crave her.

I need her so much . . .

He shook his head. "Laurel," he said simply, "was good at impressions."

"She's still good at them, Will. She's not gone yet."

That was looking on the bright side of things. Will's jaw clenched. "Maybe we could talk about something else?"

Rob looked flustered. "Sorry. I shouldn't have . . ."

Will shook his head and waved away his apology.

Rob smiled. "So how long have you two been married?"

That was talking about something else? But it was so good to be talking about anything at all that Will let it go and just answered. "Three years. We met just as I was finishing dental school."

"Oh, so it's *Doctor* Tavish." Rob leaned back. "Do you have a specialty?"

So normal. So mundane. The sort of question a new acquaintance might ask at a party. "Just call me Will, Rob. I'm just a regular guy out of the office." Small talk had never felt so wonderful. He could feel himself relaxing. "I'm an orthodontist. Now if Laurel had just broken a tooth when she fell . . ."

But she didn't, did she?

The tension that had haunted him for the last two weeks came flooding back hard. Everything that had happened came back. Not that he could ever forget, but for just a moment, he had been thinking about something else, and the memories came back that much more harsh. The corner of his mouth twitched and fell. He shook his head. "I'm sorry."

"Will." Rob sat forward again. "Whatever happened to Laurel wasn't your fault."

"Wasn't it?" The words slipped out. Will clamped his jaw shut, but the corner of his mouth continued to twitch. He rubbed a hand across his face, scrubbing at it. "No. I'm sorry, Rob. You don't need to hear this."

"But maybe you need to tell it."

Maybe he did. The truth of it, not just the same story he had told the police.

No!

Some part of him rebelled against the idea, the same part that held his attention on that mad moment in Bachelor's Grove. He fought it away. There was a word for that intrusive, persistent voice, and that word was paranoia. He let his hand fall away from his face and settle to the table. Where to begin?

Nowhere, he warned himself. Don't begin anywhere. All you need to tell him is the same thing you told the police.

No. He needed to get it all out, needed someone to tell

him he wasn't crazy. But he had told one story to the police so many times that it seemed easiest to start there again.

"You noticed that Laurel is pregnant?" he asked Rob. Stupid question—it was impossible not to notice. But Rob nodded, so he continued, describing the fascination with family that the baby had roused in him. "Two weeks ago, on Saturday afternoon, Laurel and I drove out to Midlothian—my grandmother was born there—to check out a cemetery. Have you ever heard of Bachelor's Grove?"

"It sounds familiar," Rob said slowly. "It's . . . supposed to be haunted, right?"

"Most haunted place in Chicago. If you believe in that sort of thing. We didn't—don't." Will's mouth twitched again.

"But. . . ." prompted Rob. He was leaning forward, focused eagerly on the story. Maybe too focused. Maybe too eager to hear.

Why? Will thought. Why does he want to know? Why is he pushing? Don't trust him. Don't tell him anything.

Will thrust back the wave of panic. He forced the words out of his mouth—again, the same words he had spoken to the police.

"But we got spooked anyway," Will confessed. "While I was wandering around poking at gravestones, Laurel went down to look at this lagoon at one end of the cemetery. All of a sudden she screamed and said something in the water grabbed her. I told her it had to be a leaf or something, but she wouldn't believe me." He picked up his coffee cup and began to swirl the liquid inside. "But then the wind blew this mist that had been hanging over the water toward us and we couldn't see and we . . . we . . ."

It was as if he was there again. He could feel his heart racing, pumping adrenaline-saturated blood through his body. His paranoia was screaming at him. Why now? Why should he be so terrified now, talking to Rob, when he had given this exact same story to the police half a dozen times and walked away?

Maybe because he had never even tried telling the police the whole truth. What difference did it make if Rob heard the real story of what happened in Bachelor's Grove? He was just a well-meaning stranger. There were things you could say to a stranger. Like the truth. Like—

"Will!"

Rob was reaching out and grabbing his hands. Will blinked and the coffee shop seemed to come back into focus around him. People at nearby tables were staring at them. Rob nodded at all of them. "It's all right," he said. "He's okay." Slowly they turned back to their own business. "You are okay, aren't you?"

No. No, I'm not. The words floated in Will's mind, strangely disjointed and separate from the paranoia that made his ears ring. But he didn't speak those words. Instead he nodded, and Rob let go of his hands. The muscles in them were weak and aching, as if he had been trembling hard. He didn't remember trembling.

"Yes," Will lied. "I'm okay. Sorry."

"I pushed."

"No, you didn't." Will took a deep breath and picked up where he'd left off. "This cloud of mist blew over us and we ran like school kids. We shouldn't have. There was long grass and broken gravestones all over the place. Laurel tripped and fell." He drew another breath, ragged and harsh. He could do this. It wasn't that big a deal. Now or never, Will, he told himself. Now or never. Now or . . .

Never.

He couldn't do it. He didn't have the strength of will to fight. His head throbbed, his heart was pounding, and he could feel a tingle in his fingertips, as if they were falling asleep. The paranoia was a barrier all around him, cutting him off from the hope that simple confession would offer. He was too weak to break through that barrier. He looked at Rob, looked into his open, earnest face and told him the same lie he had told the police.

"She hit her head on a rock. I know I shouldn't have moved her but I panicked. I picked her up and ran all the way back to the car with her." He managed a twitchy smile. "It must have been half a mile. I had a cell phone in the car, and I called 911. They put her in an ambulance and sent her straight here." He shook his head at Rob's look of surprise. "The police were there. They had to investigate. It didn't take long for them to realize it was an accident."

Now that he had given in to it, the paranoia was receding. He felt confident now, maybe more lucid than he'd been in days. It was more of a relief than confessing to Rob could ever be.

Rob nodded and said, "I can see why you would be reluctant to go to a support group, though."

The paranoia was back in a flash. "What do you mean?"

Rob gave him an odd look, and Will realized there had been an unintentional growl in his voice. He cleared his throat and gulped some coffee before repeating, "What do you mean?"

"Well, a police investigation?" Rob shook his head. "That doesn't look good, even if nothing came of it."

"Oh. No. No, it doesn't." Will relaxed again, but this time the paranoia didn't go away. It coiled up just inside his ear, fretting and worrying.

You got lucky, he thought. End the conversation. Get away.

But he liked Rob. He seemed like a solid, sensible guy. If he had met him a few weeks ago, he might have seen if Laurel wanted to invite him over for dinner.

The thought of Laurel brought back the image of her lying in the mist, her head beside that deadly stone. He hated himself, hated his weakness. He slid his coffee cup away and said, "I should be getting back up to Laurel."

Rob blinked. For just a moment, he looked startled, but an easy smile washed that away. "She'll be fine, Will. Stay."

"Aren't I keeping you from your work?"

"Hey, I'm the boss." Rob pushed the remaining danish toward him. "Here. That needs eating."

"You have it. I'm not hungry." Will stood. "Thanks, Rob. This has been good."

Rob stood up with him. "Listen, anytime you need a break from the bedside vigil, let me know. We can get a drink, or maybe we can catch a game sometime. Basketball? You a Bulls fan?"

"Sorry. Bears."

"Yeah, how are they doing this year? Didn't I hear something about . . ."

Rob looked past him, out through the glass wall of the coffee shop. Will glanced over his shoulder in the same direction. Rob's assistant, the old Asian man, stood on the other side of the glass. For a moment, panic swept through him. Someone else to confront? He felt a crushing urge to flee.

No. He had given in to the paranoia and held his tongue with Rob. Was he going to start being afraid of everyone? He forced back the paranoia and nodded to Rob's assistant. The old man smiled and nodded back. Thankfully, Rob was talking again, and he had an excuse to turn away. It felt as if he were turning his back on some menacing thug.

Rob had a business card out. "If you need to talk—about anything, anytime—you give me a call." Will took the card a little numbly. It was very stark, very minimalist, just a phone number printed in fine, raised black type. Rob smiled and asked "Have you got a card on you?"

"Oh, sure." Will fumbled for his wallet and slid out a card. Next to Will's it looked like a short novel, its face crammed with information. It had ridden around in his wallet so long the once crisp cardstock was crumpled and dog-eared. He tried to smooth it out, then gave up and just handed it to Rob. "It was great talking to you. Thanks."

"You're welcome. And take care—I hope Laurel gets better real soon."

He walked out, and his assistant joined him outside the coffee shop door. Will watched them turn toward the lobby doors, then glanced down at the card in his hand. The paranoia urged him to destroy it immediately. Instead he slipped the card into his wallet, into the place his own card had occupied. It made him feel a little bit stronger, knowing it was there.

"Did you learn anything?" Ngan asked as he came out of the coffee shop.

McCain let out a slow breath. "That I feel really dirty right now," he said honestly. Will seemed like a genuinely nice, genuinely troubled man. He didn't deserve to be lied to and manipulated. "Where's Jeane?"

"She's going to be staying on to examine the ventilation system in more detail." Ngan ushered him toward the lobby doors and a line of waiting taxis. "What did you learn from Mr. Tavish?"

"Bachelor's Grove Cemetery." He repeated what Will had told him about the events in the cemetery. "That mist sounds familiar. It might be nothing, but I get the distinct impression he was holding something back."

"He seemed disturbed when he saw me."

McCain blew out a breath and shook his head. "Ngan, he's disturbed all around. I don't think he's handling all this very well." He hesitated for a moment, then asked, "A ghost?"

"Are you backing away from your initial assessment?"

"No, but . . ." He sighed. "Isn't there someone at the Institute better qualified for this assignment? I don't know about you, but Jeane and I have never dealt with this before. We don't know anything about ghosts."

Ngan stopped. "Michael, this is our investigation."

"But doesn't the Institute have a spook squad or something that should be handling this?"

"No," said Ngan. There was an edge to his voice. "The Institute has us. We were assigned to Chicago to take care of investigations of all kinds—ghosts included."

"Hey, easy!" McCain snapped back defensively. What the hell had gotten Ngan's back up? "All I'm saying is that this is outside our areas of expertise."

"Then you will have to learn something new. You might want to start with Bachelor's Grove Cemetery. I want you to go there tomorrow."

McCain opened his mouth to protest, but Ngan turned away before he could say anything. "I will let Jeane know. Consider yourself debriefed." He walked on toward one of the taxis, then paused. "I almost forgot. You learned something else today. Dr. Doyle asked me to give you this."

He flicked a business card through the air as though it were a bit of steel. McCain caught the card. It was the doctor's hospital business card, but on the reverse was another telephone number together with a very brief message:

Call me Shani.

He looked up. Ngan was already inside a cab and pulling away from the curb.

Damn!"

The ductwork caught Jeane's curse and sent it echoing though miles of metal tubing. She bit off her next words and pulled her head and shoulders carefully back through the access port and closed it behind her. Once she was safely out of the duct, she gave her frustration full vent.

"What next?" she snarled finally.

Harry Fenn, one of Presbyterian-St. Luke's maintenance supervisors, scratched his forehead and made a mark on the diagrams he carried. "There's one more junction we could check, then you're looking at a main shaft. That might be a bit much for such a localized problem."

"Let's check it."

She followed his directions through the gloom. They were on an interstitial floor, built between the other floors of the hospital. Cables, pipes, and ducts

55

paraded in neat formation along the walls, color-coded like a chaotic rainbow. The interstitial was a dim, cramped place, built to provide maintenance access, not easy passage. Still, it was better than most of the places where Jeane had carried out investigations for the ATF. Nothing was burned here. Nothing was going to collapse on or under her. It smelled industrial and a little stuffy but no worse than that.

At least the interstitial was clean. Most service access areas tended, in her experience, to be dirty places. There was barely a speck of dust here. "Regulations," Harry had said when she commented on it. "All the air gets treated to minimize dust so it can't foul up the medical equipment. The interstitials get the same air as the rest of the hospital." He'd looked at her a little bit funny, and Jeane had realized she'd slipped up.

After McCain had led Will Tavish away, she, Ngan, and Dr. Doyle—"Shani," she had said, "I think you can call me Shani now"—had slipped back into room 923. Jeane had immediately gone to work inspecting all of the visible aspects of the hospital's ventilation system. Shani had watched her for a few minutes before quietly placing a few calls. When Harry had shown up, Jeane had barely been able to contain herself. What had Shani thought she was doing? Ngan's sharp gaze had kept her calm long enough for her to realize that the doctor had done her an immense favor. Harry knew the ventilation system inside and out and was perfectly willing to play tour guide for a consultant on the trail of an apparent problem. To Harry, she was Jeane Stand of Windy City Ventilation and Climate Control, and she suspected she was actually winning points for her choice blue language and her willingness to peer into the dirtier corners.

Unfortunately, while her arson investigation training filled in most of the major elements of how a large scale ventilation system worked, it was the small things that could trip her up. She was finding a whole new respect for the way McCain so easily assumed new identities.

Harry stopped and pointed to a new hatch. "Here," he said, opening the hatch for her.

Jeane turned her flashlight back on, then put one arm and shoulder through the hatch and slipped her head in after them. The warm air rushing through the duct pushed on her and caught at her hair. It carried the antiseptic smell of the hospital already, courtesy of the building's air conditioning systems at the head of the network.

She looked downwind first, back toward the hatch she had just inspected and, ultimately, to room 923 and Laurel Tavish. There was nothing she could see: no obstructions, no breaks or tears in the skin of the duct that might alter the air flow and produce anomalous events. There was nothing but smooth, carefully seamed metal. The same thing she had been seeing since starting her inspection. She twisted around awkwardly, blinking against the air that blew into her face. About five feet away the duct ended, opening out into one that was even larger, a main supply duct for this part of the hospital. The whole wing fed from that shaft. Jeane sighed and pulled herself out. Harry closed the hatch behind her.

"Well?"

"Nothing," she admitted. "Like you said, anything beyond this is going to be too generalized to create such a local problem."

"So what do you want to do now?"

Jeane caught Harry's eyes sneaking toward his watch. They had been at this for several hours now, and she could sympathize with him. He probably wanted to go home. So did she. Her stomach was starting to complain of lack of attention. The case, though, demanded priority.

"Give me a minute," she said, then turned away, leaning

against the broad, blue-painted girth of the duct as she thought.

On the surface it had all seemed so easy. There was plenty of information. Shani had turned over all her notes concerning the strange events. They were good notes, too: what had happened, when it had happened, and who saw or heard it happen. The only events that didn't suggest a flaw in the ventilation system were the blue glow under Laurel Tavish's door and the apparent force in the mist.

And no offense to Shani, but Jeane was more than willing to ascribe the mysterious force to imagination. Mist and smoke could create optical illusions that the mind could build on. In the course of her arson investigations, she had come across more than one firefighter who swore he had seen and felt things that later turned out to be just billows of smoke. She had seen things herself in similar situations, though she never let herself think too much about them, especially that one time in particular. . . .

Snap out of it, Jeane, she told herself.

As for the lights, Jeane suspected that Shani had been right all along that they were just reflections from something outside. The mist, the odor of earth and leaves, and the sound of children, though, she could trace. If she could find the cause of one, she was more than willing to bet she could find the cause of the others.

It hadn't been that easy.

The simplest explanation for the sound of children was eliminated first. She had suggested that the sound was echoing through the ducts from the pediatrics ward. Harry had pulled out his diagrams and shown her conclusively that there was no way that could happen. Pediatrics was in another wing entirely and though the maternity and neonatal wards were closer, just two floors down from intensive care, the connection was indirect, and Shani was adamant that it was always clearly children, not babies, that were heard.

Harry hadn't been able to prove quite the same thing when it came to the odor that Shani had recorded. He had, however, been able to show Jeane where the odor was *not* coming from: The intakes for the hospital's air supply drew across the roof of one of its lower wings. There was no wet dirt or dry leaves in sight of them and the internal filters were inspected and cleaned regularly.

That left the mist, which in itself actually presented two problems: What was it and how was it getting onto the ICU? Without a sample (something Shani had tried to collect but without any luck), the first question was the thorniest. The eyewitness accounts gave a few clues. The mist was consistently white-grey, odorless, cold, and apparently heavier than air since it had a tendency to stay low to the ground and to resist drifting apart. Those characteristics had allowed her to eliminate a number of possibilities immediately, including a whole range of gases and vapors that were either colorless or had a distinct aroma. Shani's direct exposure to the mist with no apparent side effects also ruled out a number of corrosive and toxic gases.

It was possible that the mist wasn't actually a mist at all. It could have been a dry particulate suspension like smoke or a dust cloud. But if it was a particulate suspension, it would have left a residue behind, and there was no residue visible. Just to be certain, Jeane had taken swab samples from various surfaces for more detailed analysis in the Institute labs. In light of the immediate evidence, though, she had to admit that the mist appeared to be exactly what it seemed: plain, ordinary, condensed water vapor.

But if that was the case, what was doing the condensing? Water vapor didn't just condense for no reason. Something somewhere was chilling the air.

That left her with the second question. Where was the mist—whatever it was—coming from? At least the eerie spill of the mist from room 923 into the hall that Shani had noted was easily explained. Intensive care hospital rooms were almost always kept at a positive pressure in comparison to the surrounding hallways. Air blew out when the door was opened, protecting the often vulnerable patient within from airborne microbes that might be circulating in the hallway. The same pressure would force mist in the room out into the hall, where weight and temperature would keep it low.

Unfortunately, that didn't fully explain the instances Shani had recorded of the mist being away from the door of Laurel's room. Nor did it explain the speed with which the mist appeared and disappeared. Jeane had decided that she would worry about explaining those points once she found the mist's source. She tried not to think about the chain of unanswered questions her investigation was leaving behind.

Her initial disappointment, however, had led her to consider other possible sources. The gas supply system? There were supply valves mounted beside Laurel's bed, one connected and feeding oxygen to her, the others capped and securely sealed. A malfunction in the life-support equipment? Shani assured her it was working perfectly and that none of it had the capability to generate anything like the mist unless it burst into flames and poured smoke into the room. There would certainly be evidence if that had happened.

On the other hand, Jeane wasn't quite sure exactly what she had expected to find, either. Damage to the duct that would indicate something being introduced into it from outside? There was no sign of any break in the metal surface. A hidden mechanical device as a source either for the mist or for the kind of cooling effect that would produce a mist in normal hospital air? Some substance lodged in the ventilation system? No, that was just letting her imagination run away with her. Such a solution also implied that there was a motive behind the events, and that was something on which she did not care to speculate.

In the end, there had simply been nothing else she could do in room 923 for the moment. She had given the swabbed samples to Ngan to take back to the Institute offices, and he had gone to the lobby to collect McCain. Shani had departed, and Jeane had followed Harry into the echoing dimness of the interstitials and an endless maze of ducts. An almost endless maze—they were almost through them, and still there was nothing.

Jeane closed her eyes for a minute. Okay, she told herself, think about this from another perspective. The thought reminded her of Ngan's advice about clear and open minds. She ignored that. An open mind was one thing but accepting some nebulous force as the cause for strange events was another. She wanted to work the scientific explanations to exhaustion first.

Exhaust. She opened her eyes. "Harry, is it possible to run the exhaust system in reverse?"

"What?" he blinked. "Well, I suppose so."

"Where would the exhaust vent in room 923 lead?"

Harry rubbed his forehead. "To a decontamination system first, then through a heat exchanger so the exhaust warms up fresh air. Then it's drawn up an exhaust stack by an impeller and ejected. But to reverse the entire system? Jeez." He shook his head.

"What if part of the system was just turned off—or was broken?" Jeane clapped her hands together as she thought. "You've got a source of cold air and maybe some extra humidity. The supply of air entering the system might increase with the right wind." During the day, a broken system might produce nothing more than a draft of untreated air, but night winds changed and night air would be colder. The backward flow of air might even cause some of the simpler machines in the exhaust system to move and produce unusual sounds that might be mistaken for laughing children. She glanced up at Harry. "How about it?"

"Nope."

She frowned. "No?"

"Well, for one thing, you're looking at the same problem as the fresh air system—it branches." He rapped on the duct. "A break at the end would send air into all kinds of rooms. If that was even possible, which it isn't. We have all kinds of monitors up in those stacks to keep track of what's going out. If one of them was broken, we'd know about it."

"Maybe something is broken deeper inside the system?"

Harry shrugged. "Maybe, but like I said, something like that would get noticed. You know how the ICU rooms have positive pressure? Well, things like the laundry rooms and washrooms have negative pressure. Air blows into them from the halls. When the exhaust system breaks—and it has happened—you notice it there first." He hesitated for a moment, then added. "Jeane, it's getting late. If there's more that you want to look at it, do you think we can do it tomorrow?"

Jeane looked at her own watch. It was after eight. They'd been working on this far longer than she'd expected—with nothing to show for it. Even her last brilliant insight had been nothing. She groaned and gestured for Harry to show her the way out.

A cool autumn night had fallen during her investigations. As she waited at the traffic lights to make the turn from the hospital parking lot onto West Congress Parkway,

Jeane looked up at the building. Presbyterian-St. Luke's was lit from below with floodlights that swept up from the base of the building. It gave the windows and ledges a deeply shadowed look—like a kid making a spooky face by holding a flashlight under his chin. Jeane clenched her teeth. Too bad the events in the ICU didn't have such a convenient explanation.

A little way down Congress, she made a right onto Damen Avenue. Her apartment in Ukrainian Village was actually relatively close to Presbyterian-St. Luke's. Thank God. She was looking forward to putting the day behind her. There was one thing she should do first, though. One hand dipped into her purse and came up with her cell phone. Without looking, she dialed Ngan's office number. As much as she disliked her lack of success, she would have to report it. She might as well leave the message now and get it over with.

To her surprise, Ngan answered. "What are you doing there at this hour?" she asked.

"Wrestling with the demons of paperwork," he replied. There was just a trace of weariness in his voice. "May I ask why you are calling so late?"

She sighed. "I couldn't find anything wrong with the ventilation system at the hospital."

"I'm sorry to hear that. It was a reasonable hypothesis."

"It still is a reasonable hypothesis," Jeane pointed out. She slowed to a stop at a red light. "When the analysis on those swabs is done, I'm going back. If there's a residue in the room, I might be able to pick it up in the ducts. That will give me a trail."

"As you wish. In the meantime, Michael has picked up a trail himself. You're going out to Bachelor's Grove Cemetery with him tomorrow."

Jeane scowled at the phone in disbelief. "You're pulling me off the hospital?"

"By your own admission, there's nothing to find there. The cemetery is where Laurel was injured. Her husband told Michael they saw a strange mist there. I believe it merits investigation."

"Ngan!" Jeane slapped her free hand against the steering wheel. "A cemetery? That's the most ridiculous . . . You've bought into this whole ghost thing, haven't you?"

"I wish to see all avenues of investigation explored," Ngan pointed out. "Every one of those avenues should be subject to skepticism, however, and I value yours."

"Thanks." The light changed from red to green. The driver of the car behind her leaned on his horn almost immediately. Just what I need, buddy. Jeane flipped her finger at him through the back window as she stepped on the gas. "I'm glad you decided to let me know about this little field trip."

"I left you a message at your apartment. Wherever you were was interfering with your cell phone."

The steel of the ducts and trusses of the interstitial. Jean sighed. "Sorry, Ngan. It's been a long, frustrating day."

"My sympathies," he said sincerely. "Speak with Michael. Perhaps you can make it a late morning meeting." He paused and added, "Jeane, try to keep an open mind. Would you have believed in the Greys before Washington?"

"No," she confessed. "But I did believe in the scientific plausibility of alien intelligence."

"Then try to believe in the plausibility of other phenomena."

Jeane smiled into the phone. "Bigfoot?"

"Not in Chicago." She couldn't tell if Ngan was joking or not. "Good night, Jeane."

"Good night, Ngan."

She dropped the phone onto the passenger seat and groaned loudly. There was nothing quite like having superiors tell you what to believe. That had irked her more than once while she was at the ATF—ultimately, it had actually been a pigheaded superior telling her how to interpret her evidence that had started the sequence of events that led to her dismissal from the ATF. If the same thing was going to happen in the Hoffmann Institute . . . For a moment she just watched the lights of Chicago flash by. No. It wasn't going to happen this time. For one thing, Ngan wasn't telling her what to believe, only to keep an open mind. And for another, Jeane wasn't sure of what she believed herself.

D.C. had been easy. Hard evidence, very clear. There was no question she had been right and they were wrong. Here . . . Here it wasn't so clear and she had nothing to back her case up but guesswork and gut feelings. And that only took you so far in the real world. In the television cop shows that had inspired her to pursue a career in law enforcement, sure. Gut feelings were always right and inevitably led to the collar. In the real world, you had to work. You had to follow the evidence. You had to build a case. You had to consider all avenues of investigation.

"Damn," Jeane muttered to herself.

If they were going to be investigating this kind of phenomenon, she might as well be rational and professional about it—even if the very concept of being rational and professional about ghosts made her twitch. What she knew about ghosts was limited to a string of silly horror movies and novels. A professional knew when she needed to do research.

She had seen a little-used bookstore with below-street frontage along one of the streets in Wicker Park, the trendy neighborhood just to the north of Ukrainian Village. The sign outside claimed the store specialized in occult books. It wasn't much out of her way. She swung past it, hoping that it might be closed so she could put off the unpleasant task. No such luck. The lights were still on. She sighed, parked her car, and walked down the steps to the front door. The name of the shop was painted in faded blue on the glass: **Devromme's**.

The distorted, broken sound of a badly tuned television set engulfed her as soon as she opened the door. The shop's clerk sat behind his counter on a high stool, his attention riveted to a tiny black-and-white TV set. Jeane caught a glimpse of a chubby, laughing face with pouting lips and a famous beauty mark. Marilyn Monroe. Jeane had never liked the actress and didn't understand her enduring appeal. That the clerk should be so intent upon her didn't bode well for the quality of the shop. She cleared her throat and asked "Occult books?"

One skinny arm came up, pointing to the far back corner of the shop. The clerk's eyes didn't move from the television screen.

"Thanks," said Jeane.

The aisles of the store were ridiculously narrow and the shelves tall and frail. Jeane was glad there was no one else in the store. Trying to pass another person in the aisles might have started a chain reaction, knocking down bookshelves like dominos. More importantly, though, someone might actually have seen her in the place. She had been in slums where the housekeeping was better. One entire long wall was dominated by dog-eared pornography. A thin grey carpet lay over the floor like compressed lint. It probably hadn't been vacuumed in years. A stale odor, possibly oozing out of the carpet, lingered in the air and mingled with the cloying stink of old incense. The static of the clerk's television pursued Jeane through the shop, the announcer drooling inanities about Marilyn's life.

There wasn't much she could do about the atmosphere of the shop but there was something she could do about the noise. She walked back up to the front.

"Excuse me," she said, "could you turn that down?"

That got the clerk's attention. He turned a jaundiced eye toward her for a second, then spun the volume knob down so low it was barely audible. Feeling rather righteous, Jeane went back to the far corner of the store.

Behind her, the volume on the TV set began to creep up again. She clenched her jaw and ignored it.

She found the occult books easily enough. It was actually surprisingly easy. There were shelves upon shelves of them, with only one battered rack groaning under the trashy popular paperbacks she had been expecting. Most of the books in the section were hardcovers, ranging from volumes with colors so bright they must just have been published to dusty, ragged tomes faded by time. She began skimming through them. There didn't seem to be any sense to the organization of the books. Everything was mixed up together: Glastonbury and the Holy Grail, Atlantis and Freemasonry, jaguar cults and were-hyenas, John Dee and Alistair Crowley. By the time she reached the end of one of the shelves, she had spotted only a few books on ghosts, and only one of them, about the specters of New Orleans, had ended up in her hands. She peered around the corner of the shelves. More books lined the back wall of the store— except for one section just at the corner that was covered with a heavy curtain of deep purple velvet. She brushed it aside to look at the books behind.

Abruptly, a hand reached past her and plucked the cloth from her grasp. "Hey!" she protested. She spun around sharply, hands up, ready to defend herself.

A large man with a scruffy beard and messy black hair glared at her. "These books," he said with a slight accent she couldn't quite place, "are available by invitation only." He twitched the curtain back into place with one hand. In the other, he held a greasy piece of fried chicken. He pointed it at her. "I don't recall inviting you."

Jeane glared right back at him. "Who the hell are you?"

The man gave a little bow. "Ned Devromme. You might have noticed my name on the door." He studied her as if he were evaluating a bargain-brand deodorant. "My dinner is getting cold. Is there something I can help you find before you leave?"

She met his gaze dead on. He wanted to help her? Fine. "Ghosts," she said imperiously. "I need a book on ghosts."

He gestured to the rack of paperback trash. "There."

Jeane gave the pile a cursory glance. "You know, if no one else is buying those, why should I? How about something with more substance?"

Ned pulled a thick, water-stained book out of the middle of the rack. "Here. This has substance."

"So does your breath." She shoved the book on New Orleans back in his face. "Got one like this on Chicago?"

Ned's eyes narrowed, and one bushy, black eyebrow rose. He reached out without looking and took a thin hardcover off a nearby shelf. "This one's good for stories at Halloween." Jeane didn't even take it from him. His other eyebrow rose. He put the book back. "You're a picky one, aren't you?"

"Yes," said Jeane bluntly. She dropped the book on New Orleans into his hands. "I want a book that tells me about ghosts and related phenomena in as much detail as possible. It doesn't have to be just one book—I'll take several if it's necessary. First-hand accounts are preferable. I don't want to wade through any New Age feel-good crap about spirit advisors."

The New Orleans book went back onto a shelf together with the thin Halloween book. Ned produced a thicker book that shed flakes of paper. "Take a look at chapter five."

Jeane opened the book, leafing through the brittle pages to a chapter that started opposite a gruesome illustration of three men in Puritan clothing being hanged. Whether the chapter was what she wanted or not, she couldn't immediately tell, but she nodded to Ned and tucked the book under her arm. Ned nodded in return.

"So," he said. "It's the raw stuff, then." He set his chicken down on a shelf, wiped his hands on his pants, and began walking along the shelves. He pulled another book off and passed it to her. "Be careful. Some of the pages are stuck together in that."

"Funny, I would have thought your private collection would be on the wall with the other magazines."

He snorted and gave her another book. "Oh, you are the wit. When we're finished here, let me get you a book on hags and crones. You'll identify." Another book went onto the stack in her arms. "Is there anything specific you want beyond just nasty stories, you bloodthirsty minx?" He turned and flashed her a smile. A really nice smile actually. Ned Devromme had a beautiful mouth.

Jeane's stomach spun into a knot. That was one observation she hadn't needed to make.

"Not really," she said. "I just need to research actual details of ghost sightings."

Ned passed her yet another book. Their fingers touched for just a moment. Ned's fingertips were warm. Jeane made a note to wash her hands as soon as possible. "Books on Bachelor's Grove Cemetery would be best, if there are any."

Ned stopped. "*The* Bachelor's Grove Cemetery?"

"There's another?" Jeane shot back defensively.

"Not that I know of." Ned stepped close and began taking back some of the books that he had given her before. Jeane forced herself not to flinch. "You should have said."

He replaced the books with others, then stepped away down a side aisle and came back with a large green book.

"History of the Chicago area," Devromme said. "You might find it useful."

He looked through the books in her arms, then glanced up and into her eyes. Jeane almost jumped at the suddenly unnerving strength of his gaze. Ned nodded, not so much at her as in some kind of inner satisfaction, as though he had just come to some important conclusion.

"One more," he said.

He walked back to the purple curtain and pushed it aside, reaching down to pull one book off a lower shelf. Jeane caught only a glimpse of the other books behind the curtain before it settled back into place. They didn't look any different from the other books in the store, except perhaps that a few seemed far older and more ornately bound. The fat book Ned put in her arms was old, too, though still modern looking. It had a navy blue binding with the title stamped in gold: *World Unseen: Unexplained Events of the Later Nineteenth Century* by Brian Desmond.

"Take good care of that one," he said. "It has truth in it." He cocked his head at her. "You're going to see a lot of truths in your life."

"Yeah? Here's one for you: Lay off the fried foods."

Jeane turned and marched quickly up to the front desk. On the little television screen, Marilyn Monroe was crooning Happy Birthday to John F. Kennedy. She dumped the books on the counter with a bang hard enough to throw the television into static.

"Cash," she snapped at the clerk.

"Half-price on the Desmond, Kaz!" called Ned.

Jeane looked back. He was standing at the end of the aisle by the purple curtain, the cold and dusty fried chicken back in his hand. Jeane desperately hoped he wasn't going to start eating it again. She paid the clerk without flinching at the price that came up on the cash register and waited impatiently as he counted out change and shoveled the books into a plastic grocery bag. He muttered something thick that might have been "Thank you for shopping at Devromme's" but she didn't stay for him to repeat it. Jeane was out the door in a second, her skin still itching from the repulsive encounter. Her apartment was only five blocks away, and she set off briskly.

She was four blocks away and turning onto her own street before she remembered that her car was still parked outside the shop.

cCain pulled his car over to the side of 143rd Street, in the Chicago suburb of Midlothian, Illinois. He looked around. A few houses, some trees, lots of fallen leaves. It wasn't one of the best streets he had ever seen, but he could think of worse places to live. The street was pretty much the edge of town. At the western end of the block, 143rd turned north to become Menard Avenue and join up with the Midlothian Turnpike. The turnpike itself angled down from South Pulaski Road and 294 past Cicero Avenue. A little more than half a mile west of Menard, it turned to run east-west again in a continuation of the straight line of 143rd Street.

Between Menard and the curve in the turnpike, though, the woods had taken over. Rubio Woods Forest Preserve squatted here. In the summer it would probably be quite a pleasant, green place. In the late fall, under a cold, cloudy sky, the trees stripped of their leaves and turned as grey as the sky, it was just another starved landscape.

McCain looked at it glumly and scowled, "I wore the wrong shoes."

"Told you so."

Jeane got out and slammed the car door behind her. She was wearing sturdy hiking boots.

McCain sighed and got out of the car as well, wrapping his overcoat around himself. Jeane looked at him without commenting. McCain was grateful for that. Naturally she had worn her heavy fleece jacket with a cap for her head and gloves for her hands. She'd be warm.

"I hate November," muttered McCain to himself. He went around to the trunk of the car, unlocked it, and pulled out two camera bags. The smaller one he threw to Jeane. "For you."

"Too kind." She unzipped it and peered inside. "A 35mm." She looked vaguely disappointed. "I do have my own digital camera, you know." She tapped the pocket of her jacket.

"Film seems to be a little more traditional for this sort of thing. The camera is loaded with high-speed film, the ghosthunter's option of choice." He opened his bag and pulled out a small camcorder with a built-in liquid crystal display screen. "I tape the whole thing, you shoot anything suspicious."

"And you say you did all of your research on the internet." Jeane shook her head. "Amazing."

"Better than lugging those books of yours around." McCain jerked his thumb at the pile Jeane had left in the backseat of the car. She had spent most of the forty-minute drive from downtown Chicago reading from one of them or another. She had been rather dismayed to learn that McCain had done research on Bachelor's Grove Cemetery as well—just by going on-line. When she tried to argue that she had depth of information and reliability on her side, McCain had just glanced at the publisher of one of her books. Yellow Bird Society Press, 1929, sounded very reliable to him. He had flashed her the color photos he had downloaded and printed. They were five or six years old at most. That had sent her into a snit.

He grinned at her now and said, "You're sure you don't want to take them with you?"

"Ha ha." She pointed to the woods and the gravel trail that was all that was left of the old route of 143rd Street. "You can lead."

Ten minutes later, they were standing outside the rusted chain link fence of Bachelor's Grove. Jeane looked around with distaste. "This is supposed to be the most haunted place in Chicago?"

"It's not exactly what I expected either. And I have pictures."

McCain turned on the camcorder and panned slowly across the cemetery, watching as what was basically an overgrown field scrolled across the little screen. Only the few surviving gravestones that still stood upright suggested anything different. Even the fallen gravestones could have been mistaken for building debris.

"With the kind of rep this place has and after forty years of being abandoned," McCain said, "you've got to figure it's going to end up a little run-down."

He slipped through the hole in the fence that was now the cemetery's main entrance. Jeane squeezed in after him.

"If it's been abandoned for that long," Jeane said, "I'm surprised it looks as good as it does. I'd have expected a few more trees to take hold. Someone's looking after it."

McCain shrugged as he turned around in a full circle to capture a sweeping view of the cemetery. It was easy to see how Laurel could have tripped. The ground was treacherous with half-hidden stones and tangled, matted grass.

"Could be the forest preserve," he guessed, "could be Midlothian's public works department. Could just be relatives and genealogists like Will." He had told Jeane about Will and Laurel's visit to the cemetery on the drive out. "I'm pretty sure there's a law that says even inactive cemeteries have to be kept up to certain minimum standards."

"Even when they're in the middle of the woods?"

"Respect for the dead." In the silence of the cemetery, the words sent a chill up his back. He looked up from the camera and asked, "How do you want to do this?"

"Your call. Wasn't this whole trip your idea?"

"I guess so, but you're the professional investigator."

Jeane closed her eyes for a moment and sighed. "Okay. What are we looking for?" She held up a finger before he could reply. "I'm not answering this one for you. If you think there's a connection between the cemetery and the hospital, you tell me how we prove it."

"Well . . ." McCain drew a breath and let it out slowly. He looked across the dry brown grass of the cemetery. "Will and Laurel were surrounded by a mist here. Now Laurel is in the hospital, and the same mist is manifesting there."

"So why aren't we back in the hospital or investigating Laurel?" Jeane asked. "She's the obvious link."

"But when the mist appeared in the cemetery, Laurel was fine, so presumably it's not some extension of Laurel's being injured."

McCain rubbed the bridge of his nose between his eyes with one hand. Making the connection would have been a lot easier if one of the stories about the cemetery had said *something in the lagoon touched her, then she was suddenly engulfed in mist*.

None did. Both his research on the net and Jeane's in her dusty books had agreed on that, even though the variety of sightings associated with this one small cemetery was startling.

He and Jeane had compared notes on the drive out. A farmer dragged into the pond by his plow horse was seen calmly guiding his plow through the water. A phantom car was seen on the turnpike near the cemetery. A woman, the White Lady or Madonna of Bachelor's Grove, was seen carrying her baby among the gravestones under the full moon. A white-robed, monklike figure was seen standing near the lagoon on occasion, and a monstrous, two-headed figure was said to emerge from the lagoon. A nonexistent farmhouse could sometimes be seen from the path, light burning in its windows. Not ghostly, but still sinister, were the tales of black magic rituals and opened graves that also clung to the cemetery.

Of all the stories about Bachelor's Grove, though, there were only two with associations to the lagoon, one with a baby, and none at all with mists or manifestations in broad daylight. There were photos that had been taken in the cemetery and apparently showed lights and patches of glowing mist, but they were small and isolated and were never visible to the naked eye. The mist connected the hospital and the cemetery, but there was nothing to connect the events at the hospital with the cemetery's history. They had to start somewhere, though. McCain sighed in frustration.

"If we look around in the cemetery," he suggested, "we may be able to find something that will at least prove that the two appearances of the mist are the same."

"And that something would be . . . ?"

"Damn it, Jeane, I don't know," he snapped. "I've never tried to do this before. Do you have any ideas?" She was silent. "*Do* you?"

"None," she admitted finally.

"Wonderful."

In the end, they divided the cemetery up into a rough grid and methodically went through each section looking for anything, anything at all, that was "unusual." McCain

kept an eye on the screen of the camcorder in case something revealed itself. Jeane flicked aside the long grass and
poked around gravestones, occasionally snapping photos of
what came to light: old chalk pentagrams and graffiti scrib-
bled on fallen stones, with the stubs of candles half-buried
by years of dirt nearby. A hole that had been dug down into
an unmarked grave and loosely filled again—some time
ago, Jeane observed, to judge by the way grass had grown
over the little pile of excavated dirt nearby. A whole nest of
empty beer cans and discarded cigarette packs. A very
weathered brassiere.

"Suspicious?" McCain asked Jeane as she prodded the
undergarment with a stick.

"Not particularly. I'd guess someone was just being
kinky and lost it in the dark." She brushed grass back over
the bra and stood up. "She should be seriously slapped for
having sex in a cemetery, though."

That left only one section of the cemetery still
unsearched. McCain looked down the length of Bachelor's
Grove to the leaf-choked waters of the lagoon. From the
look of the fragmented gravestones nearby, it lay in the oldest part of Bachelor's Grove. And to judge by Will's story,
everything had started with Laurel dipping her hand in that
black, still water.

McCain glanced at Jeane. "Well?"

"It does seem to come down to this, doesn't it?"

Together they walked over to the edge of the lagoon and
stared into it for a moment.

"So," Jeane said finally, without taking her eyes from the
water, "what do you make of this two-headed monster
story?"

McCain didn't look up from the water either. "Sounds
like someone had too much to drink and passed out in the
wrong spot." He scanned the camera across the pond. "How
about the farmer with the plow?"

"Maybe," Jeane said with a shrug. "But I mean, dragged in and drowned by a plow horse?"

"If the horse went in with the plow and was drowning, the farmer might have gone in after it to cut the ties to the plow." McCain shook his head. "In swimming class, they told us never try to grab a drowning person to save them. They can pull you under, too. Imagine what a panicky horse could do."

He kicked a twig into the water. It bobbed about for a second then sank. The water barely seemed to ripple.

"Our cat got stuck in the banister rails on the stairs when I was a kid," Jeane said. "I got these two huge scratches down my arm trying to get her— Oh, this is ridiculous!" She stepped back from the water. "You touch it, Fitz."

"Hey, just because Laurel did it doesn't mean we need to do the same thing." He glanced up from the camera. "On the other hand, if we're going to be thorough we probably should. And since you're a woman, too . . ."

"No way." Jeane dug a hand into her pocket and came up with a quarter. "Flip you for it?"

McCain snorted. "This is silly. Look, it's just water. Nothing's going to—"

"Call it." Jeane spun the quarter in the air.

"Tails."

Jeane caught the quarter and slapped it onto her wrist. "Damn."

She walked forward, knelt down beside the lagoon, and asked, "Ready?"

McCain took a few steps back and to the side so that he had a perfect view of the lagoon and Jeane. He zoomed in on her, then looked up to watch the whole scene with his own eyes. "Ready."

Jeane pulled her sleeve up, baring her right arm to the elbow. McCain watched her inspect the dark water carefully, then draw a deep breath.

"All right," she said, "Let's do this on three." She stretched her hand out to hover over the glass-still surface of the water. "One. Two." She drew another deep breath. "Three." Her hand dashed down and splashed through the water, in and out like a leaping fish.

She looked up. "Nothing."

McCain realized that he had been holding his breath and let it out. Jeane reached into the water again, more slowly this time, letting her hand rest in the water then stirring it around. After several long moments, she pulled it out.

"Nothing at all," she reported, shaking water droplets everywhere. "The water's damn cold but no more than you'd expect."

"Damn it!" McCain cursed.

He stopped the tape in the camcorder, rewound it a little way, then played back the scene again. The camcorder had captured a perfect shot of Jeane getting her hand wet.

"Were you really that eager to have something grab me?" Jeane asked wryly. She dried her hand off on her coat and started back through the cemetery to the hole in the fence.

"Having something to show for an afternoon of wandering around in the cold would have been nice," he told her. "Where are you going?"

"I'm going to have a look around on the outside of the fence and see if I find anything. If anything grabs me, I'll let you know."

McCain grunted and sat down on the nearest fallen gravestone. Jeane did have a point. What had he expected to happen? As he had said himself, he didn't know what they were looking for. How did you investigate a ghost? He chuckled ruefully as he rewound the tape all the way back to the beginning and started it playing. He had even already started thinking of the target of their investigation as a ghost. Not even Will Tavish had gone so far as to call it a ghost, and he had experienced the entire attack.

Of course, Will didn't work for the Hoffmann Institute.

The videotape had played forward to the point where they had found the pentagram and candle stubs when suddenly Jeane called out from the woods, "Hello! We have something!"

McCain twisted around to see her walking up to the fence with a paperback book in her hand. He got up and went over to her.

"What is it?"

"*Macbeth*. I found it back there behind a tree, half under a bush. It's probably only been there a couple of weeks." She flipped through it. "It's not too weathered, but it was sandwiched between layers of fallen leaves."

She held it up so he could see. The edges and corners had been wrapped in wide transparent tape to protect them but not before they had seen some serious damage from use. It looked as if the book had been used fairly heavily even after the tape was put in place. "High school text book?" he guessed.

Jeane checked the first few pages. "Right you are. Senior year, local high school. Looks like it's been passed around for a few years." There was list of names on the inside front cover. She tapped her finger against the bottom name. "Van Dimitriat."

"Interesting. I wonder—"

"Good afternoon, folks."

Both McCain and Jeane turned sharply at the sound of a new voice. Standing at the entrance to the cemetery were two police officers. Well, thought McCain, the internet did say the cemetery was heavily patrolled. A cover story was already unraveling itself in his mind. He took a quick breath, prepared himself, and started toward the officers, not too slow, not too fast. Just casual, both hands loose and plainly visible.

"Afternoon, officers," McCain called. He stepped through the gap in the fence to join them on the other side. "Is there something wrong?"

The older of the cops looked him up and down, then nodded to his partner. "No, sir. We keep an eye out for vandals and nuisances in the cemetery, and when we saw your car parked down on 143rd, we thought maybe we should check things out." He eyed the camcorder in McCain's hand. "You're not a nuisance, are you, sir?"

"Not unless you consider movie location scouts a nuisance. My name's Wade Maxwell. I'd be pleased to give you my card." McCain reached into his pocket slowly and deliberately. He passed one of his anonymous cards to the older cop. "I take by 'nuisances' that you mean people who come out looking for ghosts, Officer—" he glanced at the man's name tag—"Jessop."

Jessop nodded as he examined the card. "Exactly. And we saw the books in the back seat of your car."

"Research." Jessop started to hand the card back, but McCain waved him to keep it. He nodded toward Jeane as she came tramping out of the brush, the copy of *Macbeth* just poking out of her jacket pocket. "My assistant is thorough. We're looking for background material for a movie, and Bachelor's Grove has quite the . . . Well, I'm sure you're familiar with its reputation." He turned and held up the thumb and forefinger of his free hand to frame the cemetery. "Do you actually get that many vandals coming through? I'll bet the local teenagers are more of a problem."

"Not really. They all know better than to mess around out here."

McCain turned back and smiled. "And do people really see ghosts around the cemetery?"

The younger man laughed, a short snorting sound. Jessop just smiled and said, "We get reports once or twice a year."

"But we can usually trace them back to a bottle in a brown paper bag," his partner added.

McCain laughed, too. That's right, it's all just a big joke. He grinned at the young cop. "What about the times you can't?"

The young man snorted out another laugh. "We had one guy try to off his wife by bashing her with a rock, then pin it on her falling after they got spooked and tried to run out of the cemetery."

McCain forced himself to keep his face neutral. If that's what the police thought had happened, no wonder Will wanted to keep their investigation of the accident a secret.

"Greene!" snapped Jessop, with a frown. He looked back to McCain. "I hope you'll ignore that Mr. Maxwell. The case was investigated, and the man was cleared."

"There's a distinct difference between cleared and believed, Officer Jessop," Jeane chimed in.

Jessop looked at her for the first time, and McCain caught the look that passed between them. He had seen that look before: between two cops, between senior partners in a law firm, between dogs meeting for the first time. It was the reaction to a threat to dominance, probably unintentional but definitely unwelcome. McCain pulled Jessop's attention back to himself.

"Officer Jessop," McCain said, "I don't suppose I could call on you sometime to hear about some of those brown-bag reports, could I? It would be great background for the movie."

Jessop shrugged, safely distracted. "I don't see why not. What would this movie be about, anyway?"

"Oh, horror, of course," McCain improvised swiftly. "Something like three teenagers investigating stories about a ghost get lost in the woods, then the ghost starts hunting them. We'd do the film as if it were a documentary."

This time it was the younger officer that frowned. "I

hate to burst your bubble but I'm pretty sure that's already been done."

"Of course, it has," smiled McCain. "We're not talking big budget here. This would be strictly direct to video." He rubbed his fingers together. "Pure money."

"Ah." Jessop looked distinctly less impressed. "Well, if you're going to be back out here doing any more scouting, you might want to let us know. It saves the hassle."

"Absolutely. Say, how about at night? If we want to come out and have a look around after dark, is it okay?" His smile just got bigger and brighter as Jessop's frown got deeper. "It is okay, right? We just need to get a feel for what the place looks like at night."

"Yeah," agreed Jessop reluctantly. "But you're definitely going to have to make special arrangements. The cemetery is strictly closed after sunset."

McCain nodded. "No problem. In that case, we're done for the day. Thanks very much for your help." He shook hands with the two officers and gestured for Jeane to precede him back down the path. "One other thing." He indicated Jeane's 35mm camera. "Is there a one-hour photo nearby? We need to get this developed ASAP."

"How come when you come up with these aliases, I'm always your assistant?" demanded Jeane. They sat in a doughnut shop in the same strip mall that contained the one-hour photo Jessop had recommended. They'd managed to get themselves a corner table—not a difficult task since the only other people in the shop were a pair of old men wearing faded bowling jackets and playing checkers.

"Because I'm the one who buys." McCain set a coffee in front of Jeane, then took a seat himself. He sipped at the coffee and made a face. "Weak." He pointed at the camcorder.

They shared the table with it and several of Jeane's books. "What do you think?"

Jeane was holding down the fast-forward button, watching herself zip through the speed-blurred landscape of the cemetery.

"There's not much to think about, is there?" she said. "You've got lots of scenes of me and of the cemetery and not a hint of anything else." She juggled the camcorder into one hand so that she could pick up her coffee. "Let's hope the camera caught something, or this is going to be a wasted day."

"Mmm," mumbled McCain into his coffee. "Not entirely a waste. At least we made contact with the local cops. They're always good to have on your side." He looked at her over the rim of his cup. "What was that comment to Jessop about anyway?"

Jeane returned his gaze. "I wanted to know if they thought Will really attacked Laurel or not."

"We already knew they did. Their investigation might have cleared Will, but Greene wouldn't have made a joke out of it if they believed him." He looked at her sideways. "Why? Do you think Will attacked Laurel?"

Jeane shrugged. "I don't know."

McCain gave her a curious look, and she made a noncommittal face.

"Head injuries can be funny things," she said, "but for Laurel to fall and hit herself hard enough to put her in a coma without also inducing early labor . . ." She shrugged again, then shook her head.

"Naw," she said, taking a sip of her coffee. "That's a pretty simple investigation. Even Jessop looks like he would have a hard time screwing—" She was interrupted as the door of the doughnut shop banged open, accompanied by the whooping calls of a crowd of teenagers. "Damn. School's out. There goes the neighborhood."

The teens poured into the restaurant, five boys and three girls. Jeane was talking again, something about angles of impact. McCain didn't really hear her. He was watching the teenagers. In a way, he missed high school. Sure it had seemed like a tremendous pain at the time, but compared with adult life, that was nothing. Just as these kids had the doughnut shop, there had been a pizza place near his school where he and his buddies from the football team had hung out. Some of the boys were wearing school jackets and he glanced at them, idly curious if any of them were on the football team.

It took a minute for the fact that he was staring at the name of a local high school to register.

He turned back to Jeane sharply and said, "Can I take a look at that copy of *Macbeth*?"

"Here."

Jeane reached into her jacket pocket and pulled out the book, along with a thick wad of crumpled old cash register receipts. McCain snorted and knocked several more out of the book itself. "Some people throw these things out, you know."

"I don't like to litter."

McCain swept the receipts to the back of the table and opened the book to the page that listed the students who had used it—and the high school they attended. He looked up at Jeane and a smile spread across his face. "How much do you think this Van Dimitriat knows about the cemetery?"

She blinked. "He has to know something. The woods outside a cemetery are a pretty strange place to read Shakespeare."

"Good. Back me up."

McCain got up from the table, straightened his collar, and approached the tables where the teenagers sat. "Hey, kids."

That shut them up instantly as they examined the stranger—the adult—who had walked into their midst. McCain had figured they would. It was certainly what he and his buddies would have done. He kept right on talking, flicking copies of his card across the table.

"My name's Wade Maxwell, Angel Station Productions. I'm in town doing location research for a movie. I'm wondering if you can help me out with some information." He caught the eye of the woman behind the counter and passed her a twenty dollar bill. "I'm paying for them."

One of the girls looked at him suspiciously. "What do you want to know?"

And we have a bite. He should have thought of this earlier. He grabbed a free chair from a nearby table and spun it around so he could straddle it backward. "Bachelor's Grove Cemetery."

That got them a little more interested. "What about it?" asked the same girl.

He smiled at her. Good girl, keep feeding me those lines. "See, me and my assistant—Jeane, can I have my coffee?— were out there today looking around. There's not much to see, as I'm sure you know."

Jeane tapped on his shoulder and handed him his coffee. She didn't look impressed. McCain shared his smile with her as well before sipping his coffee and continuing, "We ran into a couple of local cops, and I asked them if they had problems with teenagers out at the cemetery. They said you all knew better than to mess around out there. Of course, I know what that really means." He looked around the table, then reached into his pocket and pulled out a wad of ten dollar bills. "Who's got stories?"

That started them all talking at once, of course. McCain had to shout them down. "Hey! One at a time, and here's the deal: ten bucks for every good story that we haven't heard before. And don't try to make one up because I deal with bullshit every day and I can smell it a mile away." He cocked a finger at a big kid with a wide grin. "You first, hotshot."

Most of the stories that came out were repeats of what he and Jeane already knew, of course. The Madonna, the monk, a ghost car on the highway. A couple of times, Jeane had to open up her books and point out stories that were being repeated word for word just to shut up the ones who challenged them. Sometimes McCain gave a kid money even for a story he had heard—it kept them interested. But there was some new information to be learned, even if it was mostly just new wrinkles on the old stories. One girl who claimed to have seen the Madonna with her own eyes got ten dollars for a new detail: She swore that the ghost was crying as she cradled her baby. A couple of other kids had seen lights moving in the cemetery, blue among the stones, red out along the path. The kid with the grin supplied a tale about the ghostly farmhouse sometimes seen near the cemetery. Anyone who dared to approach the house, climb the steps to the well-lit porch, and pass through the door never emerged again.

Jeane had raised a skeptical eyebrow at that. "I don't suppose you've ever heard of anyone who actually did go into the house?" The kid had shaken his head. "Then how do you know they never come back?"

But the biggest surprise actually came from one of the old checkers player. As the kids were winding down, he stood up and came over with a story of his own. When he was a young man in 1952, he had seen the legendary ghost car.

"A big, black Ford Model A from the late twenties. A mob car," he said. "One of the Chicago gangs used to drive down to dump bodies in the lagoon."

The part about the bodies had caught McCain's attention during his research, but the information on the car was new. Not very helpful but new. McCain gave the old man his ten bucks and paid for his coffee, too. He turned back to the teenagers.

"How about that lagoon?" he asked, watching them all closely. "Anybody ever heard anything about something in the water grabbing people?"

The kids glanced at each other, then shook their heads almost in unison. Almost. At the end of the table, two boys exchanged sharp looks. McCain remembered them: When the other teenagers had been spinning tales, they had remained strangely quiet. One had offered an old chestnut about the white-robed monk. The other, a tall blond kid with a patch of a beard on his chin and a Chicago Blackhawks cap, had said nothing at all. McCain looked away from them and shrugged for the benefit of the other kids.

"Too bad," he said. "There's something about seeing people get pulled into water that makes an audience go nuts."

The big kid with the grin waved his hand. "Hey, my uncle told me about this two-headed monster that's supposed to come out of the lagoon. Maybe it could pull somebody into the water."

McCain squeezed his eyes shut. "Don't ever go into the movie business, hotshot." He stood up. "Thanks for your time. We have to go. If any of you come up with anything else, you've got my number. Give me a call." He went back over to his own table and helped Jeane gather up her books and the camcorder. "By the way, do any of you happen to know a Van Dimitriat?"

All of their eyes shot to the tall, blond boy. He shifted uncomfortably for a moment. "That's me," he said finally in a voice that was surprisingly deep, "I'm Van."

McCain looked at Jeane. She nodded and handed McCain the copy of *Macbeth*. As they left the doughnut shop, he slapped it down on the table in front of Van. "We found that out by the cemetery. Bet you're glad to get it back."

Van stared at it like it was alive. "Yeah." His big deep voice came out more like a whisper. "Real glad."

He knows something," Jeane told McCain bluntly as the door of the doughnut shop closed behind them.

McCain smiled and said, "I know he knows, and I'll bet that he knows we know he knows. If he doesn't, he at least suspects it." McCain unlocked his car, then held open the back door so she could pile her books inside. "Now we wait for him to decide that he wants to tell us what he knows."

Jeane groaned. "You're kidding, right?" She stood up and turned to face him. "He knows. We know. Why don't we just take him aside and ask him?"

"Keep it down."

McCain looked around the parking lot. She followed his gaze. They were alone. It was starting to get dark, and the cool greyness of the day promised a wet night. No one else was around.

"First," he said, "you're not a federal agent anymore, remember? We don't have any legal right to take someone down to the Institute and shine a bright light in their face until they talk. Second, Van is a kid in the middle of a crowd of his friends. Do you think they're going to let us take him aside for a little chitchat?" He opened the passenger side door and held it for her. "If we let him come to us, he's going to be happy to spill everything."

"And if he doesn't come to us?" asked Jeane. She remained standing outside the car. "We've lost a lead."

McCain sighed. "If he doesn't call us then we find out where he lives, and I'll let you use the battering ram on his door. Happy?" He let go of the car door and pointed to the other end of the strip mall and the one-hour photo store. "I'm going to go pick up the pictures. Promise me you won't bust his ass before I get back?"

"I'll try to restrain myself."

McCain strode away across the parking lot. Jeane got into the car and pulled the door shut. It was cool inside. Her breath made short-lived white patches of condensation on the windshield. From where she sat, she could see back into the doughnut shop. Van and his friends had taken up talking and kidding around again. No, she realized, Van's friends were talking and kidding around. Van seemed quiet in a way that he hadn't when the crowd first entered the shop. He was focused on his coffee, stirring it relentlessly. Occasionally one of his friends would say something to him, and he would react briefly, interacting for a few moments before lapsing back into silence.

"What do you know, Van?" Jeane murmured to herself. "What have you seen in Bachelor's Grove?" She watched him finally stop stirring his coffee and lift it to his mouth.

The sudden opening of the driver's side door made her jump. "Jesus Christ, Fitz!"

"Sorry." He dropped down into the driver's seat and

pulled the door shut behind him. "Let's see what the camera saw."

He turned on the overheard light. The world outside the
car vanished in reflected light. McCain pulled a thick stack
of photographs out of a green-and-white envelope and
began flipping through them. Eager anticipation quickly
faded from his face. Jeane leaned over to look at the pictures shuffling between his hands. They were good, clear
shots with sharp detail. On any other investigation, she
would have been proud of them. This time, though . . .

"Nothing?" she guessed.

"Nada." McCain handed the photos to her and leaned
forward to rest his head on the steering wheel as she
looked through them. "I don't suppose I should be surprised."

"I'm pretty sure ghosts don't give command performances." Jeane slid the pile of photos back into the envelope.
"Look at it this way, Fitz, we've got complete photographic
documentation of the scene. That's a reasonable start to
any investigation."

McCain grunted into the dashboard. "I was kind of hoping that we'd be a little further along than just the beginning by this point." He sat up and looked at her. "I want to
go back out to the cemetery. Tonight."

"You're joking." She turned to look back at him. The
overhead light cast his face into sharp, earnest angles.
"You're not joking. Fitz, it's going to rain."

"I've got an umbrella in the glove compartment."

"It's dark."

"That usually happens at night." He reached under the
seat and brought up a long, black flashlight.

Jeane held back a growl of frustration. "Boy scout," she
snarled. "Look, in a few days it will be a full moon. The
Madonna appears on the full moon. You can either go out
and get wet tonight—or you can wait a few nights, hopefully

get nicer weather, *and* have a statistically better chance of actually seeing something." She raised one eyebrow. "Well?"

McCain just stared out the windshield. After a minute, he sighed and confessed, "I'd rather not get soaked just to round out a day of big disappointments." He switched off the overhead light, turned the key in the ignition, and backed out of the parking space. "I do want to drive along the turnpike and look at the cemetery from the other side of the lagoon, though."

"Did I mention that it's dark out?"

"I've got it covered."

"That doesn't surprise me."

Jeane put on her seat belt and spared one last glance at the doughnut shop. Van's crowd of friends was starting to break up. Time to go home for dinner. Van was looking out the window, watching McCain's car pull away. He was flipping something in his hand, maybe one of the cards McCain had flicked around the table. For just a second and in spite of the distance between them, Jeane felt as though their eyes met. It sent a strange, electric shiver through her. There was something odd about the young man, something she couldn't quite define.

McCain turned onto the street, and the moment was broken. The strip mall—and Van—disappeared beyond the rear window. Jeane glanced over at McCain. Had he seen Van at the window? It was hard to tell. The orange illumination of the streetlights under which they drove flickered over his face, throwing shadows on top of shadows and obscuring his features. Only when an oncoming car caught them squarely in its headlights did his face come clearly into view—and even then the headlights cast new shadows.

For all of McCain's talk about not being able simply to walk Van into the Institute for questioning, Jeane couldn't help but wonder how he himself saw Van. Was the boy just another contact to him, another source of information? Was he just another person for McCain to mislead with his endless parade of aliases? Wade Maxwell. Robert Neil.

Michael McCain?

'Fitz' is the only name that he doesn't wear like an alias, Jeane realized.

In a few minutes they had left most of the lights of Midlothian behind and drove through the semidarkness of the suburban night. The houses and lights became fewer and fewer as the road cut through the southern fringes of Rubio Woods Forest Preserve. They thinned out even more as McCain turned north on Ridgeland Avenue, right up through the heart of the preserve. Jeane watched the transformation pensively. The night was very dark, and a breeze sent the arms of the trees swaying. If the woods around Bachelor's Grove had seemed innocent and harmless during the day, they had matured rapidly with dusk.

"I've been thinking about the stories those kids told us," she said suddenly, her voice breaking the silence. "Especially the one about the Madonna crying over her baby."

"What about it?"

Jeane settled back down in her seat. "What if she's mourning?" McCain shrugged and she elaborated. "Think about all of the other apparitions that are associated with the cemetery. What reason would they have to strike out at Laurel and Will? The Madonna is, or was, a mother. She lost her baby. Laurel and Will come into the cemetery, just about to give birth to a baby. Could she be jealous? Maybe the force we're looking for is the Madonna trying to take some kind of revenge against the living."

McCain was silent.

"Well?" she prompted.

"Aside from the fact that no story ascribes anything like the events at the hospital to the Madonna, it's not a bad theory."

"Thank you for that overwhelming vote of confidence."

McCain turned again, heading back east on the Midlothian Turnpike. "Look, there's even less evidence linking the Madonna to this than there is linking the hospital and the cemetery. And there's the question of why now? How far back do reports of the Madonna go? You can't tell me that Will and Laurel were the first parents to walk into that cemetery. There must have been babies and children in Bachelor's Grove before now."

"You have a better suspect?"

"Not really." He glanced over at her. "I can't believe you're the one proposing this."

Jeane grunted and rubbed her forehead. "Neither can I. But it's the only thing I can think of that makes any sense. At least it makes sense right now. Ask me again in the morning, and I'll deny everything."

McCain slowed down abruptly, looking across the seat and out of the window beside her.

"Hey!" Jeane snapped. "Keep your eyes on the road. What are you looking for?"

"A landmark. There was a big old forked tree near the highway on the other side of the lagoon."

Jeane peered out the window, cupping her hands around her eyes to block out the reflected lights of the dashboard. "Nothing. Nothing. Whoa! There it is."

McCain braked sharply and pulled over onto the shoulder. "You're sure?"

"As sure as I can be in the dark. Just how do you intend to see from here?"

"Get out," he said, "and I'll show you."

He opened his door and hopped out. Jeane sighed. She zipped her jacket tight, turned up the collar, and got out of the car. McCain already had the trunk open, pulling something out of a box inside. He pushed the trunk lid down and held up his prize, a pair of night-vision goggles. Jeane looked at them doubtfully.

"Are they going to be good enough over this distance?" she asked.

"Absolutely," McCain replied as he carefully fitted the goggles over his head. "Warn me if there are any cars coming. I'd rather not get high beams blasting into these things."

He began fiddling with the goggles, focusing the lenses. After a few moments, he stopped and began slowly scanning the darkness.

"See anything?" asked Jeane. Even with her eyes adjusted to the darkness, she couldn't make out any real details.

"The lagoon. A couple of the bigger, whiter stones. The goggles work better without a heavy cloud cover." He pressed a button on the side of the goggles, and the long lenses spun and extended like binoculars. "Better," McCain grunted.

"You've got something?"

"No," McCain admitted with a sigh. "It doesn't look like there's anything mov—wait . . ." His arm came up, pointing. "There. There's a dark streak, and everything has gone kind of hazy. It's very faint, kind of like it's only half there."

Jeane held out her hand, then looked up at the sky. A fat drop of cold water hit her squarely on the forehead.

"Fitz? Does this haze disappear if you close one eye?" She dug the cap she had been wearing earlier out of her pocket and pulled it on.

McCain's face wrinkled beneath the goggles as he closed first one eye then the other. "Um . . . yeah."

"You've got water on one of your lenses, genius. It's starting to rain."

"Damn!" He tugged off the goggles and ran a hand through his hair. He contemplated the goggles. "For a second I thought I really had something."

"Nice try." More rain was coming down now, and several drops hit Jeane in rapid succession. She opened the car door, letting light spill out into the night, and sat back inside. "Maybe we can try them again the next time we're out here."

"If there is a next time." McCain sighed again. "Like you said, ghosts don't give command performances. We didn't see any today. I didn't see anything tonight. How many times do you think we're going to have to come out before we spot something? How long do people who are really interested in hauntings hang around in cemeteries before they catch a glimpse of anything even remotely—"

"Fitz, shut up for a second." Jeane sat still in her seat with the door open. She stared out into the darkness. "Do you hear anything?"

He cocked his head. "No."

"Exactly." She stood up and looked all around them. Everything was perfectly, utterly still. There was no sound. The breeze had died away into the night. The rain was falling gently, yes, but it fell onto the leaves lying on the ground and onto the metal hood and roof of the car. It should have made *some* noise.

Jeane turned and looked at McCain. "When was the last time you saw a car come by?" she asked.

"Not since well before we pulled over."

"There should be more traffic coming past than that. It isn't that late."

"Do you think . . . ?" McCain nodded toward the cemetery.

"No," Jeane said instantly.

But as soon as she said it, her breath caught in her throat. The stillness and silence were, if not unnatural, then at least unusual. Wasn't that exactly what they had just spent the entire day looking for? The rain started to fall more heavily—not harder, just heavier and with the same eerie silence. Jeane climbed back into the car, shutting the door behind her.

"No," she said again.

She stared straight ahead through the rain-streaked windshield. This was what they wanted. Something to investigate. But . . .

She realized that she had her fists clenched. Slowly and deliberately, she forced her hands open.

"Do you think we should hang around and check it out?" asked McCain as he got in. He set the night-vision goggles carefully on the back seat, then turned back to her.

Yes. No. "I—"

A flash of light in the rearview mirror interrupted her. Both she and McCain twisted around at the same time. A pair of headlights was coming up the road, moving rapidly.

"Well," breathed McCain with relief, "there you go." He turned back around. "There's someone else on the road."

Jeane stared at the lights. There was something not quite right about them. They were too high off the road for one thing, and too close together for another. They were dimmer than normal and diffuse, too, as if the car were driving through fog.

She blinked. It was foggy. A thick mist had come up out of the rain.

"Fitz," she said, her voice low.

"I see it." He was already reaching forward and twisting the key in the ignition.

Nothing. Jeane watched the lights come closer and listened to a sound like distant thunder. McCain turned the key again and again.

Will Tavish blinked and refocused his eyes on the newspaper for what seemed like the hundredth time. The text of the day's *Tribune* crept along the page, the words and sentences slipping away from him. He blinked again and sought out the paragraph he had been reading.

"Sorry, Laurel," he muttered over the paper, "I didn't get much sleep last night."

The apology was habit more than anything else. Laurel didn't respond, of course. She was as silent as she had been since the hospital orderlies first laid her down in the bed. Will fought the urge to glance over the top of the paper and look at her. He knew nothing would have changed.

The paranoia was the reason he hadn't slept last night. Ever since his talk with Rob Neil yesterday, it had been there, murmuring in his ear. It had kept him up all night, it kept him from reading, it even kept him from watching television. And he thought it had been bad before he met Rob. He had only found peace for a few short minutes today, and that had been when he let down his guard and the paranoia had overwhelmed him. He hadn't meant to do it. The paranoia was madness, and he would not give in to it. Not consciously, anyway. But around eleven a.m., the caffeine buzz from an extra-large coffee slowly fading, his feeble attention had wandered. He had shaken himself awake, alert with sudden horror. Fifteen minutes had disappeared during which all he could remember was the murmuring presence of the paranoia.

He had fled to the only sanctuary he knew: the hospital. Somehow the paranoia seemed to ease during the time he spent beside Laurel's bed. Even here it didn't give him much respite, though what it did yield was a blessing. He still couldn't sleep, but he could at least relax. He filled the time reading to Laurel. Dr. Doyle encouraged it, actually—she said the stimulus was good for Laurel, that it might help bring her out of the coma faster. Will wasn't so sure of the accuracy of that. Or maybe the paranoia wasn't sure. Sometimes he wasn't sure where he ended and it began.

Will forced that thought away and bent his attention back to the paper. He blinked yet again, found his spot, and began to read. The article was some ridiculous bit of fluff on blending your own potpourri. Laurel would have hated it if she had been able to—

The text of the newspaper leaped off the page with a sharpness and clarity that took Will's breath away. It was as if he had suddenly been fitted with glasses that he never knew he needed. Maybe a hearing aid, too, because abruptly the room was alive with little noises he had never noticed before.

The constant presence of the paranoia was gone. He lowered the paper slowly. "Laurel . . . I'm . . ."

The slack mask of Laurel's unconscious face had been replaced by a particular tightness he had seen too many times on patients in his dentist's chair. Pain.

Her body moved, too. Small movements, tiny stirrings, a slight shifting of joints. They only lasted a moment. Behind the tape that held her eyelids closed, her eyes began flicking rapidly back and forth. Will stood spellbound, watching.

Laurel made a noise, a low keen that crawled out from the back of her throat. That broke the spell. He reached out and slapped the call buzzer for a nurse, then slapped it again. Nothing. Nothing! He jumped for the door and tore down the hall to the nursing station. He almost slammed into a nurse and Dr. Doyle running toward the room.

He grabbed Dr. Doyle and shouted, "Laurel's waking up!"

The doctor shrugged him off and pushed her way into Laurel's room, the nurse and Will right behind her. Dr. Doyle glanced over Laurel, then went straight to the machines that monitored her life signs. She frowned. Turning back to Laurel, she peeled off the tape covering one eye, then pulled back Laurel's eyelid. Laurel's eye continued to dart about as if controlled by some unseen puppeteer.

"Rapid eye movement. She's dreaming, but there's no change in her vital signs." Dr. Doyle looked up at Will. "This shouldn't be happening."

"Fitz!"

"I'm trying!"

Jeane stared at the lights. There was clearly something behind them, a car maybe but taller and thinner than any car she was familiar with. It was the source of the distant thunder as well, now a roar that echoed in her head and shook through her bones—she couldn't tell for sure whether she was hearing the sound or simply feeling it. The thick mist made it hard to tell how far away the lights were. For a moment, she thought that maybe the lights would just race right past them. McCain's car was pulled far over on the shoulder and well out of range. Then the lights swerved abruptly. Bright beams flashed her straight in the eyes.

"Bail!" she yelled, grabbing for her door.

"No!" McCain snapped back, "I've got it!"

The ignition roared to life, and McCain slammed his foot on the gas. For a second, the tires spun, kicking up muddy gravel and squealing like a wounded animal before catching traction. The car shot forward and onto the road. Jeane braced herself as the acceleration pressed her into the seat. Something big and black rushed past the rear bumper and plunged off the road.

The lights were gone as instantly as if someone had flicked off a switch.

McCain stepped on the brake and brought his car to a bone-jarring stop. The night vision goggles slid forward off the back seat and onto the floor of the car with an unpleasant crack, but McCain paid no attention to them. He was staring out the rear window.

"What the hell was that?" he asked.

Jeane opened her door and jumped out. The mist was so thick she couldn't see to the other side of the road, but at least the rain had stopped. She followed the smear of rubber that marked the pavement all the way back to where they had been parked a moment ago. There were no other marks, either on the asphalt of the road or the gravel of the shoulder, or among the grass and autumn-dead weeds that lined the road. McCain jogged up beside her—she noticed that this time he had left the car running.

"Where . . . ?" McCain started to say.

He stopped as soon as he realized there was nothing to see. For a moment he just stared into the darkness and the mist. Then his arm came up, he pointed into the distance off the road, and said, "Look."

A pale blue glow illuminated the mist back in among the trees, moving slowly but steadily. Jeane couldn't make out the source of the glow, but she could guess. Something was moving in Bachelor's Grove Cemetery.

It wasn't the only light in the mist, though. Back down the turnpike, two more lights had appeared, the same color, height, and size as those that had vanished moments before. The only difference was that these were moving a lot faster. Jeane could already sense the beginning of the same horrible roar beating against her.

"Back into the car!" she yelled.

McCain didn't need any additional urging. He ran back, trench coat flapping, and threw himself into the driver's seat. He pushed the car into drive almost before Jeane had her door closed. She wrapped the seat belt tight around herself and held on. The car's acceleration was smoother this time, but it still sent the engine howling through rapid gear shifts. McCain kept the gas pedal pressed to the floor, pushing them faster and faster through the mist. Jeane glanced behind them.

Somehow the lights in the mist were still gaining on them.

"Fitz . . ."

"I know," he said grimly. His face was hard and his jaw

was clenched. He looked down at the speedometer and shook his head. "Damn. Look for a turn-off."

"Menard down to 143rd."

"We're way past it."

"There must be a ton of other streets. There's houses all around here."

McCain shook his head. "I haven't seen any. Look for Cicero Avenue. It should be impossible to miss." He glanced briefly up toward the rearview mirror and gasped. "Holy shit!"

Jeane looked back. The lights were right behind them and holding pace easily. She could clearly see now that they were headlights—old headlights. The car that followed them was built high off the ground, with a square grill and a narrow hood slung between rounded fenders. The headlights were mounted on the sides of the car's nose. The windshield was almost vertical and capped by a ridged cloth top that shook with the speed of the car's passage. All of the car that she could see was painted black. Even the windshield was dark—anyone, anything, or nothing at all might be behind the wheel. If Jeane had to make a guess, she'd say it was a Ford Model A from the 1920s, a "mob car" as the old man in the doughnut shop had described it.

She swallowed hard. How was an antique like that keeping up with them? There was one possible explanation, and she didn't like it. Jeane, she told herself, there's a time for scientific objectivism and a time when you just have to go with what your eyes are telling you.

The roar of the Model A changed slightly in pitch and the other car began slipping into the oncoming lane. "It's moving up!" she warned.

"Like hell it is," McCain snarled. He pulled his car sideways to block the Model A . . . and went into a short, sharp skid. Jeane felt her stomach rise and twist, and she grabbed reflexively for the door handle. Even McCain gave a yelp.

The skid probably didn't last for a second, but it was enough. The Model A was up on their right now, overtaking them with hideous speed and a fluid smoothness. The wire spokes and wide, white sides of the old tires slid past Jeane's window. She became aware of a new sound underneath the roar of the car. A terrified wailing and a hollow, irregular pounding. She knew what it was instantly. Someone or something was trapped in that car, hammering at the polished black metal and trying to get out.

The Model A began to ease toward them.

"Fitz!"

"Brace yourself!"

She reacted instinctively and just in time. A heartbeat later, McCain's foot jumped from the gas to the brake. The car screamed in protest, but it bucked and skidded to an abrupt halt.

The Model A didn't even try to stop. Before McCain's car had even given a final jerk, the Model A had been swallowed by the mist. Jeane drew a ragged breath and looked to McCain. His face was ghastly pale in the dashboard light. Except for their breathing and the muted growl of the car's engine, the night was as silent and still as it had been by the cemetery.

McCain leaned forward and cleared his throat, spitting helplessly onto the floor between his feet. "Is it gone?" Jeanne nodded silently, but something made her look back over her shoulder.

In the distance were two lights, approaching rapidly.

"Go!" she rasped. McCain slammed his foot back onto the gas pedal, and they were going again, accelerating fast. Jeane scanned the side of the road for any sign of a turnoff—Menard, Cicero, an on-ramp for 294, a driveway, anything. But there was nothing and the lights were catching up with them faster than . . .

The mist fell away behind them. The transition was so

fast it made Jeane blink and McCain start, his twitch send-ing the car swerving to the side of the road. The headlights flashed across a street sign. Jeane barely caught the name as they whipped past it. Menard Avenue. They were barely half a mile beyond Bachelor's Grove.

She looked back. The mist was nothing more than a tat-tered mass of drifting wisps, rapidly vanishing into the night, and the only lights behind them came pulling out of Menard flaring red and white. The silence was shattered by the wail of a police siren. Jeane exchanged a sharp glance with McCain.

"What the hell?" she breathed.

"I don't know."

He braked gently and pulled over to the side of the road. The police car caught up to them in a few moments, slow-ing to stop just behind them. Jeane caught the sound of a car door slamming shut a moment later. McCain flicked on the interior light and rolled down his window. Night air came streaming in, carrying with it a hundred different sounds, all the nocturnal rustling and twitching and distant noises that had been missing before. It also carried the measured pace of boots on asphalt as a figure, silhouetted by the lights behind, came up on the driver's side and bent down to the window.

"Evening, Mr. Maxwell," said Officer Jessop. "In a hurry to get back to Chicago?"

Jeane found herself exhaling in a thin sigh of relief. McCain was already giving the police officer a smile. "I'm afraid we lingered a little too long over coffee then took a wrong turn coming out of town. I've got an appointment and I guess my foot's a little heavy with the road so . . ."

"Foggy?" supplied Jessop. "I saw you come barreling out of that cloud just before it broke up. Strange place for a heavy foot."

The light inside the car cast Jessop's face into shadows,

but Jeane still caught an odd look in his eyes. An odd, knowing look.

She leaned forward to peer around McCain and said quickly, "Strange place for a fog, Officer Jessop."

McCain shot her a sharp glance.

Jessop studied the two of them silently. Jeane was suddenly aware of how McCain looked: pale and drenched in the sweat of fear. She could feel cold perspiration running down her back as well. She didn't take her eyes off Jessop, though, and eventually the officer nodded.

"Yes," he said. "Yes, it is. You don't look like the type to let anyone take a wrong turn, ma'am." He glanced back to McCain. "Funny thing—your wrong turn took you right past Bachelor's Grove."

"I guess it did."

"Some of the stories about Bachelor's Grove say the road along here is haunted, too. Did you read about that in your research?"

"It sounds familiar," McCain replied.

"A couple almost ran off the road near here back in the seventies. Said they smashed into another car, but when it was all over, they were fine and there was no sign of another car." He looked at both of them. "You two look like people who were almost in an accident."

McCain's eyebrows rose. "The ghost car?" he asked innocently. Jeane kept her face neutral. "You know, after our conversation this afternoon, that would have been the last suggestion I'd expect you to make, Officer Jessop."

"It's a suggestion that's a lot easier to make at night," Jessop replied. He caught Jeane's eye. "I think at least one of you knows it, too." He straightened up and slapped the top of the car. "Try not to let your foot get too heavy the rest of the way back to Chicago, Mr. Maxwell. And good luck on your movie."

He stepped away from the car, then turned back to his

own vehicle. After a few moments, the police cruiser turned out on the road and sped on past them.

"Well," said Jeane, "that was interesting." She looked over to McCain again. "Still think the day was a disappointment?"

He returned her gaze. "Still think the Madonna is the ghost we want?"

Hovering at the foot of Laurel's bed, watching Dr. Doyle fuss over his wife, Will gasped as a thick, horrid pressure exploded inside his head. For a moment, his vision shrank to a tiny pinpoint, and anger poured through him. No, not just anger. Burning, blinding, unthinking rage. Then the strange pressure had settled back into him and he was left gasping for air beneath the crushing weight of his paranoia.

Except that it wasn't just paranoia anymore. The pressure pulsed and seethed in his ears. It was anger. It was urgency. It was *need*.

Will stifled a cry, just as Dr. Doyle stood up sharply. "It's stopped. She's totally inactive again." She turned toward Will. "I'm—"

It was too much. He fled the room, sprinting for the elevators and escape from the hospital.

chapter
7even

For a time after Ngan had come to America in the 1950s, he had shared an apartment in San Francisco with fourteen other Tibetan refugees. Actually, calling it an apartment was generous. In his childhood, he had known Himalayan caves that were larger, more generously appointed, and better lit. The apartment in San Francisco was a dark, damp basement room with a bare bulb, a leaking sink, and a toilet down the hall that backed up every time it rained.

His new office at the Chicago branch of the Hoffmann Institute was twice as large as the entire place.

He closed the policies and procedures manual the Institute had given him to read and looked around his office. In the squalor of his San Francisco apartment, three grown men would have slept in the space taken up by his desk alone. In Chicago, the desk was

109

merely piled high with papers, stuffed with files, and weighed down by the cold new computer with which the Institute had insisted on providing him. The television and video equipment against one wall could have been moved to accommodate another man, and an entire family could have slept where the big meeting table stood. No, he realized, if there had been a table in San Francisco, the landlord would have packed in two families, one on top and one underneath. The office was too big. The corners of it were shadowed and always empty.

Ngan sat forward in his chair and scanned the mosaic of buttons on his new telephone for the one marked "intercom." After a moment, he gave up. He walked across his big office, pulled open his big door with the big, bright brass name plate on it, and stuck his head into the outer office.

"Emma," he said, "has there been any word from Michael or Jeane?"

Emma Kazmeryk, the secretary assigned to the team, glanced up. Perhaps if there was one good thing about his promotion, it was that somehow he had been fortunate enough to acquire her services. The slim, dark-haired woman was a marvel of speed and efficiency. She could, to use Fitz's words of awe, "field strip a photocopier and reassemble it blindfolded." Her desk, Ngan noticed, was small, compact, and perfectly neat. No matter what she was given to do, it never seemed to sit for long.

"Jeane came in about thirty-five minutes ago," Emma answered, "but she's waiting for Fitz so they can make their report to you together."

"Ah." The brushed metal clock on the wall behind Emma read 10:45. "Is she in their office?"

Emma nodded, and Ngan crossed the outer office to the door that bore the agents' names. It was closed. He knocked. "Jeane, may I come in?"

"Report's not ready." Jeane's voice was muffled.

"It will only take a moment."

There was a muted sound that might have been a sigh of annoyance, then Jeane spat out. "Yeah, okay—come in."

Ngan was always somewhat surprised that the Institute would put two agents together in such a small office when his own could so easily and comfortably accommodate all three of them. But, he supposed, there was a hierarchy in the way office space was assigned, even within an organization of such apparent good will and co-operation as the Hoffmann Institute.

At least Jeane and McCain had done the best they could with the limited space they had been assigned. They had shoved their desks together in the center of the room, leaving a narrow aisle around the room's perimeter. A filing cabinet, a short bookshelf, a coatrack, and a spare chair turned the aisle into a tight maze. Jeane was seated at the narrow computer workstation that capped the far end of both desks. There was a pencil in her mouth. She gave him a weary, sour look. "I'm waiting—"

"For Michael. Emma told me." Ngan walked into the room and squeezed through to sit on the spare chair. "I'm very curious to hear about what you learned yesterday."

"Oh, you'll love it." Jeane went back to typing, her fingers clattering over the keyboard.

"I regret not being able to go with you, but I had to attend a meeting yesterday."

Jeane didn't look up. "Really? How was it?"

"It . . ." Ngan hesitated. Was it appropriate to tell the agents that he felt some of his superiors and colleagues were petty bureaucrats whose time might be more productively spent picking their noses? Would that promote proper respect and the need for teamwork? " . . .was a meeting."

"Better you than me," snorted Jeane. "I'll stick to field work, thank you very much."

"That's a wise choice." Ngan leaned forward. "Was the trip to Bachelor's Grove worthwhile?"

Jeane paused in her typing and glanced up at him sharply. He sat back again and said, "My apologies. I'm eager."

"Ngan, Fitz and I will give you the report *together*." The pencil in her mouth bobbed with each word. "Is there anything else until then?"

"No." Ngan stood. "I'll wait in my office."

He almost bumped into McCain on the way out. The young man carried a rough-pressed paper tray with two tall cups of coffee and a small paper bag.

"Doughnuts?" asked Ngan.

"Muffins, actually." McCain gave him a level look. "I'm afraid I only have two. Sorry."

Ngan returned his gaze. "Of course."

He took long, deep breaths as he crossed the outer lobby and reached for the handle of his own office door. He was disappointed, yes, but what could he really expect? McCain shared an office with Jeane. He had been out in the field with her yesterday. Certainly they were all supposed to be one team, but the two agents did work more closely with each other than with him.

Yet he had known McCain for virtually all of the young man's life. When they had been reunited in Washington, McCain had certainly seemed pleased to see him. What had happened to that rapport?

Ngan was not looking forward to this debriefing. He would have given his promotion not to be the one conducting it.

An idea struck him, and he returned to Emma's desk. "Would you ask Lily Adler if she would be free in an hour? And pass a message to Jeane and Fitz that they will need to have their report ready for the same time." He gave Emma a smile. "Don't mention anything about Lily to them."

An hour later, he was rather pleased to watch Jeane blink in surprise as she stepped through his office door and saw the woman with silver-grey hair sitting beside his desk. McCain, just behind her, did the same double take and straightened his posture.

"Field Director Adler," McCain said.

"Mr. McCain. Ms. Meara." Chicago Branch Field Director of Observation Lily Adler nodded to both of them.

Ngan gestured for McCain and Jeane to seat themselves in the chairs in front of his desk. Jeane placed several printed pages on Ngan's desk, then reached across and gave her own copy of the report to Lily.

"Thank you," said Lily.

"You're welcome, ma'am." Jeane took her seat.

Ngan watched both her and McCain as he skimmed through their report. Both of them were now studiously avoiding looking at Lily. Ngan concealed a smile. Lily Adler was something of a legend among the staff of the Hoffmann Institute in Chicago. She carried both herself and her command with an elegant, steely grace that spoke of long hours at a blueblood finishing school. For many agents, Lily was the last sort of person they would have expected to find working for the Hoffmann Institute, let alone serving as a field director of observation. Most of them never got used to that or to her iron-willed style of management. When Lily gave an order she expected it to be obeyed, just as a grand matriarch might command her family.

Ngan had known her for years. She was one of his oldest friends in the Institute, and when he had asked for her help, she had been happy to agree.

He finished the report and looked up. "I've asked Field Director Adler to sit in today. I felt her observations on this investigation might prove useful." And, he hoped, supportive. He tapped the edge of the report on his desk. "Your encounter on the turnpike concerns me."

"It was an unexpected event," admitted Jeane. She spoke in the official "report" voice she used around superiors— with, he had noticed, the exception of him. "But it was also fortuitous." She glanced at McCain. "Just before we stopped on the turnpike outside the cemetery, we had been speculating on the possibility that the Madonna might be the Bachelor's Grove ghost most likely to be responsible for the events. The appearance of the phantom car suggests otherwise."

Ngan raised an eyebrow. "So you have accepted the possibility that a spirit force is at work?"

Jeane lifted her eyes to the ceiling for a moment as if considering the question. "It is a . . . possibility. If you accept the existence of such spirits."

"Which you don't, Ms. Meara?" asked Lily. She leaned forward, glancing toward Ngan for belated permission to intrude on the conversation.

"Under duress, ma'am. I'd register my objection to the existence of ghosts, but there doesn't seem to be much point. In this case, all available observations currently indicate the involvement of such a force, and our investigations have failed to suggest another alternative. If you'll forgive me for quoting Sherlock Holmes, 'when you've eliminated the impossible, what remains, no matter how improbable, must be the truth.' "

"Not one to jump to conclusions, are you, Ms. Meara?"

"No, ma'am," Jeane said with a little pride in her voice, "I'm not."

If Lily's orders, Ngan reflected, were obeyed as if they came from a family matriarch, then even her smallest compliments were accepted as if they came from the same source. Lily had a way for rewarding her agents with words. Or at least rewarding most of her agents. He noticed McCain sneaking Jeane a glance of disgust.

"Is there anything you'd like to add to the report, Michael?" asked Ngan.

McCain's attention snapped back to him. "Only that we continue to lack any demonstrable direct link between the hauntings at Bachelor's Grove and the events in the hospital," he said smoothly.

He was quick, Ngan had to give him that, but he did have a tendency to leap without double-checking his facts.

"What if you knew that Laurel apparently experienced a nightmare last night at the same time you were on the turnpike?" Ngan asked.

"What?" McCain looked to Jeane. She shook her head. "What happened?"

"At the moment, that is the extent of my information," Ngan admitted. He described what had happened exactly as Shani Doyle had described it to him earlier that morning. "Of course, no one knew until now that the duration of the episode coincided with your encounter in the mist."

Jeane sat back as well, a stunned expression on her face.

McCain closed his eyes for a moment and took a breath. When he opened his eyes again, he said, "I asked you this once before, and you didn't give me a straight answer. Do you think it's really a ghost?"

Ngan considered both of them for a moment. Out of the corner of his eye, he could also see Lily waiting on his answer. Suddenly his idea of inviting her to sit in for support felt like it had backfired. She had told him once that a good leader only gave his agents facts, never opinions. He wondered if that advice had ever trapped her like this.

He looked at McCain and said, "I think you think it is."

McCain's eyes flashed with frustration.

Jeane rubbed her forehead and said, "No offense, Ngan, but that's not much help. I couldn't find anything at the hospital that would explain the mist, and I can't think of anything that would reasonably explain what we saw last night unless I resort to saying that Fitz and I shared a hallucination." She threw up her hands. "Lacking any other explanation, I'm willing to accept a ghost—or some other paranormal force. Whatever it is, we need some guidance."

McCain pounced into the opening Jeane had made. "If it *is* one of the ghosts of Bachelor's Grove at work, we still don't know which one it was. Remember, the mist doesn't fit any of the stories about Bachelor's Grove, and there haven't been any reports of ghost cars driving around Presbyterian-St. Luke's. And I've never heard of ghosts following people home from the graveyard. We either need another lead or a new approach to the problem."

Ngan could feel a flush growing in his cheeks. He looked to Lily for aid, but a quick dart of her eyes told him that this was something he had to work out himself. There was nothing she could do to help him now that wouldn't make him look bad in the agents' eyes.

He fell back on the only advice he felt fully confident in, advice first given to him by an older mentor than Lily.

"Patience," he said. He laid the report down on his desk. "Jeane, continue with your research. You've made a good start, and more research might reveal something else. Michael . . ." He groped for a moment, trying to find instructions that would take full advantage of McCain's talents. "Go back to Presbyterian-St. Luke's. Talk to Dr. Doyle."

McCain gave a cheerful little grunt. "That's the first order you've given in a while that I like."

"Mr. McCain!" snapped Lily, and McCain blanched.

"Sorry, ma'am."

"I'm not the one you owe an apology to."

The young man turned toward him, but Ngan just waved him toward the door. "Apology accepted. You have your assignments—you're dismissed." He brushed his hand across the report. "I'll digest this and let you know if there's anything else."

He waited until the agents were out of the office and the door had closed behind them before he turned to Lily.

"I believe that went rather well," he sighed.

"Hold that elevator!" Someone inside caught the door just before it closed and McCain ducked through. "Thanks." He turned to the attractive black woman in the lab coat at the side of the elevator. "Why, imagine running into you here, Dr. Doyle—or may I accept your invitation and call you Shani?"

She smiled. "You may. And running into me on the floor of my office is hardly a co—" McCain gave her a sharp grin and she bit her tongue. "Let me rephrase that. Running into me on the floor where my office is located is hardly a coincidence. Did Ngan send you over?"

"More or less. I'm here for a follow-up." The elevator stopped and the other passengers got out. McCain glanced at the panel. "Going to the ICU?"

"Checking on Laurel. After last night, we've got a new monitor set up on her, but I like to check in myself every so often. I'm worried about her." Shani leaned against the elevator wall. "Like I told Ngan, though, there's not much to add to the story."

McCain coughed discretely. "That's not actually the follow-up I had in mind, though I do have some news for you. What I really wanted was to ask you to dinner tonight."

"Your timing is perfect. I'm free tonight. How's seven?"

"You read my mind."

The elevator stopped at the Intensive Care Unit and McCain followed Shani out.

"Sounds good," Shani said with a smile. "So what's your news?"

"Something happened to Jeane and I last night at the same—"

"Dr. Doyle!" One of the nurses from the station by the elevator came running after them. "Are you here to see Mrs. Tavish?" Shani nodded. "Dr. Tavish is with her."

"Thanks, Jenny." The nurse went back to the station and Shani turned to McCain. "Do you want to talk to him?"

"I probably shouldn't. He might get suspicious if Rob Neil keeps showing up in his wife's room. How about I walk you to the door? On the way, I can tell you what Jeane and I saw."

He only hit the highlights of the events on the turnpike, but it was more than enough to keep Shani in silence while he spoke.

When he was finished, she added quietly, "I don't like it."

"*You* don't like it?" McCain grimaced. "You should have been in my car."

"It's way too much of a coincidence that this should happen to you and Jeane. Have you thought that maybe what we're dealing with knows who you are and what you're trying to do? Last night might have been a deliberate attack."

"Maybe, but I don't understand how." They stopped outside the door of room 923, and McCain nodded toward it. "How do you explain Laurel's nightmare at the same time last night?"

Shani frowned.

"Well?" McCain pressed.

"Shh." Shani tilted her head. "Listen." She pointed at the closed door.

It took McCain a moment to distinguish the sound that came through it from the background noise of the hospital. Someone was talking inside the room, a low, disjointed diatribe. McCain looked at Shani.

"Will?" he whispered.

"I guess so. What should we do?"

McCain stepped up to the door and pushed very slowly

and gently, opening it just until he could see into the room. Shani peered in past him.

He had crept back into the hospital at about one o'clock in the afternoon, slinking into the ICU and his wife's room like a disgraced dog. The night had become a blur in his memory. He couldn't remember. He couldn't concentrate. He could barely *think* with the chaos that boiled in his brain. He remembered clearly his flight from the hospital, but that was all. He had gone home at some point, he was fairly certain of that, but he had also driven around the city at random for a long, long time, from the north side to south side neighborhoods he would normally never think of going near. He had circled the Loop and the seedy streets under the L so many times that a watching cop would have thought he was looking for prostitutes. He had gone out to O'Hare and watched planes land. He had stopped at some apparently nameless twenty-four-hour diner, only to watch a cheeseburger cool and congeal untouched in front of him. He had eventually asked for it to be wrapped up to go—he still wasn't sure if he had eaten it. Exactly where home had entered into those roamings, though, he wasn't sure. He only knew that he had gone there and tried to sleep. Sleep hadn't come, and he had left again.

There had been one constant through the night, however. The whispers that he had once mistaken for paranoia were more insistent than ever. More unified, too. Sometime during the night, they had joined into a single voice that drove him on, keeping sleep away, never letting him forget the anger. The fear. The urgency.

I need her. Oh, how I need her.

Maybe it was that need that finally brought him back to the hospital. For a long time, hours maybe, he had just sat beside Laurel's bed, letting the whispering voice flow through him and watching her . . . sleep? Watching her body being driven by machines. The child shifting in the warm liquid darkness of her womb seemed more alive than she was.

He wasn't sure when the words started coming. They were simply there, welling up from somewhere deep inside him and pushing the whispers aside. Maybe Laurel would hear him. Maybe she would understand. He had to hope.

" . . . sorry, Laurel, I'm so sorry. We shouldn't have gone—I shouldn't have gone. Why didn't I leave it all alone? We were so happy. But you had to come didn't you?" His voice, he realized, had turned harsh, but he didn't stop. "You had to. And now look at everything that's happened. Look at it. Look at you!"

I need her.

He realized that he was standing, looking down at Laurel. He didn't remember rising. His hands were wrapped tight around the bed rails, the metal warm from the heat of his grip and slick with the sweat from his palms. He took his hands away from the rail, rubbing them dry on the hips of his pants. His right hand came away feeling grubbier than before. Something greasy stained his pants. The cheeseburger, maybe, nuzzled up beside him in the car.

"Look at me," he told Laurel. "Look at me." There was a little sink built into the wall on the opposite side of the bed. A mirror was mounted above it. He raised his head and looked into the mirror.

Will Tavish stared back, almost unrecognizable. The twitch that had begun to manifest when he had been talking with Rob had gotten worse—every so often, his lips would twist and frown. His eyes were very, very bright, their fevered sharpness highlighted by the dark circles of insomnia. At least his hair was clean and he had shaved. His shirt looked clean, too, though he had still managed to pull a pair of dirty pants back on. Unless they had been clean when he put them on, and he had gotten the cheeseburger after he had been home. He couldn't remember.

"I need you," Will whispered.

He touched her arm through the rough hospital blankets, slid his hand all the way up to her shoulder and her neck. Where the blankets ended, her skin was cool. He touched her ear and brushed her hair aside. The gauze on her head was soft against his hand. He could feel the thickness of her hair under the bandages. Spread out, his fingers could cover the entire side of her head. He pushed gently, turning her head to the side. There was no resistance.

There had been no resistance before. Bachelor's Grove welled up around him again, and Laurel was lying in the mist, the stone by her head. Will saw his own hand reaching out to take her head, turn it toward the stone and . . .

Finish it!

"No!" He snatched his hand away and stepped back from the bed, breathing hard. "I'm not listening!" he screamed. "*I'm not listening!*"

Last night he had fled without thinking. Now he fled because he knew he couldn't stay any longer. When had he given in to the voice? Just now, when he had stood and touched Laurel, or earlier? Had coming to the hospital been his idea at all? What else might he do? He couldn't stay in the same room as Laurel. The voice pounding in his ears, he grabbed his coat from the chair and strode for the door, wrenching it swiftly open. He knew what he had to do.

The hall was quiet, and if he had not been so focused on getting away from the ICU and Laurel as quickly as possible, he might have breathed a sigh of relief. What if someone had heard his outburst? What would they think?

"You're not crazy," he told himself. "You're not!"

But he did need help. He needed—

Her, supplied the voice.

"Shut up," he told it.

It didn't help.

McCain slipped his head around the corner of the cross-corridor and watched Will stalk away down the hall.

"Clear," he told Shani.

She dashed past him grimly and darted into Laurel's room. McCain followed a little more slowly, alert in case Will came back. There was no sign of him. He slipped into Laurel's room after Shani.

"Is she okay?" McCain asked.

The doctor was checking Laurel and the machines that surrounded her. "She's as good as she was before."

"Good." He sagged back against the wall for a moment. Will's sudden cry had given him and Shani barely enough time to scramble away from the door and out of sight before the other man had come out of the room. "Any idea what set him off?" he asked her.

"Stress? Trauma finally catching up with him? You saw him. He looks awful."

"I heard him, too." McCain shook his head.

Maybe Will was just traumatized by Laurel's ordeal, but there had been something in his voice that was particularly disturbing, a tone that shifted too quickly from apology to anger. McCain knew that tone. When he had been a child, a friend's parents had gone through a very bitter divorce that centered on a string of affairs his friend's father had been having. When his friend's parents argued, though, his father never accepted the responsibility—insisting his friend's mother had been the one who drove him to the affairs.

"Will's not blaming himself for what happened," McCain said. "He's blaming Laurel."

Shani shrugged. "Believe it or not, that's actually not an uncommon reaction to trauma. It's easier to blame the person who got hurt. It'll pass."

"Maybe," said McCain doubtfully. His cell phone rang. "Hello?"

The voice on the other end was mostly calm with only the slightest edge of tension. The anger that had shaken it a few minutes ago was either gone or well-concealed. "Rob? This is Will Tavish."

Shani said, "You're not supposed to use those in—"

McCain waved her to silence. "Will!" he said as cheerfully as he could.

Shani's eyes went wide when he said the name, and she darted to the door, glancing out into the hall. When she looked back, she shook her head and shrugged.

"How are you doing?" McCain said into the cell phone. "How's Laurel?"

"Not great—either of us that is."

There was quite a bit of noise in the background of Will's call. "Hey, where are you calling from? A mall?"

"Actually, I'm in the lobby at Presbyterian-St. Luke's. I've just come from visiting Laurel." His voice caught for a moment, then he cleared his throat. "Will, I was wondering if I could take you up on your offer to talk some more."

McCain could have choked. "Sure I can talk. When's good for you? I'm not far away from the hospital. I can be there in a few minutes."

"No!" Will coughed and repeated more calmly, "No. I don't think I can talk right now. I need some time. What about tonight?"

"Tonight?"

McCain really did choke this time. He looked pleadingly at Shani. She shook her head and pointed sharply at the phone. Her meaning was clear: Talking to Will was more important. McCain groaned silently to himself.

"Yeah," he said to Will, "tonight should be fine. Where?"

"There's a place just around the corner from North and Clybourn, down the street from the Golden Ox. It's an old bar called Ellie's. I'll meet you there at eight o'clock. I figure maybe we can have something stronger than coffee this time. I know I need it." He gave a bitter laugh.

"That sounds okay to me. I'll see you there."

"Thanks, Rob."

"No problem. See you tonight." McCain broke the connection. "Damn!"

Shani crossed her arms. "Unhappy with your work?" she asked sarcastically.

"There was something else I was looking forward to doing tonight." He slid the phone back into his pocket and smiled hopefully at her. "Can we reschedule our dinner for tomorrow?"

"I'm on duty Thursday nights."

"Friday? Maybe with something after dinner—I've found a club that has really good live bands on Friday."

"Done. But if you're not meeting Will until eight tonight, we still have time for a quick dinner. My treat unless you object to hospital cafeteria food."

"As long a I can buy you something better Friday."

"It's a deal." She stepped in close and gave him a quick kiss on the cheek. "Just leave your work at home."

chapter
8IGHT

When the Institute had assigned the team to Chicago and Jeane had gone looking for a place to live, part of what sold her on the apartment in the big old Victorian in Ukrainian Village was the neighborhood. When she was growing up in Parma, Ohio, her mother's best friend had been Ukrainian, and while Jeane had never been a real talent in the kitchen, she had fallen in love with Ukrainian cooking and culture. Chicago's Ukrainian Village, with its little ethnic food stores and restaurants was like a bit of her childhood come back. Since she moved in, she'd made a point of shopping in the local groceries rather than the big chain stores. She was starting to get to know the strengths of each shop. Ann's Bakery had the best bread and pastries, Corona had the best meat, and Teslenko's was the best all-around for fruit, vegetables, and general items. And the best pre-cooked, ready-to-go food to take home was at a big, crowded place called To The Table.

It was almost embarrassing to admit that she was starting to become a regular there. In spite of her mother's best efforts, Jeane still had no talent in the kitchen. Then again, her mother hadn't had a job outside of the house with a crosstown commute and the paranormal thrown in.

Jeane walked down the canned goods aisle, considering the range of soups on offer. After an afternoon of reading and research, soup sounded good. She picked an old favorite then paused at the end of the aisle to contemplate a bag of sourdough pretzels. When she looked up, Van Dimitriat was watching her from the other end of the aisle.

She blinked and looked again. It *was* Van, though he was turning away now as someone out of sight caught his attention. Jeane stepped quickly in the direction he had gone and looked up the next aisle under the guise of examining a display of imported wafers. Van was trailing behind a woman who bore a strong resemblance to him. His mother, maybe? That answered the question of what he was doing there, anyway. The woman looked as if she was doing some shopping—Dimitriat sounded like it could be a Ukrainian name, and Jeane doubted if there were many Ukrainian specialty stores in Midlothian. Van must have been dragged along for the ride.

So why did she get the feeling that he didn't seem surprised to see her? The memory of meeting Van's gaze as McCain pulled away from the doughnut shop rose unbidden in her thoughts, and an eerie prickle touched the back of her neck. Jeane shook her head sharply. No—something odd might have happened to her last night, but she wasn't about to let herself go all New Age sensitive just yet. McCain had said Van would come to them. Fine. Let him come. The next time Jeane caught Van peering at her, she very deliberately looked up, made eye contact with him, and promptly stepped around a corner out of sight of both him and his mother. She waited there, surrounded by tins of soup and packets of boil-in-the-bag dumplings.

Aside from the setting, it actually wasn't all that different from flirting with someone at a party. Tease them, play hard to get, and they'll come right—

Exactly on cue, Van stepped around the corner and into the aisle.

"Hello, Van." The boy almost jumped out of his pants, and Jeane felt a certain guilty pleasure in having gotten the drop on him. She gave him the same smile she had given cocky rookies in the ATF—friendly but with just a hint of teeth. "Imagine meeting you here."

"Uhh . . . yeah. Hi." She could almost see him struggling to regain the confidence she had just scared out him. "You're Wade Maxwell's assistant, right? Jane?"

"Jeane. Jeane Meara." She didn't see any point in making up another false name.

She held out her hand. After a moment's hesitation, he reached out to take it. As soon as his hand was in hers, Jeane squeezed. Not hard enough to hurt him, but hard enough to let him know she was in control. He let out a little gasp of surprise.

"You're following me," Jeane said simply.

"No!" The word came out as little better than a squeak. Van glanced around nervously. Looking for mommy, Jeane guessed. "I wanted to talk to you."

She didn't let go. "Why not call Wade? You had his number."

"He was so in your face at the shop it made me nervous. I didn't want to call him. But you were less threatening . . ." Jeane raised an eyebrow slightly, and Van backpedaled furiously. "I mean you seemed less threatening, and I knew you were going to be here tonight."

The prickle returned to her neck. "You . . . knew?"

Van nodded, and the prickle became a shiver.

He reached into his pocket and pulled out a fistful of receipts, once crumpled, now neatly folded and Jeane felt the eerie prickle on her neck turn into a very mundane burn of embarrassment as she recognized them. She wondered which of Van and his mother had really been dragged along for shopping at To The Table tonight.

"You left these on your table at the doughnut shop," Van said. "You've shopped here every Wednesday night for the last three weeks." He looked her straight in the eye, or at least tried to. He ended up staring at her chin. "You're not scouting Midlothian for a movie location, are you?"

The boy was perceptive. She considered stringing him along, but that was definitely McCain's way and not hers.

"No. We're not." She let go of his hand. "How did you guess?"

He looked around again, then dropped his voice low. "Because you asked about a mist in Bachelor's Grove." This time he met her eyes. "You want to know about the couple that were there in October, when the woman fell and hit her head."

Jeane just looked at him for a moment. They hadn't said anything about Laurel the other night. "You saw it," she said.

Van nodded. He didn't look happy.

"Do you want to talk about it?" Jeane asked.

"More than you'd believe," Van replied miserably. "I would have talked to you in the doughnut store yesterday except that my friends were around. I don't want them to know about this—or my mom."

"Fine. Outside?"

"Give me a minute to ditch my mom, and I'll meet you there." He ducked back into the other aisle.

Jeane took her purchases up to the checkout and waited impatiently as the line crawled forward. The store was always busy at this time of the evening, but it had never bothered her quite this much to wait. Then again, she had never had to rush out before. They had a witness. Finally she was through and stepping out into the cool night air. Van was waiting for her already, pacing back and forth in a tight little circle.

"Sorry that took so long," Jeane said.

He shrugged casually, but Jeane could see a nervous tension in his shoulders. "S'okay. I thought you would beat me outside—I told my mother I wanted to get outside for fresh air, and she decided to give me a lecture. She's been paranoid about letting me out of her sight since my dad left."

"I'm sorry to hear that." She nodded toward a sidewalk bench. "Sit. I'm not going to stand here with groceries. How long have we got?"

"Fifteen minutes at least. Ma's just getting warmed up, and some of her friends are shopping tonight. She'll stop to talk to them." They sat down, and Jeane dug into her coat pocket for a little notepad she kept there. She flipped it open, pulled the cap off her pen, and looked to Van.

"So," she asked, "what did you see?"

Van shifted and gave her an uncomfortable look. "A couple of weeks ago, me and some friends were out in the woods near the cemetery. We saw a man and a pregnant woman poking around the cemetery and stopped to watch them. All of a sudden, a mist came up out of the lagoon. The man and the woman got scared and started to run. I didn't see what happened next because the mist was so thick, but I heard a sound like somebody falling. The next thing I knew, the man came running out of the cemetery carrying the woman. Her head was bloody."

Jeane tapped the pen against her teeth and contemplated Van for a moment. He wasn't wearing the ball cap he'd been wearing the day before, but his blond hair was pressed down as if the cap was a semipermanent fixture on his head. That hair and the patchy beard on his otherwise smooth face belonged to someone young. The guarded eyes didn't.

"That's a pretty simple story to want to hide from your friends—especially if they were with you when you saw this."

"Those were different friends. One of them was with me at the doughnut shop, but he doesn't believe the same thing I do about what happened."

"And what's that?" Jeane asked. Van just looked down at the scarred wood of the bench. She waited a moment, then added, "Van, you were the one who wanted to talk about this."

"Yeah, it's just that . . ." He stuffed his hands into the pocket of his coat. "You're not a cop," he said bluntly, "or you wouldn't be sneaking around getting stories about the cemetery. And I don't think you're a private detective or something like that because you'd be asking about that couple and you're not." He looked up. "I think you want to know about that weird mist. And I think you know it's not natural."

"Maybe," Jeane said carefully. "Does that make a difference?"

Van almost looked relieved. "Yeah. It does. Because I think I'm the one that caused it."

Finding Ellie's had been difficult. Following Will's directions had been easy—Clybourn and North was a busy enough intersection, and the Golden Ox was a local institution. Ellie's, clearly, was not. McCain walked right past it twice before realizing that the grubby frontage actually concealed an operating bar.

Ellie's was a throwback to a time when what was now called the Clybourn Corridor had been a light industrial zone. Some of the industry still lingered, but most of it had left in the eighties, replaced by developments catering to the young and trendy. In stark contrast to the bars that had opened to cater to the area's new inhabitants, Ellie's was old-fashioned. Or maybe just old. Rather than being dim or strategically underlit, it was just plain dark. The flickering neon signs above the bar advertised beers McCain remembered his father drinking. There was an obnoxious haze of smoke in the air. The floor was uneven, most of the chairs needed mending, and McCain was certain that some of the myriad old photos that served as decoration also covered over patches and holes in the walls. Ellie's wasn't just a throwback, it was a throwback to a throwback.

He found Will sitting at a corner table. There was a half-empty pint glass on the table in front of him. To judge from the slackness of Will's face though, he had drunk far more than just half a pint. McCain slid into the chair across from him, grimacing as he touched the tabletop. The old varnish had gone soft and sticky with age and humidity.

"Evening, Will."

"Hey, Rob."

Will reached for the partial pint and drank deeply from it. When he put it down again, the half glass had diminished to a quarter. He stuck his hand up in the air, two fingers raised. The bartender saw him and nodded.

Will glanced at McCain and said, "One of those is for you."

"I'm glad to hear that." For this, thought McCain, I skipped an evening with Shani. He cleared his throat. "This isn't exactly the kind of bar I'd expect to find a professional man hanging out in, Will."

Will finally looked up, a brief smile flickering across his face. "Actually, 'professional' men did hang out here a lot at one time. It was a popular mob bar from the twenties until about World War II."

McCain looked at Will appraisingly. "So just how did you end up finding out about it?"

"It's kind of ironic actually." Will lifted his glass and took a long drink of his beer. "Remember I said I was interested in genealogy? Well, it's my paternal grandmother's family that's buried in Bachelor's Grove. The Harveys were one of the leading families in Midlothian. But even the best families have their black sheep, and for the Harveys it was Nana's twin brother, Jack. Nana moved to Chicago when she married into the Tavish family. Turns out Jack moved to Chicago too, except he joined the mob as a small-time goon." Will gestured around them. "I did some research on him, and apparently he used to hang out here, so I dropped by once to check it out. It seemed like a good place for a quiet drink tonight."

A waitress came up to the table with two fresh beers, thin and watery heads slopping over the rims of the glasses. Will smiled at her, drained off the rest of the glass he was working on, and passed it to her. McCain noticed that Ellie's didn't bother with such niceties as coasters.

"It might look a little rough, Rob, but the people are friendly," Will assured him.

"I'll keep it in mind for my niece's birthday party." He watched Will suck back another mouthful of beer. "Will, how many of these have you had?"

Will shrugged. "Enough." He set his glass down with a thump that brought bubbles frothing out of the amber liquid.

"Enough?"

"Enough to get seriously drunk. Liquid courage, Rob. Car's parked at home. I took a cab here, and I'll take a cab back." He drew a deep breath, then cut loose with a thunderous, stinking belch.

McCain looked at him narrowly. "Will, I know dealing with Laurel's accident is stressful, but this isn't the way to cope. Therapy . . ."

"Don't lecture me, Rob." Will's eyes went dark and hard. "I don't want to hear it."

This wasn't the Will he had had coffee with at the hospital, the man whose vulnerability had made McCain feel guilty for manipulating him. There was something harsh and ugly in him now, as though he had been pushed to the wall.

"All right," McCain agreed. "No lectures. You said you wanted to talk. Let's talk. Why are you drinking? To forget?"

Will's laugh was as hard as his eyes. "To remember, Rob. I'm drinking so that I *can* talk."

"You don't have to."

"Hey, do you know what's going on up here?" Will tapped on his temple. "Do you? Have you ever had a secret so big that just the thought of telling it to someone else made you want to piss your pants, and yet you knew you had to tell someone or you would go crazy?"

More than you know, thought McCain. He stared into Will's eyes. "Drinking is not going to help. Keep it up and it will only make things worse."

Will raised his glass in a mocking toast and said, "This is a one-time prescription. I'm going to feel like hell tomorrow, but I know I'll feel worse if I don't get this out of me."

He swallowed some more beer then set his glass down, carefully this time. He leaned forward. McCain could smell the beer on his breath.

"I didn't tell you everything that happened in the cemetery, Rob," Will went on. "I haven't told anybody. Every time I tried, something held me back. At first I thought it was just because I was afraid. Then I thought it was paranoia. Now I think it's something more. I've been drinking tonight to make it quiet, just for a little while."

His hand shot out and grabbed McCain's arm. His grip was tight with desperation. "There's a voice in my head, Rob. It started in Bachelor's Grove. When the mist surrounded us in the cemetery, when Laurel fell, something spoke to me."

The bar receded around them as McCain looked into Will's face. There was a mad, terrified desperation there. "What?"

"Something was there in the mist, whispering to me. And it's still here." He tapped his head again. "It's what kept me from telling you everything before."

"It . . . this voice . . ." McCain searched Will's drunken face. "What did you hear in the mist, Will?"

" 'I need her.' " Will drew a long, shuddering breath. "Whatever was in the mist, it wanted Laurel. It wanted her any way it could have her. Even dead."

Jeane gave Van a long look. "What do you mean, you 'caused' it?"

She would have liked it if the answer involved large quantities of dry ice dumped into the cemetery lagoon, but she had a nasty feeling that it didn't.

Van swallowed. "Look, you know that the cemetery has a big reputation for being the most haunted place in Chicago, right? Everybody in Midlothian knows the stories—and not just the kids, either. You heard Mr. Hendricks in the doughnut shop. I bet everybody who has grown up in Midlothian has sneaked out to Bachelor's Grove sometime."

"So that's what you did?" Jeane guessed. "You went out to the cemetery to try to see a ghost?"

"Sort of," Van admitted. "Except we didn't want to just wait around. So back in the summer when my mother dragged me into Chicago to go shopping with her, I ducked into a used bookstore and found a book on séances."

Jeane, just putting pen back to paper, started so badly that her pen left a streak of ink across her notepad. She glanced up sharply.

"Not a basement store in Wicker Park," she said.

"No, just around the corner from here." He jerked his thumb vaguely over his shoulder. "Why?"

"Never mind." Jeane drew in a relieved breath. "So you held a séance in Bachelor's Grove Cemetery?" she guessed.

"In a way. Nothing happened." Van shivered and Jeane had a suspicion that it wasn't just because of the cold. "At least, we thought nothing happened."

"But now you're doubting that?"

"Wouldn't you?" His brow furrowed for a moment then he looked up at her. "We decided to try the séance a second time," he said firmly. Jeane recognized the sound of decision in his voice. There was no going back for him now. He was letting everything come out. "So we went out in the afternoon to hide the stuff we'd need at night. That's when the couple came up the path, so we hid. And we saw what happened."

He described again what he had seen that day in the cemetery, though this time in more detail. Most of it agreed with what Will had told McCain. Some details were new though. The way the mist stayed so perfectly within the borders of the cemetery. A stillness very much like what Jeane and McCain had experienced the night before. Finally, the sounds that had occurred in the mist: a gasp, a thud, and Will's crying out.

When he was finished, Van was breathing hard, his breath making big white clouds in the cold air. Jeane considered her notes, then looked up at Van. "So what did Dave, Tawny, and Boone make of all this?"

"We were all scared at first and we ran. Nobody said

anything, and we all just went home. But the next day, Dave and Tawny were already laughing about it, and saying that they couldn't believe how scared we all were of a little fog." He gave her a lopsided grin, trying to look confident. "But I've noticed they haven't told anybody else around school about it. Boone's pretty creeped out by the whole thing. I don't think he really knows what to think."

"But he's keeping it quiet?" Van nodded, and Jeane made a note on her pad, then studied Van for a moment longer.

"When did you . . ." She hesitated.

Was it really possible that Van and his friends had roused one of the legendary spirits of the cemetery? Come on, Jeane, she chided herself, at least try to stay objective here.

"When did you make the connection between your séances and what you saw?" she asked.

"A few days later," said Van miserably. "I was cleaning out my backpack looking for my copy of *Macbeth,* and I found the séance book. The more I thought about it, the more it was the only thing that made sense. We were trying to summon a ghost in Bachelor's Grove, and something answered. Only we didn't know it. Or *I* didn't know it. I was the one who led all the séances."

He sat back against the bench. Jeane sighed.

"You know, this might not be a ghost at all," she said. "There could be a perfectly rational explanation for everything that's going on."

"Everything?" Van looked up instantly. "There's more?"

Damn. "Sharp, aren't you?" she asked, dodging his question. "Where are you going to college next year?"

He shook his head. "I'm not. My parents were saving up, but my dad took the money when he left. Now we can't afford it. I don't qualify for the right kinds of assistance, and I don't quite have the grades to get a scholarship."

"Oh." Jeane grimaced. "Sorry."

"I'm over it. " Van stretched and pointed at her note-book. "So did what I know help you?"

Jeane nodded slowly. "Possibly. I'm going to have to talk to my partner and sort it all out. Is there a way we can get in touch with you if we need to?"

"I have my own phone number." He gave it to her, then paused. "The couple from the cemetery. Are they all right?"

"No," Jeane told him bluntly. "The woman—her name is Laurel—is in Presbyterian-St. Luke's in a coma. Her husband is nuts with worry."

"I'm sorry. Really."

"Don't be, Van. Even if you did start this, it wasn't inten-tional. And telling me was the right thing to do." She tucked her notepad back into her pocket and gathered her groceries.

"I should go," she said. "Your mother is going to be out soon. Thanks for your help." She shook his hand and turned to go.

"Jeane," Van asked suddenly, "who do you work for? Who really wants to know about Bachelor's Grove?"

"Nobody," lied Jeane. "Just me and my partner."

"Dead?" Rob asked, leaning forward. "How do you know?"

Somewhere in the depths of Will's mind the voice seethed.

He doesn't believe you! Why are you telling him this?

The voice was virtually impotent now though, mired in beer like an angry wasp in mud. Will let go of Rob's arm and gave him a sharp smile.

"Ever read a book where someone looked at something and just knew it was evil?" Will said. "It was like that."

The words came out a little slurred. God, he hadn't been

this drunk since college. How desperate was he? Really desperate. He had to get this out.

"Remember, I said I wondered sometimes if it was my fault Laurel hurt herself?"

Rob answered slowly. "Yes, but it was just an accident." He paused for a moment. "It *was* an accident, wasn't it?"

He's scared.

Will ignored the voice. He knotted his fingers tightly together and pressed his joined hands against the tabletop. He was going to say it this time. Inside his head, the voice was wailing dire warnings and threatening him. He couldn't shut it out but he could talk over it.

"I think Laurel fell and hit her head. But I keep having a vision of something else happening. I see her falling—"

You're shouting. Do you want the whole bar to hear this?

"Shut up!" he snapped.

Rob sat back suddenly, surprise on his face, and Will realized the warning hadn't been the voice trying to trick him into silence. It had been Rob trying to calm him down. He jerked his hands apart and grabbed for his beer.

"Sorry," he whispered into the glass.

He took a long, long swallow, keeping his mouth full while he fought for control. Was the voice breaking free? It couldn't be.

Will set the beer down, put his hands flat on the table, and said again, "I see Laurel falling . . ."

He could see it all as if he were still there in Bachelor's Grove. Laurel was on the ground. The fall had shocked her, maybe knocked the wind out of her, but she was okay. They could still get away.

No! I need her now!

The desperation of the thing in the mist was over-whelming. Invasive. Laurel couldn't be allowed to leave. There was a stone near her temple. Will watched his hand spread itself gently across her head. Did Laurel look up?

Did she know what he was doing? Did her eyes beg him to stop? He didn't. In one fast motion, he slammed Laurel's head against the stone.

Will forced himself to describe the vision aloud. Every terrible moment of it. When he finished, he was almost choking. He stared down at the dark, cloudy varnish of the tabletop as if his gaze could burn right through it.

"It's so real, Rob. As real as what I think I remember about Laurel hitting her head."

For several long moments, Rob was silent, and in that awful, guilty void, all Will could think was that he had said too much. Rob was scared. Rob thought he was a monster. Will's stomach churned in terror. *What have I done?*

Finally, Rob drew a long breath and said, "Will, does . . . does the voice still want Laurel dead?"

"The voice still wants *Laurel*, Rob," he said tightly. He was sweating and shaking. "I would never hurt her!" He squeezed his eyes shut. It was a bad idea. Suddenly everything was spinning. He forced them open again. When he talked, his voice sounded disembodied. "I'm worried that it's waiting now. Waiting until I'm vulnerable."

Rob just looked at him. "Why are you telling me this, Will?"

Will reached for his beer and swallowed yet another mouthful. "Because you offered to listen. Because you don't really know me from Adam. Because I had to tell somebody!" He caught Rob's gaze and held it. "What should I do, Rob?"

Rob was silent again, then he pulled out one of his cards and wrote a name and number on the back.

"Will, I'm saying this because I really mean it—you need to see a professional about this right away." He pushed the card over in front of Will. "This is a psychiatrist I know."

Will glared at the card. "Well, I guess that answers the question of what you think."

"I'm sorry, Will. I am. But you can trust her. I want you to call her first thing in the morning, as soon as you're sober." He looked into Will's eyes. "Are you going to be all right until then?"

"I'm not going to break into the hospital and try to kill Laurel if that's what you mean." Will took a deep breath and stood up slowly "I think it's time for me to go."

"I'm sorry, Will."

"Yeah. So am I." He pulled out some cash and threw it on the table. "That will cover everything."

He turned, staggering toward the door. At least the voice was silent.

As soon as Will was gone, McCain whipped out his cell phone and punched Shani's number. It seemed to ring forever before she picked it up. "Shani—it's Fitz."

"Hi!" Her voice was sunshine. "How's Will?"

"Bad . . ."

He gave her a synopsis of what had just happened.

"I gave him the number of an Institute psychiatrist. Can you find a way to keep a guard on Laurel's room without letting Will know something is up?"

"I'll make the calls." She hesitated, then added, "Fitz, I don't know if the doctor who examined Laurel for the police looked for the kind of bruising that an attack like that would leave."

"Would it leave any at all?"

"Maybe," Shani said doubtfully. "Laurel had thick hair that would have cushioned her scalp. And you make it sound like the motion used was relatively gentle."

"Can you look?"

"The attack in the cemetery was over two weeks ago. If there was any bruising, it will have faded."

He clenched his fist in silent frustration. "Thanks anyway."

"You sound rough."

"Don't worry about me, Shani." McCain glanced toward the bar door. "Worry about Will."

McCain pulled into the decrepit parking lot of the Institute branch office hard on Jeane's bumper. She glared at him as she got out of her car.

"What gives?" she asked. "You've been tailgating me for the last five miles."

She had to shout over the rumble of one of the innumerable jets passing overhead on approach to O'Hare. Institute branch offices were supposed to be inconspicuous, but Chicago's, buried in the labyrinthine industrial parks of Schiller Park, took it to extremes.

"I've got news," McCain shouted back.

Jeane looked him over as she reached back into the car and pulled out several of her books. McCain's face was neutral, but his body was as tense as a just-wound clock spring.

"Well," she said, "you're not the only one."

She hipchecked the car door shut and stepped up onto the cracked sidewalk that ran across the front of the building. McCain fell into step beside her.

"Want to share?" he asked, opening the front door for her.

"Only if you share first."

Jeane breezed past him. The receptionist stationed at the desk in the tiny public lobby nodded at them, then went back to her work. Jeane juggled her books for a moment while she waved her key card over the electronic lock on the inner door. She paused on the other side to give McCain a chance to do the same.

She favored him with a smile when he came through and asked, "So what have you got?"

"What have *you* got?" He closed one eye and squinted at her with the other as they walked down the long hall to their offices. "No, wait. Let me guess. You brought the books, so I'll say that you've found some information for us."

"Not as such. The books are just research. Want to try again?"

The hallway opened out into the outer office. Emma looked up as they entered. She had a fax machine broken down into pieces and laid out across her desk.

"Ngan wants to see you," the secretary said. McCain's eyebrows went up in surprise, and his finger wavered between himself and Jeane. Emma gave him a weary look. "It's not always about you, Fitz. He wants to see both of you."

"When?"

Emma was already picking up her telephone. "ASAP." She dialed Ngan's extension

"Oh, well, Fitz," Jeane chided, "looks like you won't get to play twenty questions after all."

Jeane juggled books again and reached for the knob on

the door of their office. McCain snaked his hand past and opened it for her.

"Would it have been worth it?" he asked.

"Absolutely." Jeane smiled again.

It was actually a surprisingly pleasant feeling: She had beaten McCain at his own game. McCain might have predicted that Van would come to them, but she was the one who had made contact with him. What was better, a dive through the books from Devromme's suggested that the young man might actually be right in his suspicions. At first Jeane couldn't quite bring herself to accept that a high school séance could produce any real effect at all. It was too much like a bad movie. But after she'd left Van she had gone back to her apartment and started checking through her books. There was actually some truth to the power of séances it seemed. Of course, with what she had seen since joining the Institute, that shouldn't have surprised her.

More importantly than simply one-upping McCain, it also gave them a fresh lead in the investigation. Jeane had all of the relevant research flagged. Perversely, she was as eager to present it to McCain and Ngan as if it were carefully gathered hard evidence for a more mundane, scientific explanation.

"Don't you want to know what I found out?" McCain asked.

He seemed a little put out. Jeane turned her smile on him as she pulled off her jacket. "Maybe later."

It was hardly the attitude of a good investigator, but for now she wanted to savor the moment of her own triumph. She picked up the books again, ready to face Ngan, and nodded toward the door. "After you," she invited McCain.

Ngan, though, was already coming out of his office as they stepped out of theirs.

"Good," he said, closing the door behind him, "you're here. I have news."

McCain grunted. "It seems to be the morning for it." He jerked a thumb toward Jeane. "If she makes you guess at what she's got, I'd pull rank."

"Fitz," said Jeane smugly, "I can't wait for you to hear what I've got." She turned to Ngan. "I—"

He held up a hand, gesturing for her silence. "Let me tell you my news first. After the debriefing yesterday, I started thinking about your encounter on the turnpike and about something Michael said in the hospital when we first started the investigation. Michael, you were right: None of us have dealt with something like this before. There is someone in the Institute who is more qualified to deal with what we seem to be facing."

McCain's eyes went narrow. Jeane felt her own heart skip a beat. She had a nasty feeling she knew what he was about to say. "Ngan, don't tell me you've—"

"I've called in a specialist."

For a moment, there was utter silence in the outer office. Even Emma paused in her repair of the fax machine. All Jeane could do was look at Ngan. His face betrayed nothing. It never did. She was the first one to say anything.

"You did what?" she asked slowly.

"I've asked a specialist to step in. He's not one of our regular agents, but he is attached to the Institute." Ngan turned to his door and put his hand on the handle. "Come in and meet him."

"Wait a minute." Jeane could feel the blood rushing in her head. "I thought we were just getting a grip on this investigation."

"And what happened to learning while we work? Did we miss a pop quiz somewhere?" spat McCain. "Don't tell me we got into a chase with a phantom car for nothing."

Ngan looked at McCain then back at Jeane without removing his hand from the handle.

"It is exactly because of your experience with the ghost car that I called him in," Ngan explained. "What would you have done if the mist hadn't fallen away? And as your meeting with Will last night indicates, Michael, the ghost presents a clear danger—both to you and to others."

Jeane shot McCain a glance. A meeting with Will? Was that his news? And he had told Ngan first? She clenched her jaw.

"Would you care to elaborate on that last bit, Fitz?" she asked sarcastically.

At least McCain looked a little bit embarrassed. Ngan just shook his head and told her, "In good time. For now I want to know that you understand why I did this."

Jeane took a deep breath. Back in the ATF, "specialist" had been a dirty word. When one got called in, it meant someone was going to be taking control of your investigation. She knew—she had been the specialist often enough. No matter how courteous she tried to be, she was always unwelcome from the start. Now she knew why. It hurt right from the moment your chief told you a specialist was coming.

Yet Ngan was right. They were fumbling their way through the case. They needed guidance. Especially if evidence had turned up that things were getting ugly. She was going to have a talk with McCain about that. In the meantime, though . . .

She took another deep breath, swallowed her pride to make room for professionalism, and said, "I understand."

Ngan looked to McCain. The young man was unusually silent, but he finally nodded stiffly.

"I'll accept that," Ngan sighed.

He opened the door and led them into his office. A large, heavy man in a black blazer sat at the big meeting table. He looked up as they entered. A beautiful smile cut through his scruffy beard.

"Well," said Ned Devromme. "Isn't this a coincidence?"

Jeane flinched, sucking in a sharp breath. "No . . ."

Ngan raised an eyebrow as he walked around to the head of the table. "Since it appears you two know each other, I'll skip that introduction. Ned, this is the third member of my team, Michael McCain. Michael, Ned Devromme."

"A pleasure." Ned shook McCain's hand without bothering to get up. "You must be the 'Fitz' I heard Jeane snarling at on the other side of the door."

"Michael," corrected McCain coolly. He turned to Ngan. "I want to talk about this."

"There is nothing to talk about. Ned will be joining your investigation." Ngan sat down.

While McCain glared balefully at Ngan, and the old man took it all with the unyielding strength of a mountain, Jeane steeled herself and stepped up to the table as well. There were two free chairs—right beside Devromme or directly across from him. It wasn't much of a choice, but Jeane opted for having the width of the table between them. She moved for the chair beside Ngan.

McCain, still glaring at Ngan, beat her to it. Before she could sit, he pulled the chair out and sat down himself. Jeane fought back a hiss and looked up to see Ned smiling at her. He jumped up immediately and gallantly drew out the chair beside him. Jeane looked around for another chair—any chair—that she could draw up beside McCain.

"Jeane," said Ngan wearily, "please sit down."

That didn't leave her much choice. Feeling pretty baleful herself, she edged around the table and slid into the chair that Ned held.

"Ngan has told me something about you and your investigation," he whispered as he took his seat beside her. "I should have guessed you were involved when he started talking about Bachelor's Grove."

"I should have guessed you were the specialist when I slipped on the trail of slime in the lobby."

Ned shivered. "Ooo. You know, I don't think you need me at all—the dead may be the only ones who can properly appreciate your subtle wit."

He smiled at her again, and if his shiver hadn't been real, Jeane's was. Why did such a repulsive man have to have such a beautiful mouth? Set against the rest of him, it was almost obscene. In fact, it brought a kind of disturbing sensuality to the whole package of him. His eyes were sharp and challenging. His broad belly and hefty frame spoke of someone who enjoyed life's pleasures. His hands, resting lightly on the table, were big and heavy, his fingers thick and strong. The image of him giving her a shoulder massage flashed through her mind. She shook her head violently. That was an unwholesome image!

"I can't work with him," she snapped at Ngan.

"You have to."

"Why?" demanded McCain. "Why do we have to have another person involved?"

"News flash, pretty boy. I'm already involved." Ned reached across in front of Jeane to tap her books. "Who do you think got you as far as you've come? These came from my bookstore . . . Fitz." He savored the nickname while McCain flushed sunburn red.

Jeane shoved Ned's arm away and said, "Your bookstore maybe, but we did the work."

McCain spun around to look at Ngan. "Your specialist owns a bookstore? Why does that not inspire my confidence?"

Ngan frowned. "Would you have been happier if he had been a lawyer or perhaps a former government investigator?" he asked gently.

Jeane caught the irony in Ngan's voice immediately—and the tension. She even saw them register on Ned, his mouth snapping shut and his eyes focusing on Ngan. McCain, though, didn't seem to notice anything.

"I would have been happier if you had asked us before you called in a specialist," McCain said, gesturing dismissively toward Ned. "Who is this guy, anyway?"

"Enough, Michael." This time Ngan's voice, though still quiet, was hard enough to break through even McCain's anger. "First, I am in charge of this team, and I don't have to ask your consent before bringing in outside help. Please remember that."

Under the force of Ngan's voice, McCain was slowly sitting back in his chair, the anger draining out of his face. Ngan, on the other hand, was leaning forward, his voice as perfectly controlled as sharp steel in the hands of a master swordsman.

"Second, your complaining—and—" he shot at Jeane and Ned—"your bickering, have not left me the opportunity to introduce him properly."

Ngan drew a tight breath and said, "Ned is the best psychic working for the Hoffmann Institute in Chicago."

McCain was flat back in his chair, silent but clearly not cowed. His eyes were harsh, his jaw tight. His gaze flickered from Ngan to Ned.

Jeane looked at Ned, too, giving him new consideration. A psychic? Him? "You're kidding."

"No," Ngan said flatly.

He sat back, his face as inscrutable as always, his voice calm and uninflected once more. Ned coughed modestly.

"Actually, he is being remarkably unflattering in his accuracy." A smile tripped on the corners of his mouth and sharpness came back to his eyes. "The best psychic in Chicago doesn't work for the Institute. She's a reporter for one of the alternative papers. The best psychic working for the Institute . . . ah, well." His smile came on full. "That's a matter for debate, but I like to think I'm in the top five."

Oh, so humble! Jeane bit back her sarcasm and said, "So tell us—why do we need one of the Institute's top five psychics helping us?"

Ned spread his hands. "Because you're dealing with a ghost—a psychic presence—in the most haunted place in Chicago. Because you've gotten as far as mundane investigation is going to get you. And—" he glanced at Ngan— "because I understand that what you're chasing is getting violent."

"So you're our psychic bodyguard?" muttered McCain.

"Not just yours, Fitz," said Ned with a sneer. "I believe there's a matter of a lady in a coma."

Laurel. Jeane ground her teeth together. Was he implying that they had forgotten Laurel?

"Ned," she said through her teeth, "I think you might want to reconsider that statement."

"Touched a nerve, did I?"

McCain was sitting upright again. "Does he know about Will?" he demanded of Ngan.

The old man nodded. "Ned, my agents do know what they're doing."

Jeane could see McCain bristle at the concept of being one of Ngan's agents, but she was bristling herself.

"You mentioned Will before, Fitz," she said. "What about him?"

Ngan and McCain exchanged glances. "You haven't told her yet?" Ngan asked.

"You didn't give me a chance." McCain folded his arms on the table. "Will and I got together for a drink last night," he explained. "In a nutshell, there's a voice in his head, one that he's been hearing since the first attack in the cemetery. It wants Laurel. Will thinks it might actually have prompted him to injure her when she fell."

She caught his meaning immediately. "She didn't hit her head on a rock?"

McCain shook his head. "Will isn't sure. She might have—or Will might have listened to the voice and done it for her while she was down, just like the cops suspected. I can't tell if he did or not. Even if he didn't, though, the voice is still hounding him. It still wants her." He looked around the table. "I think it's the ghost."

"Either that," Jeane pointed out flatly, "or schizophrenia. There doesn't have to be a paranormal cause. He is going through a very rough time. That could have been the trigger."

In spite of her frustration with McCain for talking to Will without her, she found a strange reassurance in his discovery. She had dealt with the consequences of mental illness before. Schizophrenia was real. It was treatable. It was, in some ways, predictable.

Yet none of those ways predicted impossible fog and vanishing Model As on high-speed chases down the Midlothian Turnpike. Jeane realized that she was biting on her thumbnail and quickly pulled it out of her mouth. She glanced at Ned. He was staring at her. Their eyes met, and he smiled.

"Are you asking *me*?" He touched a hand to his chest. "Are you asking *my* opinion?"

Jeane glowered at him with narrowed eyes. The sleazy, arrogant bastard. The . . . the . . . *specialist*! She let her silence speak for itself.

Ned just twitched his eyebrows at her. "Well? Are you asking?"

"Fine," she growled. "What do you think? That's assuming you're capable of thought, of course."

"Ever the gracious one, aren't you?" Ned sat up to the table as though settling in behind a lectern. "Jeane does have a point," he said to McCain and Ngan. "It could be schizophrenia. But in this case, I'd go with Fitz's opinion. There's a good chance that it's the presence. The initial attack in the cemetery points to its interest in Laurel, as do the events at the hospital. If both the presence and the voice want Laurel, there's a good chance they're the same."

"Is it trying to possess Will?" asked Ngan with a frown.

Ned shook his head. "Contrary to popular belief, ghosts don't possess people."

"Ah-ha!" Jeane pounced on Ned's words. She grabbed her books, flipping through them to find the passages that would prove him wrong. She found the first. "*Vodun*— voodoo. Practitioners believe spirits possess them."

Ned shook his head again and said, "*Loa* aren't ghosts."

"All right." She flipped to another spot in the same book. "Automatic writing. It was popular in the twenties. Ghosts possessed people and guided their handwriting."

"Sorry," smiled Ned. "Not possession. Not even ghosts actually."

Jeane growled and reached for another book, the big blue one Ned had pulled out from behind the velvet curtain in his shop.

"1876. A newly ordained priest in Boston officiating at his predecessor's funeral greeted each parishioner by name and proceeded to give the final sermon that the late priest had written but never delivered." She slapped the book on the table and pushed it in front of him. "How about them apples?"

Ned studied the passage, flipped a few pages forward and back, then looked up. Jeane was surprised to see respect in his eyes.

"You've only had this book for a couple of days," he said.

"I'm thorough."

"So it seems." He pushed the book back to her and corrected himself. "*Most* ghosts don't possess people. But when possession does occur—whatever the source—it is fast and complete. The host is either possessed or it isn't. There's none of the continual urging that Will's experiencing." Ned scratched at his beard. "It's more like the presence is simply talking to him."

"A sustained whisper can be a very effective psychological weapon," observed Ngan.

Ned tapped his fingers on the tabletop. "But that would mean the presence is manifesting in some form in three different locations: at Presbyterian-St. Luke's, in Bachelor's Grove, and with Will. I've never heard of such a thing." He looked over at Jeane. "Unless you want to surprise me with something, all the ghosts I'm aware of have been linked to a place, or occasionally to a specific thing, or even more occasionally to a specific person. Call it their focus. To appear in three places implies three foci."

"Or a single one that we haven't identified yet," Jeane suggested.

"Or that," Ned agreed. "Either way Bachelor's Grove is where the presence originated, and that's where the answer will be. It might even be possible to settle this question of which of the cemetery's spirits is at work. Ngan, we need to go back out to Bachelor's Grove."

McCain made a strangled noise. "*We*?"

"Michael, would you just do it?" sighed Ngan. "The idea might not have been yours, but it's still a good idea." He nodded to Ned. "Go this afternoon."

"No." Jeane looked up at Ngan. He might have surprised them by calling in a specialist and McCain might have gotten to him first with the information about Will, but she still had her news. She had started off the day excited about it, and she was damned if Ned's unexpected presence was going to ruin *that* surprise. "Tonight."

Ngan did not look happy. "Jeane, please don't make this difficult."

"Trust me, Ngan, I have a good reason." She smiled at

McCain. "Remember Van Dimitriat? Well, you weren't the only one to run into someone with a secret last night."

She described Van's confession of a séance in Bachelor's Grove and his fears about what he had seen of the attack on Will and Laurel.

"I think he should be there, too," she said, "but he'll be in school this afternoon. We have to go tonight when he can come. He may be able to fill us in on something important."

Ngan put his elbow on the table and rested his chin on his fist. He looked at her for a long moment, and Jeane could see weary frustration in his eyes. She felt no guilt at all. It served him right for springing a specialist on them, even if the specialist was turning out to be rather useful. Finally Ngan turned to Ned. "What do you think?"

The psychic shrugged. "Frankly, I'd rather go at night anyway. It's a better time for this kind of work."

"Do it, then. This meeting is over. I'll see you tomorrow." Ngan stood up and gestured for them to go. "Jeane, can you ask Emma if she'll give me a few minutes before she brings in the next round of paperwork."

"Will do." Jeane stepped up to McCain as they filed out of the office. "So what do you think? Was my news worth the wait?"

He made a sour face. "Would have been better if I didn't want to bust Ngan's chops so bad." He took a deep breath and smiled. "It was good, Jeane. Didn't I tell you Van would come to us?"

"You didn't expect him to confess to raising the ghost though, did you?"

"Gloating does not become you anymore than command becomes Ngan." He glanced back over his shoulder. Ned was just emerging from Ngan's office. "What do we do about our psychic specialist?"

Jeane cringed inwardly at what she was about to say. She forced herself to remember Laurel and Will and the cold fear of the phantom car pursuing them through the mist. "The only thing we can do now—put up with him."

Once they were all out of his office, Ngan slid into the big leather chair behind his desk and covered his eyes with the palms of his hands. It wasn't supposed to be this way. He had listened to and weighed McCain's complaint that they knew nothing about spirits, then acted on it, but McCain just seemed more resentful than before. Jeane clearly loathed Ned on some personal level, while the big man took inordinate delight in taunting her. To cap it all, he had all but told the agents directly that he was concerned about their safety. The concept seemed totally lost on them.

At least Jeane appeared willing to accept Ned's help, however grudgingly. The cases she had so quickly presented to refute his argument had somehow impressed Ned as well. His voice had lost its sharp edge when he talked to her, as if he had accepted her as something approaching an equal.

That just left McCain. Ngan groaned and pulled his hands away to stare up at the shadows of his office ceiling. What was he going to do about him? Twice now on this investigation, McCain's constant pushing had almost made him lose his temper. That wasn't a thing that happened easily, though it seemed to be happening more easily since the transfer to Chicago, since he had been shut away in this room, doing paperwork and attending meetings instead of being out in the field where he belonged. He rolled his head around to look at the shadows and empty places of his office. Getting out to Presbyterian-St. Luke's at the start of the investigation had felt good, but that blessed respite had been three days ago.

The longing to be out with his team in the cemetery tonight filled him up and for a moment he let himself wallow in it. Only for a moment, though. Then he put self-pity away and reached for the newest pile of folders. Longing did no good. He had his own work to do now. He opened the first folder and settled in to a tedious report.

The phone on his desk rang before he was halfway through the first page. He glared at the phone. The flashing light and the insistent, incessant buzzing ring reminded him too much of McCain. He took his time answering it, a petty vengeance.

"Ngan Song Kun'dren," he said wearily.

"Ngan, it's Shani Doyle."

There was urgency in the doctor's voice. Ngan sat up. "What's wrong?"

"The decision has been made to deliver Laurel's baby by cesarean section." From Shani's tone, Ngan guessed that she had not been a part of that decision. "The operation is scheduled for this evening."

Ngan frowned into the handset. "Will the baby be all right?"

"The obstetrician and the neonatologist think it'll be fine. They barely even consider it to be premature—it was practically at term when she went into the coma." She sighed. "I'm more concerned about Laurel."

"You don't think she'll make it?"

"It will be hard on her, but I can see where the OB is coming from. Laurel isn't showing any improvement, and her nightmare episode the other night doesn't put a good face on things. We may need to start prescribing drugs that could hurt the baby. If her body doesn't have to support the baby, she might recover that much more quickly, but until she does, she'll be weak. Very weak."

Shani's voice broke off as she lapsed into abrupt silence. It didn't matter. Ngan had heard enough to hazard a guess at the reason for her urgent call. "You think the spirit may try to take her tonight."

"Yes."

"Is Will going to be present?" It was almost a ridiculous question. Of course he would be there. It was the birth of his first child, no matter how unconventional. He asked the question he should have asked in the first place. "Is she under guard?"

"Someone is watching her, but I can't keep Will away from her without having a good reason. McCain's say-so might be enough for me, but it wouldn't be enough for hospital security." She hesitated, then added, "What about the ghost itself? It did push me. Could it attack Laurel directly?"

"It hasn't attacked her yet," Ngan pointed out, "and she has been vulnerable for some time."

Still, Shani's fears were reasonable. More than that, he had a strong premonition that they were correct. He had learned long ago to listen to his premonitions. They might not have been as reliable as some of the other mental and physical disciplines he had mastered during his youth at the Monastery of Inner Light in Tibet, but when they manifested, they were invariably accurate. Someone who knew what was going on needed to be at the hospital to watch over Laurel.

He hesitated to reassign either McCain or Jeane. The cemetery needed to be investigated again and the sooner the better. Ngan's eyes fell across the folders and papers piled on his desk. They needed to be looked after, but Laurel's need was greater.

"What if someone from the Institute was present?" he asked Shani. "What if I was there?"

"You won't be able to stay after visiting hours."

"Never mind that."

There would be a way, he was confident of that. And he

was growing more confident as the idea of leaving the office for real work grew stronger. His head felt more clear than it had in weeks. Even McCain's sullen moods seemed like trifling things.

He said, "I'll be there."

The police cruiser came up from behind, passed them, swung around at the end of 143rd Street and came back, then slowed to a stop beside McCain's car so that the driver's side windows were facing each other. McCain rolled down his window and nodded to the driver of the cruiser.

"Hello, Officer Jessop," McCain said. "Checking up on us?"

Officer Jessop returned his nod. "Thought I might, Mr. Maxwell. I didn't think you'd still be cooling your heels on the street when you seemed so anxious to get into Bachelor's Grove tonight."

"Still waiting for my assistant to show up," McCain replied with a cheerful grin.

Hadn't he told Jeane that having the cops on their side was a good thing? One of the first things he'd done after leaving Ngan's office was put in a phone call to Officer Jessop. Wade Maxwell wanted to do a little location scouting in Bachelor's Grove after dark. Jessop had been reluctant at first, but McCain was able to talk him into it. There wouldn't be any surprise visits from the police or the forest preserve rangers tonight.

There had been an unexpected side benefit as well. When Jeane had called to arrange Van's attendance, his mother had insisted on knowing where her son was going. Van told her that location scouts for a movie wanted information from a local teenager. She was suspicious until McCain told her to call Officer Jessop.

"Did Anna Dimitriat get in touch with you to check us out?" McCain asked the cop.

"Yeah. I vouched for you," Jessop replied. he peered past McCain to the passenger seat. "Who's this?"

McCain turned to introduce Ned, an alias rolling up in his mind, but Ned leaned forward himself before he could say anything.

"Edward Wells," Ned said quickly. "I'm the producer. Or I will be if this lump ever gets his butt in gear. Flew in today from L.A."

Ned shoved his bulk in front of McCain and thrust a hand through the window toward Jessop. His fingers barely cleared the window frame. Jessop just waved at him.

"Nice to meet you."

His voice implied he'd as soon be scraping something noxious off the bottom of his shoe. Ned withdrew in a sulk. McCain rolled his eyes in annoyance and not entirely just for Jessop's benefit. Jessop gave him a little smile of sympathy.

"Just let me know when you've finished in the cemetery, Mr. Maxwell," Jessop said. "Have a good night."

"Thanks. You, too."

The cruiser pulled away, and McCain rolled the window back up. "Producer?" he asked.

Ned looked down his nose at him. "You think I'm going

to be another one of your assistants? Forget that." He plucked a box off the dashboard and opened it up. "Want another doughnut?"

"No, thanks."

McCain slouched back down in his seat, staring up through the windshield at the almost full moon that glowed in the sky. Smooth, impassive, and swollen—just like Ngan's head. The old man didn't wear command well. He was pushy, annoying, and interfering. He had grabbed the biggest office and he never did the dirty work in the field anymore. Paperwork and meetings, my ass, McCain thought.

There was the whole matter of Ned, of course. Of all the arrogant things Ngan could have done, bringing in the fat man "in the team's best interest" had been the most insulting. How had he expected them to react to that? With gratitude? It was like a vote of no-confidence in their first investigation as a team.

It didn't help at all that, as Jeane pointed out, Ned might actually be the right man for the job. McCain flicked a harsh glance at him. Only to find that Ned was already staring at him.

"What?" McCain growled.

"Nothing," Ned replied with a shrug. He wiped powdered sugar from his beard. "You remind me of somebody, and I was trying to figure out who."

Oh, that was all he needed. "John F. Kennedy?" he snapped sourly.

Ned snorted sharply and dipped back into the doughnut box. "Don't flatter yourself, pretty boy. I was thinking of my uncle Wally. JFK? Please." His hand emerged with a doughnut frosted in a pale pink. He looked at it with suspicion. "The man has been dead for almost forty years. Let him go."

McCain could only stare at him in amazement. For virtually his entire life, everybody who looked at him had almost instantly come up with "you look like JFK" or, at the very least, "you look like a Kennedy." To be compared to Uncle Wally was an astonishing new feeling. Even more astonishing was to be *insulted* for even suggesting that he might look like the assassinated president.

Ned must have mistaken his stunned silence for shock and anger, because he rolled right along, gesturing with the doughnut. "I mean the significance you people attach to this guy, the myths you've built up—it's a national obsession. Get over it. The world couldn't care less."

McCain managed to find his voice again. "'You people?'" he asked.

"There are advantages to being Canadian," Ned said, "and one of them is getting to snicker at some of the stupid things you lot do."

He consumed half of the doughnut in one bite, then made a face. "By the way," he mumbled around the mouthful, "you also make lousy doughnuts."

Several crumbs sprayed out of his mouth and landed in his beard. He brushed them away absently with his free hand.

McCain sat back. "So you don't think I look like JFK?" It felt strangely good to say that. Maybe he would have to rethink his evaluation of the psychic.

"Only as much as Uncle Wally does." Ned swallowed. "Now Jeane, on the other hand—have you noticed how much she looks like Marilyn Monroe? Without the blond hair and mole, of course, and with about fifteen extra pounds and a lot more attitude."

Now it was McCain's turn to snort in derision. "Uh-huh. How long has it been since you've had a date, Ned?"

"That was an observation, not a statement of intent."

"Sure." Headlights cast sudden illumination on them as another car pulled up behind and parked. McCain twisted around. It was Jeane's car.

"You know," McCain said, "I don't think I'd repeat that observation to Jeane if I were you."

"Trust me," Ned agreed, "I won't."

Getting out of the car was a shock. In addition to being an extraordinarily clear night, it was also bone-chillingly cold. The temperature had plunged with the setting sun. This time out, however, McCain had come dressed for it in a warm jacket and stout boots. He had also come equipped for nighttime investigation. The chase with the ghost car had left his night vision goggles busted, but he had an infrared camera for himself, another camera equipped with high-speed, low-light film for Jeane, and flashlights for the whole group. He hauled everything out of his car and back to Jeane's.

"Nice of you to join us," he told her. He smiled at Van as the young man emerged from the passenger side door. "Hi, Van. If we're going to be working together, you might as well call me Fitz."

"Sure," Van said, sounding more than a little uncertain.

He carried a heavily stuffed backpack with him—his séance gear they'd asked him to bring. He looked at Ned, a rather sinister figure in the half-light, and McCain introduced them. They shook hands without saying anything. When Van released his hand, Ned turned away toward the woods.

"Jeez, he's cold," muttered Van.

"I would have thought he'd be friendlier, too." McCain looked after Ned for a moment, then turned back to Van. "Did your mother give you trouble about coming out tonight?"

Van gave the same noncommittal shrug McCain was sure he'd used himself at that age. "Not really. When she called the cops and they said you were legit she settled down a lot."

"We're also paying him five hundred dollars to act as a

consultant and we have to get him back by midnight." Jeane glanced at her watch. "We should get going."

The walk in to Bachelor's Grove was silent. It was surprisingly peaceful in the darkness of the woods. The gravel path was quite clear, and one by one they turned off their flashlights to follow it by moonlight alone. With no leaves on the trees, the only shadows cast in the moonlight were the narrow spiderwebs of the bare branches. Their own thicker shadows slipped along the ground like intruders. The cemetery, when they reached it, was even brighter. The soft light erased the ravages of neglect and vandalism, and made the cemetery seem almost timeless in its ruined beauty. Ned hooked his fingers through the links of the fence and looked around.

"So," he said, turning to Van. "This is where you decided to try and contact the Other Side?"

Van nodded hesitantly.

"Ah," said Ned. He looked back to the cemetery—then spun suddenly and grabbed Van by the front of his jacket with both hands. "What did you think you were doing?" he screamed into the young man's face.

"Ned!" McCain tried to push him away from Van, but Ned was fast with his elbows and knocked McCain back. He gave Van a hard shake.

"What were you going to do if something answered you? Eh?" He shook his captive again. "Were you going to ask it a question maybe?"

Van, stunned by the swift attack, nodded dumbly.

"What would you have done if it wanted to be paid?" Ned insisted. "What would you have given it? Well?"

Van tried to answer but only managed a terrified choking sound.

"I thought so," spat Ned. "Ever heard of Gabriel Collins? He was a spiritualist in New York in the 1930s. One night he made contact with a ghost. A real ghost. It refused to answer him, and he didn't have the willpower to force it to. Know what it did? It ripped out his tongue, then it reached down his throat and tore out his vocal chords, too."

"Christ, Ned," McCain said. "You're terrifying the kid."

He tried to step forward again, but this time Jeane held him back.

"Wait," she hissed. "Do you see what he's doing?"

All of the color had drained from Van's face. He didn't look away from Ned's face though and his struggles to free himself were weak.

Ned pushed at him harder, his voice like a whip. "That's assuming you make contact with a ghost and not something else—because there are more than just ghosts out there, you know. Oh, yes." His voice dropped to a terrible whisper. "There was a group right here in Chicago that managed to summon up something much worse than a ghost. No one knows what they summoned because only one person survived. All the rest were just . . . gone. And the person who survived, the leader, she had her mind totally burned away. All she does now is scream and babble, and if she gets free for even a second, she attacks anyone who comes near here."

He pulled Van in very close and said, "I presume you don't want that to happen to you?"

Ned shoved him, and Van scrambled away. The fence stopped him, and Ned stomped after him, anger written across his face. Then, as abruptly as he'd grabbed the boy, Ned put out a hand and helped Van to his feet.

"You're never going to try something like this again, are you?" he asked.

"No!" Van said emphatically. He was trembling like a dog in a thunderstorm.

Ned nodded and said, "Good. Now pull yourself together. We're going to need you in the cemetery." He passed Van to Jeane, then caught McCain's eye. "Can I talk to you for a second?"

Ned led McCain a short distance away then said, "Sorry about elbowing you like that, but I wanted to put the fear of . . . well, *something* into that kid before he did something stupid."

"Well, I think it worked." McCain looked back at Van. His skin had the pale and waxy look of a corpse. McCain shuddered. "The stories make it. Tell me what book they're in, and next time I want a good scare, I'll come buy it."

"They're not in a book, Fitz. They're real."

"You're kidding."

"When it comes to amateurs messing around with summoning and conjuration, I never kid," Ned said seriously. He sighed. "There was another reason Ngan tapped me for this job, Fitz, one that he didn't tell you. Because of the rumors that linked Bachelor's Grove to black magic rituals, he wanted someone with a background in the arcane as well as the psychic."

Ned spread his hands wide and said, "Before my psychic skills emerged, I was a member of a group that practiced diabolism—black magic."

"Woah." McCain flinched away.

Ned caught him. "Stop that. It's not like it's contagious. Besides, I don't do it anymore. I'm a very good psychic, but I was a very, very bad diabolist." He gestured toward Van. "He reminds me too much of me at his age. If I can give him a good scare now, he's not going to go screwing around with something dangerous."

McCain looked at Ned, re-evaluating his dark presence. "So those stories . . ."

Ned shrugged and said, "Just what I said. They're real. Gabe Collins was actually an Institute operative. I met him back in the eighties. Tough old bastard."

Ned led McCain back over to join Jeane and Van.

"The other group was my old circle," Ned continued as they walked. "Not long after I left they stretched themselves a little too far. Nobody knows exactly what happened."

Jeane caught the words and looked at Ned curiously.

"Never mind," McCain told her. "You okay now, Van?"

The teenager nodded and McCain gestured toward the hole in the fence.

"Let's go then," McCain said.

Ned stepped through and McCain followed him. Jeane and Van brought up the rear. Ned sauntered slowly through the cemetery, leading them along like a little troop of ducklings. Finally he stopped near the cemetery's center and turned.

"Nothing," he reported.

"What?" Jeane looked around. "Weren't you going to . . ." She gestured vaguely, hands in the air beside her head. "Do whatever it is psychics do?"

"I've already done . . ." Ned imitated her waving gesture. ". . . what psychics do." He gave her a disparaging look. "What were you expecting, Jeane? A little glow, maybe one of those sci-fi sound effects? Because, you know, until I had them plug the hole in my head, my brain made a whistling noise every time I used my skills."

He turned to McCain and said, "Since your partner is apparently laboring under a bit of a misconception, let's try telling this to you: I don't feel anything here."

McCain looked around the moonlit dimness of the cemetery, shook his head, and admitted, "Sorry, Ned. I don't get it either. What don't you feel?"

"A presence." Ned swept his arm around. "If there is anything active here, I should be able to sense it. There's nothing. All I can feel is the same impression I feel any time I'm in a cemetery: old sorrow, the last lingering attachment to bones. Even those are old and faded."

"So you're saying Bachelor's Grove isn't haunted?" asked Jeane. Ned shook his head.

"You experienced something here. So did Van. So did Laurel and Will Tavish. But if something was here, it's not here now." He frowned. "The only strange thing . . ."

"What?"

Ned shrugged. "This cemetery was never consecrated. It's an old sense I picked up from my . . ." His eyes darted to McCain for a moment. " . . . previous training."

He shrugged again and said, "Bachelor's Grove originally served a rough community of immigrant workers, so it's possible the cemetery just started as a burial ground, and its use continued without ever being properly consecrated by the church. It's not uncommon for frontier cemeteries." He looked to Van. "However, it does mean that trying to contact a spirit here is more dangerous than in most cemeteries, so you're going to have to be careful. Where did you try your séance the first time?"

"Wait a second." Van looked so confused that he seemed on the verge of panic. He took a step back, stumbling a little on a piece of gravestone. "You want me to do it again? After the rant you just gave me?"

"I wanted you to know that you shouldn't try it without knowing what you're doing," Ned snorted. "If I say you should try it again, then you should try it again. If you need help, I'm here. If something you did was what called or awakened the presence in the first place, we need to duplicate it."

Van looked to Jeane and she nodded. He slid his backpack off of his shoulders and went over to kneel in an open patch of ground. The first thing out of his backpack was a large square of purple velvet. He spread it carefully across the ground, then looked up.

"I have incense," he said. "We were going to use it the first time, but the matches got wet and we couldn't light it."

"Do everything as close as possible to the way you actually did it the first time," Ned instructed him.

McCain watched Van stab the unlit sticks of incense into the ground at the corners of the velvet. He turned to Ned and asked, "If there's nothing here, what good is this going to do?"

"Like I said, there's nothing here *now*. I'm hoping Van's little séance will draw it back from wherever it's gone."

Jeane's eyes narrowed in the darkness. "You mean it's at the hospital now."

"Or whispering in Will's ear," Ned replied, "or wherever it goes when it's not active. If nothing else, we'll see what Van's ceremony . . ."

Ned's voice faded away as he looked toward Van. McCain followed his gaze. Van had taken a small triangular object from his backpack and now was removing, and unfolding, a large square board.

"Van," snapped Ned, "tell me that's not what I think it is."

Van looked up. "It's a Ouija board."

"Oh, dear God!" Ned stalked over and plucked it out of his hands to examine it up close. "It is."

"What's wrong?" asked McCain.

"A Ouija board? That's a kid's board game. It has nothing to do with spirits at all. It's all people pushing the planchette unconsciously. You can't actually make contact with one of these things."

Ned squatted down and grabbed Van's whisker-covered chin with one hand, forcing the young man to look up and meet his gaze. To McCain, it looked like Ned was just glowering at Van, but then the psychic grunted in surprise and let go.

"Or," Ned added, "maybe you can."

"What?" Van blinked and rubbed at his eyes.

Ned handed him back the board and said, "Never mind. Sometimes the words and motions are more important than the paraphernalia. You'd just better not have a crystal in that backpack." He sat back on his heels as Van set out the Ouija board. "How many people did you have with you the first time?"

"Three."

"Perfect."

Ned gestured for Jeane and McCain to join them around the velvet and the board. McCain couldn't help noticing that Jeane very deliberately sat on the far side of the board from Ned. Ned reached forward and put his fingertips on the triangular planchette. Van shook his head.

"We have to join hands first."

They did it, though McCain saw Ned give Van a suspicious look. He could guess what the psychic was thinking: how were they supposed to use the Ouija board with their hands linked? He also noticed that if the incense Van had laid out had actually been lit, their joined hands would have been toasting over the glowing sticks. He looked at Jeane. She didn't seem at all impressed.

After a last look around the circle, Van cleared his throat and took a deep breath.

"Hail, spirits of Bachelor's Grove," he said loudly. "We, the living, the walkers in the sun, salute thee, the dead, the dwellers in Paradise. We crave thy forgiveness for intruding upon thine eternal rest—"

From Van's first words, McCain had felt Ned's grip on his hand squeeze tight in frustration, but now the psychic choked outright.

"Stop!" He closed his eyes for a moment and groaned. "What the hell is that?"

"The ritual of the séance?" Van asked meekly.

"Did you get it out of a green book with a picture of two hands joined over a glowing crystal?"

Van nodded without speaking, and Ned groaned again loudly. "McLellan."

"Who?" asked Jeane.

"Let's just say you won't find any of his books in my shop. He doesn't even understand how to use 'thou' properly in a sentence." Ned clenched his teeth. "Right. Start again and keep going."

Van started again, pouring through a droning monologue of appeals and apologies. McCain could feel Ned flinching with practically every sentence. He tried to ignore him, instead waiting with a growing sense of anticipation for the first drift of mist. And waiting.

After several long minutes, the only unusual thing that he felt was a growing chill as the night air slowly stole the heat from his immobile body and the slight dampness of the ground soaked through the knees of his pants. He risked a frustrated glance at Jeane, who rolled her eyes in sympathy, then at Ned. The psychic just gave him a deep frown, but at least he'd stopped flinching. Van continued to chant. The young man's eyes were closed, and all of his attention seemed devoted to the séance. McCain sighed quietly. He forced himself to relax, closing his eyes as well and letting his mind drift. That seemed to help. The ache of cold slowly diminished until all he was aware of was a clean, frosty bite. Sound receded as well. Van's chanting was distant, fading into a stillness—

McCain's eyes snapped open. He knew that stillness.

"Ned!" he whispered.

"I feel it."

Ned's eyes were open, but he stared off into the night. Jeane and Van were looking at the psychic as well, Van still chanting relentlessly.

Ned gave him a slight nod and said, "Keep going, I feel something." He lapsed back into silence.

"Talk to us, Ned," Jeane said.

Ned's face knotted in concentration, but he said nothing more. McCain risked a fast glance around the moon-shadowed cemetery. Nothing had changed. No floating objects, no spectral figures. No ghostly Model As. But the stillness remained, as did the cold—and maybe something else. Tiny pale blue specks flashed in the darkness. McCain blinked and they vanished. A moment later, they were back again, shifting away whenever he tried to focus on them. A trick of the eyes in the dark? No. The blue specks clung to things. They flickered on surfaces for half a heartbeat, then faded away. He could feel the hair on the back of his neck standing up.

Van's chanting faltered. "Ned?" he asked. "What—"

"Keep chanting!" the psychic snapped and Van, startled, picked up the droning invocation once more.

McCain thought he could see the blue specks reflected in Ned's unfocused eyes. He was, McCain realized, staring in the direction of Chicago.

"There's a distant presence," Ned murmured. "Very distant. The séance isn't doing any more than drawing some of its attention, and that's only because we're at the source of its being. We're nothing. We're . . ."

He clenched his jaw, and his lips pulled away from his teeth. He squeezed McCain's hand hard—then relaxed. At the same moment, the eerie stillness and sharp cold vanished. The blue specks winked out.

Ned drew a long breath, blinked, and said, "I lost it."

"What's it doing?" McCain asked. "Where is it?"

"I don't know." Ned shook his head. "But I can tell you this—it's not happy."

In his mind's eye, Ngan stood again in the shadows of a viewing gallery, looking down into the operating room as surgeons prepared Laurel for the cesarean section. Bit by bit, they shrouded her body in blue-green sheets, then raised a curtain of the same fabric between her head and her body. When they were finished, all that remained was an anonymous patch of flesh, a distended, disembodied belly already marked for the surgeon's knife.

Ngan couldn't help thinking that this was not how birth should be. Surely a mother and child that had suffered so much deserved better.

Then the surgeon had a scalpel in his hand, and he stroked the bright steel lightly across Laurel's belly, opening a dark gash in the wake of the blade. An assistant stepped in with a broad, stainless steel instrument that reminded Ngan of nothing so much as a hoe. The instrument was hooked over the lip of skin and muscle, and the assistant drew back on it, pulling the incision even wider. The surgeon's gloved hands dipped inside, vanishing for a moment into Laurel's womb. Ngan leaned forward, alert for any sign of interference by the spirit. This was the moment. If it was going to act, surely it would act—

It was over before he could complete the thought. The surgeon pulled Laurel's child out of her body in one swift, brutal motion, passing it to a waiting nurse while he severed the thick, blue-grey umbilical cord. Ngan fell back, almost at a loss. So quickly and it was done? The child was safe now, freed from the haunted prison of Laurel's body, but it felt so wrong, so unnatural.

"Oh, Laurel," he murmured, "I'm sorry it had to be this way."

He had only the briefest glimpse of the baby before assistants moved forward to cleanse it of Laurel's fluids. It was moving weakly, wet red arms and legs thrashing against the light and air. Fine black hair was plastered against its delicate head. A warming table was brought forward, and scales for weighing, and ink to take footprints. In the background, the surgeon began to close the incision. Laurel didn't move. No one took her baby to her. Ngan bowed his head. Surely that was the most rending tragedy of all. Perhaps the child sensed the distance of its mother as well. It opened its mouth, drew breath, and . . . chimed?

Ngan snapped out of a light doze to the sound of a quiet, persistent alarm. Something was happening. Time came rushing back to replace memory. He glanced at his watch and quietly cursed the vivid dreams that had held him in sleep. Laurel's operation had taken place hours ago. He scrambled to his feet and swiftly made his way to the access door that led from the interstitial floor out into a stairwell.

Keeping watch on Laurel during the day had been simple enough. Be quiet, be still, be inconspicuous, and people's attention simply slid past you. Not even Shani Doyle had recognized his presence. The end of visiting hours had brought a new problem, though. It was much harder to trick people into ignoring you if they knew you weren't supposed to be there. The maintenance area that had given Jeane such frustration had proved to be the answer.

In some ways, though, remaining nearby might not even have been necessary. Will Tavish had not shown up to witness the delivery of his first child. There had been no sign of him at all, not before the delivery, not during, not after. And there was no way Will could get to Laurel with the hospital closed for the night.

Unfortunately, Will wasn't the only danger to Laurel.

Ngan slipped out of the stairwell and onto the floor of the ICU. The sound of the alarm was louder here. It was also overlaid with urgent shouts. From where he stood, Ngan could see the elevators. He watched as the doors of one crashed open and two big orderlies jumped out to run in the direction of Room 923. Hard on their heels, another elevator arrived, disgorging a harried-looking doctor. Quickly but silently, Ngan followed them all.

Bright light flooded from Laurel's room into the dimmed

corridor outside. The light carried shadows from inside the room as well, shadows that looked like they were fighting. Ngan glanced behind him once. No one else was coming yet, but they could come at any time. He stole up to the brightly lit doorway and peered inside.

Cold air poured out of the room along with the light and shadows, chilling the entire corridor. If the nurses and order-lies and doctor within felt the cold, they didn't show it. They were too busy struggling with Laurel Tavish as she shook in the grip of a massive seizure. For the first time since Ngan had laid eyes on her, there was color around Laurel and around her bed. Red.

A huge crimson stain spread across her gown where the cesarean incision had been torn open again. The blood blossomed on the sheets as well. It made Laurel's skin—and the hands of the nurses—slick.

Red wasn't the only color in the room, though. Here and there on the metal surfaces of the room clung tiny flashes of pale blue light, like reflections of some unseen source. None of the medical staff seemed to notice them. Ngan remembered what Shani had seen, a blue light glowing under the door of the room. He remembered what she had heard as well: children playing. He could hear them himself now, a haunting sound that was faint beneath the shouts of the medical staff. But there was something else, as well. A crying baby.

He paused, listening and trying to hear more.

The doctor chose that moment to look up. "Hey! Who are—"

He had been seen. Ngan slid back into the shadows—just in time to feel something brush past him. Not just a gust of cold, but something with substance. He snapped his head down, scanning the floor and caught a light streamer of mist snaking away down the corridor. He didn't hear the rest of the doctor's question. He lunged after the mist.

Away from the bright illumination of Laurel's room, he could see it better. Pale blue light flickered on the metal that it passed, and Ngan could feel the chill that it left in its wake. The mist sped back down the hall toward the nursing station . . . toward the elevators.

Then it stopped abruptly, hung still for a moment, and dropped straight to the floor.

No. Not *to* the floor. *Through* the floor.

Ngan knelt and touched the spot where the mist had been moments before. The tile was marked by a light tracing of frost. Shani had never described this. When the mist had disappeared before, it always just dissipated. Now it was passing through things? Why? Ngan ground his teeth together. So close and it had vanished like . . .

A ghost passing through a wall. The mist hadn't dissipated this time because the ghost was still present.

Ngan heard the elevator doors opening. They were just ahead around a corner. Anyone who emerged would see him. A door nearby opened into a stairwell. He leaped through it and eased it almost closed, leaving just a crack that he could peer through. A security guard hustled past.

They wouldn't send a security guard for a medical emergency. The doctor who had seen him . . . they knew he was here. He closed the door the rest of the way and leaned against it for a moment. The mist had dropped straight down. If he wanted to find the ghost again, it would be a simple matter of checking the floors below the ICU for the chill it left behind. With hospital security looking for him, though, he didn't have the luxury of time.

Something stirred in his memory, something from Jeane's report on her investigation in the hospital. The sounds of children in Laurel's room—they couldn't have come from the pediatrics ward because that was in another wing, and the closest children of any kind were in the maternity ward and neonatal unit.

Two floors down from intensive care.

He ran down the stairs, vaulting over the rails from flight to flight. He knew he had guessed correctly when he reached the door to the seventh floor. The desperate wails of a dozen babies and a thin draft of cold air cut through the gaps in the door frame. Ngan opened the door just enough to peer out. The narrow gap didn't give him a very wide field of vision, but it did reveal one thing: another security guard, an enormous mountain of a man, looking straight at the slowly opening door. His hand dropped to his belt and the holster that hung there.

It was too late for Ngan to simply duck back into the stairwell. With the ghost now among the babies, how could he? Ngan pulled the door wide and stepped through. He caught the guard's gaze and held it. Be quiet, be still, be inconspicuous. If you can't be inconspicuous then dominate their attention. The guard's hand stopped as he stared into Ngan's eyes. Ngan let the door close behind him. Back to the wall, he walked past the guard, holding his gaze the entire way. The guard turned with him, helplessly caught. The man who had taught Ngan the trick so many years ago in Tibet had described it as the reaction of a goat watching as a snow leopard stalked past.

Just beyond the guard was a door equipped with a punch-code lock. A sign on the door described the hospital's desire to ensure the safety of new mothers and their children. Authorized persons only in the maternity ward— apologies for the inconvenience. The barrier would be nothing to a ghost, but it stopped Ngan. Could he press the awe in which the goat held the snow leopard? He looked sharply at the guard and pointed at the door.

"I want to go in there."

The guard leaped for the door just like a skittish goat and rapidly punched in the entry code, swinging the door wide for him. Ngan backed through slowly, his eyes still holding the guard. When he was finally on the other side, his free hand came up, pointing back past the guard. The big man followed the gesture out of sheer instinct, and in the split second that his attention was elsewhere, Ngan quietly pulled the security door closed again.

For a few moments, the guard would remember only a vague sense of disorientation but he would come to his senses soon enough. A few moments was all Ngan needed, though. He followed the sound of the crying babies. Other cries had joined them, mothers staying overnight in the hospital concerned for the safety of their children. There was one tiny wail that rose above all of the others, though. Ngan followed that one, running along the corridor and around a corner.

He froze.

Down at the end of this new corridor was the big window that looked in on the nursery. Nurses ran around frantically, trying to calm the babies and wrap them against the cold that had settled in. Directly in front of Ngan, however, was another window, this one smaller, and looking in on another nursery where a number of tiny, frail infants lay in the warm embrace of incubators, crying weakly. All, that was, except one baby. It was as big as the infants in the other nursery, and it screamed loudly with healthy lungs. Under the bright lights of the nursery, the mist and pale blue lights that surrounded its incubator were almost invisible. Ngan squinted at the name card that identified the child.

Tavish, Girl.

Two nights ago, Jeane and McCain had been attacked near Bachelor's Grove. That same night, something had disturbed Laurel Tavish's deathlike sleep. The team was in the cemetery again tonight. Could it be coincidence that something far worse had manifested? There was a telephone mounted on the wall just down the corridor. Ngan snatched up the handset and dialed a number as fast as he could.

Van had almost completed yet another interminable round of invocations to the spirits of Bachelor's Grove. The boy's voice was cracking. McCain glanced at Ned.

"Anything?" he whispered.

Ned shook his head. "Just barely a stir. Not even the connection we had before. That's more activity than I'd normally expect this drivel to produce but still not enough to match what happen—"

The sound of McCain's cell phone was so sharp and loud that they all jumped. Van broke off his ritual with a yelp. McCain let go of Ned's hand to dig the phone out of his pocket.

"Hello?"

"Whatever you're doing, stop it!" Ngan's voice was frantic. "Stop it now!"

McCain looked around. Van was silent. The circle of hands was broken. The Ouija board hadn't moved an inch from where Van had first placed it.

"We have stopped," McCain said.

"It's no good . . ."

"What's no good?" He glanced at Jeane and Ned. "Ngan, what's going on? Why do we have to stop?"

"It's the ghost. It—" The connection went dead before Ngan could finish.

"Ngan? Ngan?" McCain looked up. "Something's wrong. Something to do with the ghost."

"How?" demanded Jeane. "We didn't do anything."

"We didn't think we did anything," Ned grumbled. He snatched the incense out of the ground on either side of him and snapped the sticks in half before hurling them onto the Ouija board. "Get the other ones."

Jeane grabbed and broke the other sticks as Ned stood up. He stretched his arms wide and shouted something that McCain couldn't understand. It might have been Greek. It might have been Latin. Whatever it was, it rolled off Ned's tongue with a power and majesty that Van's babbling could never have matched. At the height of the shout, Ned brought his foot down hard on the incense and the Ouija planchette, shattering it all and tearing the board beneath. He knelt and gathered up the edges of the velvet to make a bundle, knotting the corners securely.

"Stand back!" he snapped.

Ned wound up like a discus thrower and let the bundle fly—straight toward the lagoon. It landed with a splash and sank below the surface.

The supernatural chill faded, and the urgent edge of fear disappeared from the babies' screams. Ngan was fairly certain that two floors up, Laurel Tavish's seizure had subsided as well. He desperately wanted to turn around and make sure that the Tavish baby was all right, but he wasn't exactly in a position to do so. He glanced down at the pistol in the big security guard's hands. The goat had come after the snow leopard.

chapter

he sun was coming up as McCain walked through the front doors of Presbyterian-St. Luke's and up to the information desk in the lobby.

"Where can I find the security office?" he ask wearily.

The young woman at the desk gave him the directions, and McCain dragged himself off to an elevator. There were mirrors mounted along the wall, and he took a moment to straighten his clothes and hair before the elevator arrived. Too bad there wasn't anything he could do about the whiskers that stubbled his face. More than the hair and clothes— still the same ones he had worn out to the cemetery—they made him look as if he had just crawled out of bed.

Then again, he thought, maybe that's not such a bad thing. It certainly wasn't far from the truth.

The security office was down, not up, and for the first time McCain descended into the hospital's basement. Aside from the total lack of windows and a dour light-grey paint job, it wasn't too bad. He found the security office and took a deep breath, psyching himself up for the task ahead. He pushed the door open.

The security office turned out to be a large, messy room with a few desks and two separate offices at the back. A big bruiser of a security guard was sitting at the desk closest to the door. McCain gave him the best smile he could manage.

"Hi, I'm Rob Neil of Windy City Ventilation and Climate Control. You're sitting on one of my employees."

The bruiser turned around and yelled to the back of the room. "Hey, chief—the old guy's boss is here!"

A burst of colorful language emerged from one of the offices, followed a few moments later by an older security guard with grey-speckled hair and a half piece of toast piled with eggs in his hand.

"Always during breakfast," he grunted, wolfing down the toast. He picked up a clipboard as he walked up to the front of the room. "Robert Neil? Windy City Ventilation?"

McCain nodded in confirmation and the security chief grunted again. He looked over the list attached to the clipboard.

"No official job order from the hospital," the security chief mumbled. "No listed phone number. It took us a while to track you down."

"So I understand," McCain said dryly.

While Presbyterian-St. Luke's security had been trying to find him, he, Jeane, and Ned had spent most of the night trying to find Ngan. After hastily leaving the cemetery and dropping Van at home, they had raced back to the Institute branch office. Nothing Ngan had left there had produced any answers, nor had a hasty call that woke up Emma.

Presbyterian-St. Luke's had been the next logical place to look, but with the hospital closed for the night, they couldn't look for themselves. Fortunately, Shani was on duty, and the card she had given McCain included her pager number. When they got in touch with her, the only information she had was that Ngan had been planning to visit the hospital to watch over Laurel. She hadn't seen him at all.

That Laurel had even had the cesarean had left them all stunned. Shani was at a loss. Hadn't Ngan told them?

"No," McCain had replied tightly, "he didn't."

"Then," Shani had guessed, "you haven't heard what just happened here, either."

She filled them in on the strange cold, the crying babies, and Laurel Tavish's vicious seizure. Laurel had lost a significant amount of blood from the reopened incision, but once they had her restrained, the sutures had quickly been replaced.

Shani had heard nothing about an intruder apprehended during the incident, however. That news had come only in the wee hours of the morning as they wracked their collective brains thinking where else Ngan might have been. McCain's cell phone rang, and he snatched it up only to discover it was hospital security. Ngan had spent the night under watch at Presbyterian-St. Luke's. Sticking with the ventilation consultant story McCain had first invented for Will's benefit, he had given them McCain's cell phone number as the contact for his employer. McCain arranged to come in shortly after the hospital opened in the morning.

Now he looked the security chief straight in the eye. "If he gave you my number initially, why didn't you just call it right away? We could have avoided a lot of this."

The security chief met his gaze uncowed. "We had to be sure that you weren't just an accomplice who would confirm any questions we asked."

"Because, of course, someone would come up with a

fake ventilation climate control company as a way to get an old man into a hospital in the middle of the night."

The chief didn't look amused. "Lucky for you, we did get in touch with one of our maintenance supervisors who worked with someone else from your company a couple of days ago." He rapped the bottom edge of the clipboard against the top of the desk. "It still doesn't explain why your employee was wandering around the hospital after hours on a night when the air conditioning systems on two floors went haywire."

So that was how they were explaining the cold Shani had described.

McCain shrugged and said, "Working late? Lost track of time? I don't know. He wasn't supposed to be here, and he's certainly not supposed to be doing anything to the heating and air conditioning systems. What does he say about it?"

"He says you told him it would be fine for him to work after hours."

"I told him I'd *fine* him *if* he worked after hours!" McCain groaned and rubbed his knuckles across his forehead.

"Damn it," he said, then looked up. "Listen . . ." He searched across the chief's chest and shoulders for some indication of his name, something that would make him easier to deal with. There was nothing. He fell back on the next best thing. ". . . chief, we're a new company. This is our first big job, and I'm sure that my man had nothing to do with your problems last night. I guarantee that he was nowhere *near* the air conditioning controls." At least McCain hoped he hadn't been. He grinned at the chief hopefully. "Do you think we could just keep this quiet and let me look after my man by myself? It would probably save us both a lot of hassle."

If his hands had been behind his back, McCain would have crossed his fingers. This was the best deal the security chief could hope for, and McCain was willing to bet he would go for it. After all, if he was going to turn Ngan over to the cops to be charged with trespassing, he would have already done it rather than mess around trying to verify his story. Filing charges was bound to mean a ton of paperwork for somebody.

The security chief considered him for a long minute, then finally nodded.

"All right."

The chief looked at the bruiser sitting at the desk and jerked his head toward the second office at the back of the room. The bruiser unfolded himself—Lord, thought McCain, I wouldn't want to meet him in a dark alley—and went back to unlock the door.

"Just so you understand, though," the chief said, "if my men catch him, or you, anywhere you're not supposed to be again, you're both going straight to the cops."

"Gotcha."

At the back of the room, the big bruiser had released Ngan from the other office, a bare little room modified to act as a kind of cell, and was escorting him back up to the front. Something harsh passed between them, nothing more than a glance, but for a moment, McCain got the impression that the huge man was somehow intimidated by the little old Tibetan.

McCain turned his own most intimidating face on Ngan. "We'll have a talk back at the office," he said sternly.

Ngan just nodded calmly. It was enough to make McCain grind his teeth in real frustration.

McCain shook hands with the chief and said, "Thank you very much."

Ngan was silent as a stone as they left the security office and headed for the elevator. His body language spoke for him, however. Where his usual stride was subdued and economical, now he walked with a barely contained fury.

His face was still a mask, but instead of Ngan's usual calm, that mask reflected an icy control. A nurse they passed in the hallway shied away, giving him a berth so wide that she banged her shoulder into the wall. Ngan was clearly not in a good mood.

"So," McCain commented as they reached the elevator, "you got nabbed by the security goons."

If Ngan had intended to murder the elevator call button with the stab of his finger, he might have succeeded. "I was captured because I stopped to warn you of the danger to Laurel and her child," he said. "The ghost was—"

"Shani told us what happened last night." McCain stared at the blankness of the elevator doors for a moment before adding, "She also mentioned that you knew Laurel was having a cesarean and that you were going to be here to watch over her."

Ngan didn't reply. McCain waited. There was still no reply.

"Don't you think that's the sort of thing your team might want to know about?" McCain asked finally.

The elevator arrived, and they stepped inside—Ngan slightly ahead of McCain. He turned just inside the doors, taking up station beside the panel of floor buttons.

"Is it necessary that you know everything I do?" Ngan asked.

"Maybe it is. Jeane is waiting at the Institute with Ned. We can talk about it there."

McCain reached forward to punch the lobby button. Ngan knocked his hand away.

"Hey!"

"Laurel was attacked last night," Ngan said tersely. He hit the button for the ninth floor. "I want to make sure that she and the baby were not harmed."

"Shani said they're fine." The doors closed, and McCain reached for the panel again.

Ngan blocked him a second time. He turned his head just enough to catch McCain's gaze. "I want to see them with my own eyes."

McCain stared at him. "You did hear the security chief, didn't you? We . . . *you* are not exactly an honored guest in the hospital at the moment."

"I have to check on them."

He turned back to the front of the car just as it came to a stop at the lobby and a small crowd flooded in. McCain briefly considered squeezing out past them and leaving Ngan to sneak around on his own. And let Ngan know he had finally gotten to him? No way. He let the crowd squeeze him to the back of the car, packing him in beside Ngan. Somehow Ngan still found the room to keep a few inches of space around himself. He continued facing forward, not sparing another glance for McCain.

"Rough night in the holding cell?" asked McCain sarcastically.

A thin white line traced its way around Ngan's tightly pressed lips. "You will never see the rough nights I have known, Michael."

A couple of people around them shifted nervously. A glance at Ngan's face—and perhaps at his own—was enough to make them turn away again. McCain rode the rest of the way to the ninth floor in silence.

They stepped off of the elevator into anything but silence.

"Laurel has never suffered a seizure in her life and now this!" Will Tavish shouted.

He stalked the space in front of the nurses' station. His fists were clenched and shaking. His face was red. His hair was standing on end as though it hadn't seen a comb in days. His clothes were wrinkled. A nurse stood behind the counter, but Shani and another doctor stood in front of it, bared to Will's rage. From the flush on Shani's face and the pallor of the other doctor's, it looked as if they had been enduring the assault for some time. None of them paid the new arrivals the least bit of attention. McCain shrank back immediately, keeping his distance. Ngan simply stood his ground and watched. McCain hissed at him but he didn't budge.

"As I said, Will," Shani snapped, "the seizure was likely a result of Laurel's injury. I haven't had a chance to examine her fully since it happened, but head trauma serious enough to place her in a coma could be enough to—"

"Enough to what, Dr. Doyle?" Will stopped suddenly and leaned closer. "Enough to what? What are you implying?"

McCain saw fear flash through Shani's eyes. She recognized the same edge of anguished guilt in Will's voice that he did and the same unspoken question. Before she could reply, though, Will stepped back and ran both hands through his hair.

"No," he said. "I know what you mean." He looked up again. "But how do you know the seizures are connected with Laurel's head trauma and not with your unauthorized cesarean section?"

Shani exchanged a glance with the other doctor, who said, "Will, we talked about this when Laurel was admitted. We agreed that it might be necessary. You consented."

"I withdraw my consent!" shouted Will. He stepped toward the doctor, caught himself, and started pacing again. "And don't tell me again you tried to call me about it. I was home all day yesterday, and I didn't hear the phone ring once. I missed the birth of my first child, and the operation has left my wife with seizures."

"The *head trauma* left Laurel with seizures," Shani reiterated. "It's just not possible to develop seizures from a cesarean section."

"Then how come Laurel didn't have any before you took the baby?" growled Will. "How come you put her and our child in danger without contacting me? How come when I finally *do* hear that you've gone ahead and performed a cesarean section on her, I also hear that an intruder was caught snooping around my wife's room?"

This wasn't a good place for them to be. McCain pushed the call button to get the elevator back, then grabbed for Ngan's arm, trying to get his attention. Instead, the motion succeeded only in drawing the attention of the doctor who stood with Shani. He did a double take when he noticed Ngan.

"You!" Over his shoulder, he snapped to the nurse, "Call security." He pointed at Ngan. "That's the man I saw last night."

Will spun around, and his eyes went narrow, first following the doctor's pointing finger, then darting to McCain.

"Rob?" he hissed. "What's going on? Why do I keep running into you here?"

McCain took a step forward, thinking fast. "There was a major air-conditioning malfunction last night, Will. We're here to—"

Will cocked his head. "But your assistant was already here last night." His mouth twisted. "You . . . everything I told you. You tricked me."

"No."

"Yes!" spat Will. He brought up his arm, pointing. His hand was shaking. "You tricked me. You set me up."

The other doctor was looking stunned and baffled. Ngan was just standing there like a stump. Shani at least was doing something, reaching over the desk and taking the phone from the nurse before she could call security. Good. McCain drew a deep breath and walked forward another step.

"Will," McCain said, "you're not well. You need help. Have you called that psychiatrist I told you about?"

Will laughed. "Not a chance. Do you think I'm crazy?" He sobered abruptly, so abruptly it was like watching an entirely different personality wash over him. "Of course you do. That's why she introduced . . ." He turned to point at Shani—and caught her with the phone in her hand. "What are you doing? Who are you calling?"

"Will—"

"No!" Will clasped his hands over his ears. "I'm not listening anymore! I'm not listening to anybody. I don't know what's been happening here, but it's going to stop." He snatched his hands away and glared at all of them. "You're going to hear from my lawyer. And so is the hospital. Something is going on, and I'm going to find out what."

The elevator doors chose that moment to open, exposing a trio of elderly women who stared at the chaos with open mouths. Will jumped for the elevator. McCain tried to grab him, but Will slipped through his grasp and spun inside the elevator to slap at the "close door" button.

"I'm going to sue this hospital until it's forced to close!"

He was still shouting when the doors shut on him. McCain caught a last glimpse of the elderly women huddled at the back of the elevator. He grabbed Ngan and said, "We should go, too."

The old man looked down at McCain's hand then up at his face. "Not until I've seen Laurel," he said.

The calm in his voice was so vicious that McCain snatched his hand away without a second thought.

"Whoa, both of you!" The doctor stepped up to stop them. "You're not going anywhere, and you're certainly not going to see Laurel Tavish." He glanced back to the nurses' station. "Shani, I don't know what you're doing, but I want security up here ASAP! These two are—"

His words ended in a choked gasp as Ngan reached up, grabbed his jaw, and pulled his head around hard. He glared at the doctor. McCain couldn't see the old man's eyes, but he could see the doctor go very still, then very pale. In only seconds, sweat had started to bead on his forehead. He didn't make any motion to move away, though.

"What do you want?" the doctor asked in a terrified whisper.

"Your silence."

The doctor nodded as best he could. Ngan let him go, and he fell back to lean against the wall, sucking in air as though he had just run a marathon. Shani and the nurse were staring at Ngan with wide eyes. He didn't look at them, just started walking in the direction of Laurel's room.

"Michael," he ordered. "Come with me."

It was a command he might have given a dog. Anger burned a red line through McCain's brain. "No." He reached back and hit the elevator call button again.

Ngan stopped. He didn't turn around. "Michael, come with me. That's an order."

"No."

"This is no time for your little complaints. I am in command of this team!"

Ngan started to turn, and McCain caught a glimpse of his face. There was something dreadful about it, something compelling and powerful. Something predatory. McCain forced himself to look away just as an elevator opened. Thankfully, it was empty.

"You can't command a team that isn't behind you, Ngan. And you can find your own ride back to the Institute."

He pushed the lobby button and, as the doors closed he stared back into Ngan's dreadful, predatory . . . *enraged* eyes.

McCain had actually succeeded in making Ngan break his inscrutable calm. That almost made him feel pleased.

Almost.

———

Lily Adler might not have been the most powerful person at the Chicago branch office of the Hoffmann Institute, but somehow her office door managed to carry the heaviest, most highly polished brass name plate in the building. The similar name plate that was mounted on Ngan's own office door had been her gift. Ngan had never realized before how intimidating those name plates were. Solid, cold, and untouchable, their polished surface created a distorted reflection of anyone who approached the door. Maybe he should take his down. On the other hand, it had been a gift from Lily, and he didn't want to hurt her feelings. She was one of his oldest friends in the Institute, and she genuinely wanted him to succeed. He would, he knew, leave the name plate up. He reached up and knocked on her door.

"Who is it?" Lily called in her blueblood voice.

"Ngan."

"Please, come in. The door is unlocked."

He opened the door and stepped through, quickly closing it behind him. Lily was taking her lunch—several slices of cold, leftover pizza washed down with cola. She lounged in a chair in front of her version of the AV equipment in Ngan's office.

"Grab a seat," she said, shoving a chair toward him. "The office is soundproofed, and I got a tape of last night's match."

She flicked the buttons on a remote control and the big screen of the television came to life with the garish roaring and posturing of professional wrestling.

And that, Ngan knew, was the secret of Lily's success as field director of observation. Her private and professional personas were completely different. To her agents, she was never anything less than cool, aristocratic perfection, a haughty force of nature that did not take "no" for an answer. None of them ever saw this side of her. There were probably a good number of her peers within the Institute who had never seen this side of her, either. Technically, Ngan was one of her agents now as well, but he had known her for too long, had watched her build the upper-crust image that was her professional mask. He was one of the few people Lily trusted enough to see the rough and raucous side that kept her sane in an insane job.

He slid into the offered chair and said, "How do you do it, Lily?"

She looked at him over a slice of pizza thick with congealed cheese and raised an eyebrow questioningly.

"How do you separate yourself so completely?" Ngan elaborated.

Lily chewed for a moment, then shifted her food to the side of her mouth.

"You didn't come here to eat pizza and watch big men in silly tights, did you?" she asked. There was a reason she was a field director besides being good at handling agents.

"I lost my temper today, Lily."

It was good to have someone around who knew him and knew what losing his temper meant to him. Lily swallowed her food and set the pizza down.

"McCain?" she asked seriously.

He nodded.

"I noticed he didn't come back with you this morning."

When he looked up, she was the one who nodded.

"I know roughly what happened at St. Luke's last night," she said. "Why don't you tell me what happened with Fitz?"

It was tempting to give her the kind version of events at the hospital that was kind to him. He didn't. He told her everything, from his less than gracious response to McCain's arranging his release to his very ill-advised desire to check up on Laurel and her child, to his vicious intimidation of the doctor in the intensive care unit. The teacher who had taught him about the snow leopard and the goat would have been furious with him. Ngan was furious with himself.

He was, perhaps, even more furious that he would have

turned the leopard's gaze against McCain. He had known the young man as a child. McCain trusted him. After McCain had departed, Ngan turned his back on Shani and the terrified, trembling doctor and gone to Laurel's room. She'd been as silent and still as ever, the incision in her belly freshly bandaged, the sheets of her bed just changed. Confronted with the helpless woman he was trying to save, he'd felt the anger drain away from him. It had been replaced by a bleak regret and a deep feeling that he was as helpless as Laurel.

He'd stayed with her for long minutes, then slipped out of the room and away from the ICU. He'd taken the stairs, avoiding the elevators and the nursing station. He left the hospital without even trying to look in on the baby. The trip to the branch office had been a tedious ride on the L, then Metra trains followed by a long walk through the industrial wastelands of Schiller Park. Somewhere along the route it had become a pilgrimage of atonement.

When he was done, Lily picked up her pizza again, took a small bite, chewed, and swallowed before responding.

"What about Jeane," she asked, "and Ned?"

"I told them to go home," Ngan sighed. "When they're together, it's like watching two dogs snapping at each other for alpha status." He passed a hand in front of his eyes and sat back. "At the moment, I can't deal with that, too."

"What do you want me to do then?" Lily had reduced her pizza to a thin strip of crust. She dropped it onto a crinkled piece of tin foil and picked up the next slice. "Something needs to be done about this investigation."

"I know," agreed Ngan. "We will find the answer."

"Not squabbling you won't." She considered him for a moment then asked, "Should I take your team off the case?"

He knew the answer to that question immediately. "I think it would disappoint Jeane and McCain immensely. They were very defensive when I called in Ned."

"What about you?" Lily asked.

Ngan found himself blinking in surprise.

"How would you feel about it?" she pressed. "If you're concerned about the team, maybe a simpler investigation would be in order. One they can solve easily, something to make them feel good about themselves, each other, and you."

Ngan eased himself slowly back into the chair as he thought about that. A successful investigation could weld them together, really make them a team. But the ploy wouldn't fool McCain or Jeane. He knew that. They would see through it immediately. Completing the current investigation would make them a team just as surely, and besides . . . He looked up at Lily.

"The problem isn't just them," he said bluntly. "It's me. I shouldn't have gotten caught at the hospital. I shouldn't have snapped just because McCain was exerting himself. I don't know how to react anymore."

Lily snorted. "You? I've seen you hold off trained swordsmen using nothing more than a silver tea service!"

"And last night a security guard surprised me while I was on the telephone." He rubbed his hands along the smooth, polished arms of the chair. "Nothing I do lately seems to work out right. I hesitate. I analyze my every action for the example it will set. I'm thinking of Michael and Jeane as my students, not my partners."

"They are your students," Lily pointed out.

"No," Ngan said, "if you were their agent in charge, they would be your students. I can't separate myself the way you can. I envy you that. When I'm in the office, I think of nothing but working in the field with them. When I'm in the field, I think of the responsibilities and demands of the office. The agents suffer because of that. I suffer."

"Ngan, the office is your field now. Haven't you always had responsibilities in the field? Haven't you relied on a team before? Haven't other agents been your hands and eyes the way Jeane and Fitz are now?"

He looked around Lily's office. It was as big as his was and nearly as empty. Somehow, though, she had the presence to fill it. She stood alone, like a spider thriving at the center of her web. He would have to learn how to do that.

"Maybe," he admitted. "I guess I'm just not so sure how to be the brain without having my hands tear me apart."

Lily laughed. Ngan remembered that laugh because until she learned to suppress it, it always betrayed the aristocratic mask.

"I can't tell you how to run your team, Ngan." she said with a smile. "Actually, I can tell you how to run your team, but I won't because you're not me. Everyone has to find their own way of managing, of finding the field in the office. Just remember that the Institute put you in charge for a reason. We need your leadership and expertise now, no matter how we get it."

Ngan contemplated the wrestlers on the television as they grappled and grunted with each other, torrents of sweat pouring from them. So much effort for something that was just a bit of pretty fiction. A ridiculous amount of effort, really. He cocked his head suddenly and glanced up at Lily.

"May I make a suggestion?" he asked.

chapter
2WELVE

A sense of déjà vu hit Jeane the moment she stepped out of the afternoon sunlight and through the battered door into Ellie's. She knew she had never been in the bar before, but she had been in too many bars just like it while she was working with the ATF. Ellie's was like a dip back into the dirty bathwater of her old career, right down to the suspicious glance that the bartender gave her. There were some people who could smell a law enforcement agent at fifty paces. Usually people with something they wanted to hide.

Lucky for the bartender she had a new job. Jeane went up to the bar and sat down beside the only other person there and asked, "Is this a private sulk or can anybody join?"

McCain flicked a finger against the rim of the amber-filled glass in front of him. The glass rang like an out of tune chime. "Knock yourself out," he said. "How did you find me?"

"It's called 'investigation.' Strangely enough, they pay us to do it." She flagged down the bartender and said, "Diet Coke."

"This is a bar, lady."

"Wave a bottle of rum over it and charge me, then." Jeane turned back to McCain. "I figured you'd be looking for a drink, but I couldn't find you in any of your usual haunts. Then I remembered you mentioning this place, and here you are."

The bartender came back and slid her Coke across the bar. Most of the glass was filled with ice. Jeane considered complaining but thought better of it.

"You know, Fitz, it would be a lot easier to get in touch with you if you left your cell phone turned on."

"Well, that's kind of the idea." He picked up his glass and swirled the liquid inside. "Of course, so was coming here, and you managed to find me anyway. Will Tavish was right, this is a good place for a really quiet drink."

He took a tiny sip from the glass. Jeane eyed him. McCain was still wearing the clothes he had worn to the cemetery the night before and to the hospital in the morning. He had developed a major case of whisker stubble, and his eyes looked bleary.

She nodded toward his glass and said, "How long have you been sitting here, Fitz?"

"Since I left the hospital this morning."

He said it with such a perfectly straight face that she actually believed him for a moment.

"Don't be stupid," he snorted derisively. "I drove around for a long time, went down to Streetersville and sat beside the lake, then drove back over to St. Luke's but thought better of actually going in. By then it was opening time, I was close to this place, and the rest is history. I've only been here a couple hours."

"How much have you had to drink?"

He raised his glass in salute. "Just starting a second. This is sipping whisky, and that's what I'm doing." He took another drink, then set the glass down with a sigh. "I walked out on Ngan."

"I guessed that. When he finally got back to the Institute, he sent Ned and I home, then vanished. He was even more quiet than normal, almost subdued." She looked at McCain questioningly. "What did you do to him?"

"I pissed him off."

She blinked and breathed, "Wow."

Jeane stared across the bar at a mirror set behind a bank of dusty bottles while McCain described what had happened at the hospital. When he was done, they sat in silence for several minutes, McCain sipping occasionally at his whisky, she taking longer pulls at her pop.

"So," she asked finally, "you didn't see Laurel at all?"

"No, but I thought about going back to the hospital before I came here. I feel bad about walking out when she's in danger, but Ngan . . ." He clenched his fist. "Lately I just can't stand him."

Funny, thought Jeane, I get the impression he's been feeling the same way about you.

Aloud she asked, "So what's the problem?"

McCain shrugged. "I don't know. He interferes with the investigation. He pushes us in the direction he wants us to go."

"Wasn't that how he operated in D.C., too?" Jeane asked dryly.

"But at least that was discreet. He might have been manipulating us, but he was gentle about it. And it felt like he had some respect for me. Now he's just lording it over us, always in our faces so we know who's supposed to be in charge." He shrugged again. "I don't understand him anymore. It's that damn promotion."

Jeane looked him up and down. "You're jealous. You can't stand that he's the leader."

"You're insane." He raised his glass again. "I don't want to be the 'leader' of anything."

"Yeah?" Jeane couldn't hold back a snort. Everything McCain had done since she'd met him, the way he spoke and dressed and carried himself . . . "It seems to me like it's the role you were born to play."

McCain choked hard and blew a spray of whisky across the bar. Jeane jumped away from the blast. "Jesus, Fitz!"

The hand that had been closest to McCain was soaked. There were no napkins around, and she had to settle for brushing it against the edge of her stool as she sat down again.

"Touched a nerve, did I?"

"No," he lied.

He took a big gulp of his whisky, and she looked at him with an eyebrow raised. "Go on and pull the other one. What's up?"

"Nothing," he said firmly. He put the glass down. "Just let it go."

"No. You've done this sort of thing a few times lately, and that's more than a coincidence. Something's wrong. Spill it." She crossed her arms and waited, trying to remember exactly what had brought on these little fits. "You suck at basketball, but you're trying to play 'because he didn't.' You've got a picture of the skyline of Dallas, but you've never been there 'as such.' Just now I said you were born to—"

McCain sighed. "Look, Jeane, I'd appreciate it if you'd just drop the whole thing."

He didn't look at her, just stared across the bar. She could tell he was watching his reflection in the mirror there.

"I . . . found out something about myself recently, and I'm not quite sure how to deal with it."

And suddenly it all clicked in her mind, just as it should

have from the beginning. She could guess exactly what McCain was going through. She'd been there herself. She reached across and patted him on the back.

"You're adopted, right?" she asked.

McCain blinked in surprise and Jeane couldn't help smiling.

"It's a kicker when you find out, isn't it? I found out I was adopted when I was a teenager," she said. "Must be even weirder when you're an adult."

McCain nodded slowly, tearing his eyes away from his reflection to look at her. "It is," he admitted.

"It sounds like you at least know something about your birth parents, though, right? You were born in Dallas? Your birth father is the one you're rebelling against by playing basketball?" He kept nodding. Jeane turned back to her Diet Coke. "Congratulations. Not everybody gets to know that much."

"How about you?"

"Cleveland. Single mom when that was a huge problem." She sipped her drink. "I met her when I turned eighteen. She was nice, but she told me to stay with my folks. They were my real parents. I never saw her again." She looked up. "Have you actually met your birth parents?"

"They're . . . dead."

The ringing of her cell phone saved her from the embarrassment of having to respond to that. She dug the phone out of her pocket in a hurry. "Hello?"

"Jeane, it's Shani Doyle. I've been trying to get in touch with Fitz, but his phone's off."

"I noticed that myself."

"Your secretary gave me your number. Have you seen him?"

"I'm with him now." She poked McCain and passed the cell phone to him. "It's for you."

He grimaced. "Not Ngan . . ."

"No. Shani."

His face changed completely, and he raised the phone to his mouth. Jeane turned away while he chatted and took another look around Ellie's.

It wasn't quite as bad a place as she'd first thought. She'd been in worse bars, and Ellie's was no more than the low end of neighborhood blue-collar drinking holes. McCain had told her a little bit about the place's long and colorful history. It was kind of interesting to see it captured in the multitude of photographs hanging on the walls.

Jeane drained her Diet Coke, then hopped off the stool to get a better look at the photos. Many of them weren't actually of the bar itself, but they reflected a diverse and extended record of Chicago's history over the last—how long had McCain said that bar had been here?—eighty years at least. The city's historical society would have wet its collective pants in excitement. There were photos of some of Chicago's best-known landmarks past and present, from the Tribune Tower to the stockyards. There were pictures of young men posed with cars and somber older men standing by storefronts, of children with wide, toothy grins. High up in one corner she found a fascinating series of photographs from a time when the bar mustn't have been quite so grimy: laughing people posed in an array of finery from the mid-twenties through the late thirties—party photos, all labeled with a year and the names of the people who appeared in them.

She was still looking at them when McCain came up and handed her back the cell phone.

"Everything is good at the hospital," he reported. "Shani was worried that Will might follow through with his threat to sue the hospital, but there hasn't been any sign of him since this morning. Laurel—and the baby—are resting quietly, the ghost seems quiet as well, and I have been reminded that I have an overdue date tonight."

Jeane had to smile. "You're feeling better."

"I'd say it was because I know there's someone I can talk to, but that reminds me too much of something I told Will, and look where it got him." McCain grinned and wiggled his eyebrows. "And let's face it, the real reason I'm happy is because I'm going out with Shani tonight."

He leaned past her to examine the photographs. "What are you looking at?"

"A happy decade at Ellie's." She pointed out the party photographs.

"When the bar was a mob hangout," he commented. He stopped his scanning of the pictures suddenly and focused on one in particular. "Well, well. Look at this."

Jeane looked. It was a photograph of a New Year's Eve party, 1933. Two women in shimmering dresses hung on the arms of two men in dark, broad-shouldered suits. All four raised saucer-shaped glasses of champagne toward the camera, but there was clearly a hierarchy of power represented in the photo. One of the men stood in front of the other. His suit was a little better, with a rose on his lapel. His woman wore a more expensive-looking dress and a fancy hat. The other man had also been caught glancing at the man with the rose, and there was jealousy on his face. Jealousy or fear.

McCain pointed at the label on the photograph and said, "Jack Harvey. They didn't even bother identifying the other guy."

"There's something familiar about his face."

"There should be," McCain said. "He's Will Tavish's great-uncle." He frowned suddenly. "Except that Will said he was a small-time thug."

Jeane shook her head. "Maybe he just got a good spot in the photo?"

"I doubt it." He turned back to the bar and called to the bartender, "Hey, buddy, do you know anything about the mobsters that used to hang out here back in the thirties?"

205

"Some of them," the man grunted. He looked up from stacking glasses on a tray. "Why do you want to know?"

"Somebody I know was related to one, but he says the guy was small time, and this picture makes him look big time." McCain tapped the photograph. "Know anything about Jack Harvey?"

The bartender gave a short laugh. "The only time Jack Harvey would have been small was when he was a baby. He was a big man around here for a while. Don't take my word for it though." He went down to the end of the bar and opened a door to reveal a flight of stairs leading up. Warm light spilled down from upstairs. "Hey, Gran. Come down here for a minute. Some people want to know about Jack Harvey."

Jeane blinked. " 'Gran?' Your grandmother lives above . . ."

She started to gesture around her at the foul darkness of the bar, but stopped before she embarrassed herself. The bartender didn't seem to notice.

He shrugged as he went back to the glasses and said, "Why shouldn't she? She owns the place."

There was movement on the stairs, and an old woman came tottering down them. One hand held the banister securely, and the other gripped a cane. She had the slenderness of age, but there was very little else about her that seemed frail. When she reached the bottom of the stairs, the bartender pointed her over toward Jeane and McCain.

"Hi there," she said, "I'm Ellie. What did you want to know?"

McCain stepped forward. "We were curious about Jack Harvey. Did you know him?"

"Know him?" Ellie laughed heartily. She leaned against a chair and poked her cane at the photograph. "Who do you think that is sliding down his arm?"

A few minutes later, they were all sitting around a table just under another photograph of Ellie, this one taken outside the bar on the day in 1956 that she bought it. McCain had retrieved his whisky from the bar, and Ellie had joined him in a glass. Jeane had accepted another Diet Coke. Ellie had listened intently as McCain told her Will's story that Jack Harvey was nothing more than a thug. When he finished, Ellie chuckled and shook her head.

"My grandson told you right," she said, nodding at the bartender. "The only time Jack was small time was when he first hooked up with the mob. He came up fast, and let me tell you, that's a damn attractive thing to a young woman living on the shady side of the street."

McCain nodded toward the bartender. "Is he related to . . . ?"

"Oh, hell, no! We might not have had the pill in those days, but if a woman got a bun in the oven every time she kneaded the dough, there'd be a lot more people around, wouldn't there?" She laughed. "I got married long after Jack was gone."

Jeane leaned forward. "So, Ellie, if Jack wasn't just a thug, what did he do for the mob?"

That sobered Ellie up quick. "He was an enforcer," she said quietly. "He came up fast because he didn't hesitate before he pulled the trigger and because he wasn't squeamish when it came time to get rid of the bodies."

That tugged at Jeane's memory. "I don't suppose he dumped them in the lagoon at Bachelor's Grove Cemetery, did he?"

"Good guess," Ellie confirmed. "I'll bet you've heard stories about Bachelor's Grove, haven't you?"

Jeane nodded.

"Well," Ellie continued, "Jack was the first one to dump bodies there. There's a good story behind that if you want to hear it." She settled back with her whisky in her hands. "You already know that Jack and Johanna—"

"Johanna?" interrupted Jeane.

"Jack's twin sister. Your friend's grandmother." Ellie wet her mouth with a sip of whisky. "You already know that they grew up in Midlothian. So did I. Jack and me met up in Chicago later, after he'd joined the mob and I'd become a music hall girl. Anyway, there was a story in Midlothian that a corpse dropped into the lagoon at the cemetery would never rise."

Jeane frowned. "I've never heard that story."

Ellie leaned over toward McCain and whispered, "Does she always interrupt this much?"

McCain nodded. Jeane flushed. Ellie straightened up and looked over at her. "You wouldn't have heard the story, because Jack proved it was wrong. See, the first time Jack needed to get rid of a body, he remembered the story and gave it a try."

She sipped from her glass again.

"It didn't work, of course. A couple days later, the body floated up. It was never officially traced back to Jack, but everybody in the know knew about it and Jack got instant respect as a hard ass. Dumping a body in a cemetery lagoon—can you imagine?"

"So he kept using it?" McCain asked. Ellie made a gun out of her thumb and forefinger and shot McCain with an approving click of her tongue. McCain scratched his chin as he thought. "Didn't he ever get caught?"

"Not for that. Eventually he got busted for something a lot smaller—like how they got Capone for tax evasion. But when Jack went to jail, everybody lied and said he was less of a crook than he was. Maybe that's how come your friend thought he was a small timer."

"What happened to Jack?"

"Died in a prison fight." Ellie shrugged. "Like my Mama said, bad blood always shows."

"Wait a minute." Jeane couldn't keep her silence any longer. She looked at McCain and Ellie questioningly. "I thought Will said his grandmother came from a good Midlothian family?"

"Oh, they did," said Ellie hastily. Then she grimaced. "Sort of."

"What do you mean, 'sort of?' " McCain asked.

Ellie sighed. "Listen, tell me you won't tell your friend about this. It's probably the sort of thing he's better off not knowing. It's not going to hurt him, but he might not take kindly to it."

She shifted in her chair, leaning forward and pitching her voice low.

"After Jack died, I went home and visited my Mama for the first time in years, and I told her about Jack dying. She said, 'Thank God!' and crossed herself. Mama *never* crossed herself. Then she sat me down and told me an old rumor. See, Jack and Johanna were only children, and they were only born after their parents had been married about five years. The rumor was that Mrs. Harvey finally got desperate and turned to a Steiner man for help getting pregnant." Ellie rapped her hand on the table top. "You know what that kind of 'help' means. Nobody could prove it, of course, and nobody dared talk about it because Mr. Harvey was a powerful man, and he was bound and determined to believe those twins were of his own making."

"So Will isn't descended from the Harveys," Jeane said.

Ellie nodded. "What was wrong with the Steiners?"

"Oh, phew." Ellie took a gulp of whisky. "What wasn't? Have you ever been to Midlothian? Yes? Have you ever noticed that the actual center of town is a long ways from Bachelor's Grove Cemetery? Well, the Steiners lived by there and always had. They were an old Midlothian family, even older than the Harveys. They'd been there right back to the beginning. So far back that some people said that Bachelor's Grove Cemetery started as their private burial ground and was never a proper church cemetery at all."

Ned had said that the cemetery had never been consecrated. Jeane shivered and asked, "What about the lagoon?
Was it always there?"

"My gramma knew a man who helped set up the cemetery in 1864 when it was officially founded. He told her they
dug the lagoon but that there was already something there,
a little spring-fed pond, and when they were digging it out,
they found . . . things. She wouldn't tell me what."

Ellie leaned even farther forward.

"Mama said Old Man Steiner, the one that came over
from Germany and started the family, was known as a witch-
man and the family had a reputation for witchcraft in the
blood. One of the reasons nobody talked about Jack and
Johanna having a Steiner father was because they wanted to
believe the Steiner blood had died out. The man Mrs. Harvey
went to was the last of his family. He was found hanging
when Jack and Johanna were two. Everybody stopped telling
stories about the Steiners then, and by the time Jack and
Johanna were both away in Chicago, the only people who
remembered the Steiners were the old folks. They were glad
to see Jack and Johanna out of Midlothian."

Ellie went for her glass again, and the bar seemed
dreadfully quiet in her silence.

"Ellie," asked McCain, "I'm just curious: Do you know
the stories about hauntings in Bachelor's Grove?"

Ellie laughed again, the same full laugh she had met
them with. It pushed back the silence in the bar. "You can't
grow up in Midlothian and not hear *some* stories. I know
'em all." She winked. "And a couple that probably no one
else knows. One is something Mama told me about the
Steiners. The other is one I came up with myself."

"'Came up with?'" Jeane asked in disbelief. How was it
possible to come up with a ghost story?

Ellie shrugged. "It's more of a theory really. You've
heard about the car that haunts the turnpike, right?"

Jeane nodded uncomfortably. "A Ford Model A. A mob car."

"Not just any Model A," Ellie said with a snort. "And not just any mob car. Jack Harvey's car. Jack dumped his victims in the lagoon. If he did have the Steiner blood, maybe it was like he was making a sacrifice that brought back the ghosts of his victims."

"Like a memory of their final trip to the cemetery," Jeane observed. She remembered the car that had pulled up beside them in the mist. She remembered the sound of someone trapped inside. "What's the other story?"

"It's about the Madonna of Bachelor's Grove. Mama said that in life the Madonna was a Steiner woman, a daughter of Old Man Steiner himself. On the night she gave birth, her husband died." Ellie bent forward again. "Now, she really, really loved her husband, and she knew that witching would bring him back. The old man refused to help her and told her she would regret it. But she sneaked into the cemetery—or the burial plot, or whatever it was then—under the next full moon and tried it anyway. She raised him all right, but he was still mostly dead, and when she ran away from him, he crumbled back into dust. When she got home, she found her father there waiting for her. He pointed at the cradle. Her baby was dead, too. Horrified and distraught over what she had done, she ran back to the cemetery and threw herself into the pond. She drowned there, and they say her body never came to the surface. She came back as the first ghost in Bachelor's Grove, the Madonna, wandering among the stones with her baby. Her husband comes back sometimes, too, standing by the lagoon, wrapped in his shroud and waiting for her."

Ellie took a sip of her drink, as if just talking about the Madonna made her nervous.

"There's an old story that says she controls all the ghosts by Bachelor's Grove."

If the quiet had been bad before, the silence that fell when Ellie finished her story was terrifying. It surrounded them, daring them to make a sound.

Finally, Jeane cleared her throat and asked, "Do you think that's true?"

Ellie shook her head. "I don't know, but I'll tell you something else my mother never told me: No Steiner woman she heard of ever took her babies or children into that cemetery."

They emerged from the bar and blinked in the late afternoon sunlight. The wind had picked up and turned cold. Shading her eyes and turning her back to the wind, Jeane looked over at McCain. He looked back at her. Neither of them needed to say anything. They'd been right that night outside of Midlothian. It was the Madonna, but it wasn't Van and his friends who had awakened her. Will carried the Steiner blood. He'd passed it on to his child. It was the presence of the baby, unborn but so close to term, that had awakened the ghost.

A Steiner child. No wonder the voice in the mist wanted Will to kill Laurel. And the Madonna's power explained why the ghost car had pursued them.

"We need to tell Ngan," Jeane said finally. "We need to figure out what to do next."

"That's Ngan's problem." McCain turned up the collar of his coat and stuffed his hands into his pockets. "Our assignment was to investigate the events at the hospital, not play *Ghostbusters*."

Jeane stared at him as offended surprise washed over her. "Michael!"

He shrugged and said, "Don't worry. Knowing Ngan, he'll probably just make that our next assignment anyway."

"Laurel's in danger."

"And she has been since this whole thing started, but you know what? Nothing has happened to her yet. Will's spouting off this morning will have backfired on him—the hospital will be keeping a close watch on him from now on." McCain squinted into the setting sun. "We've got an explanation for what's been happening, and you can go right ahead and file it. But I don't think you need to rush in and do it."

She couldn't believe it. "This is because of your feud with Ngan?"

McCain smiled at her. "Maybe. It's not going to hurt Ngan to sweat a bit. And it's not going to hurt me if I don't have to run off on one of his errands. I have a date, and I'm going to keep it this time. We can worry about the ghost tomorrow. Call me then."

He whirled and sauntered away down the street. Jeane could only stare after him. The pig-headed, self-centered brat! Yet, there was a nagging voice that told her he did have a point. Hadn't she been fighting an internal struggle every time Ngan gave a command lately? Maybe his orders had ultimately always turned out to be in the best interests of the investigation, but the old man had changed with his promotion. McCain was right. Ngan was becoming frustrating to work with. So far, though, all of her hard-fought decisions had told her to do what was right for the team. For Laurel.

But if Laurel wasn't in danger, if they knew what the ghost was—if Ngan was only going to order them back into activity tonight—maybe keeping the news until tomorrow wouldn't be a bad thing. Jeane's cell phone was heavy in her pocket. She looked down the street after McCain. The news could wait. Nothing was going to happen.

Rob's appearance at the hospital had been the last straw. More than two weeks of fighting with himself, with the paranoia, and with the voice that murmured its unending need into his ear—then to find that things were happening behind his back. That the hospital would deliver the baby without his knowledge. That Rob was somehow in league with them. The revelation was like a stab in the back. They knew now. They knew everything. Maybe he should have listened to the voice from the beginning.

It would be over soon, though. After a day of trying to come to terms with Rob's treachery, he knew what he had to do now. The voice would go away, and everything would go back to the way it was before.

It will, the whispering voice reassured him. *You know what needs to be done.*

Will dashed across the road and up to the staff entrance of Presbyterian-St. Luke's. He ignored the tiny new whisper, taut with horror, that nagged in a corner of his mind, asking how things could possibly go back to the way they were. Could Rob's appearance at the hospital have been a coincidence? Could the hospital really have tried calling him to tell him about the plans for the cesarean? Maybe they had. Maybe he hadn't heard the telephone because he was still passed out from the previous night's drinking binge. Or maybe the voice had drowned out the sound of the telephone. Maybe the voice didn't want him to know about the cesarean.

No. That was just crazy.

The shiver that passed through him as he ducked inside the door wasn't entirely affected. He had lost track of the exact time, but it was after two o'clock in the morning and cold outside. All he was wearing was a cheap polyester technician's uniform borrowed from his dental practice with an old lab coat thrown over the top. The cold cut right through both. Never mind. He had a warm coat and blankets waiting

214

in the car. He stepped up to the security guard's window and rapped on the glass.

"Hey!" Will called.

The man behind the window looked up and switched on the intercom. "I.D.?"

"I left it in the lab," Will whined. "I went outside for a quick smoke, and the wind blew the door shut behind me."

"You know you ain't supposed to do that." The guard reached for a phone. "You got a supervisor on duty?"

"Aw, come on. Just let me in. Trust me, I've learned my lesson—I've been freezing my balls off out here."

The guard gave him a sour look but pressed a button, and an inner door buzzed open. Will nodded at him as he passed. "Thanks, man."

"Don't do it again."

"I won't."

He went straight for the nearest elevator. He could already feel a comfortable stillness settling over him. The voice was still there, but it had receded just a bit. The relief was bliss, just a taste of what was to come. It was all going to be over soon. The stillness grew until it was like a haze around him. A visible haze. A mist.

Two weeks ago, that kind of mist had terrified him. Now it would help him. As he got off the elevator, the mist drifted ahead to obscure the spying lenses of security cameras. When a locked door blocked his path, the mist seeped around it, and the door swung open. The mist was there waiting for him on the other side.

He came to her room and went in. For a moment, he looked at her helpless form, then reached down and gathered her up. "I'm sorry, princess," he murmured, "but I need you now." He turned and began to make his way out of the hospital, the mist a calm blanket of comfort embracing him.

chapter

The shrill scream of a cell phone shattered the warm, gentle darkness of McCain's bedroom.

Apparently Institute training and medical school instilled the same kind of reflexes, because both McCain and Shani shot upright immediately and groped for their phones.

There was a crack in the dark, and Shani yelped, "How about some light?"

McCain fumbled for the bedside light and turned it on. Shani found her phone before he found his. Tracking down the ringing probably helped her.

"Mine," she said.

McCain felt his stomach jump. "Laurel?"

"I do have other patients." She wrapped a sheet around herself and flipped open the phone. "Shani Doyle."

He flopped back against the mattress, his heart rate slowing down to something approaching normal.

Moron, he told himself, it's not all about Laurel and the
ghost. Yet in spite of what he had told Jeane outside of
Ellie's that afternoon, what had been the first thing to jump
into his head?

Up until that moment, he hadn't regretted blowing off
Ngan and the Institute for a second. His date with Shani
had been incredible from start to finish. He hadn't even
given Ngan a second thought. It was good to have a night
to himself. A night when he could feel completely . . . normal. He let himself lapse into a light doze while Shani
talked on the phone. He didn't quite follow the conversation, but Shani's voice was agitated and she was asking
questions of the caller at rapid-fire speed. It was too bad
she would have to leave so soon. The bed had been very
comfortable with her in it.

"Fitz, the baby's missing."

He blinked once, instantly alert. "What?"

"The Tavish baby is missing." Shani found his underwear and threw them at him. "I asked a nurse to call me if
anything happened tonight. About fifteen minutes ago,
security got a 'door open' alarm on one of the emergency
exits. It took them that long to realize the baby was gone.
There's no sign of who took her."

The look on Shani's face said that she disagreed with
that assessment. McCain's stomach twisted again as realization crashed down on him.

"Will," he breathed.

He got up and pulled on the underwear, then went to his
closet and reached into the back for the plain, durable black
clothes he kept there.

"How the hell did he get into the hospital?" he asked.

Shani shook her head. "I don't know. The nurse is only
going on what she overheard, but apparently the doors in
the maternity ward were opened from the inside and all the
security cameras showed was a white haze."

Damn. He jerked on a pair of socks "Or a white *mist*, maybe?"

Shani's lips pressed tight. "Security is still trying to piece it together. They'll think sabotage, not spirit."

"But I don't think it'll take them too long to come up with the same mortal prime suspect as us."

McCain pulled his pants up around his hips, grabbed his cell phone, and ran out into the living room. On his bookshelf was a big card file. He rifled through it until he found the crumpled card Will had given him. He dialed Will's number with one hand while he did up his pants with the other. Will's phone rang and rang and rang until finally an answering machine picked up. McCain didn't bother leaving a message. He looked to the clock on his VCR as he dashed back into the bedroom. Two forty-eight a.m.

"He's either not home or not answering," he reported. "I need to go check."

He snatched up a black shirt and pulled it over his head—then paused with it half around his chest. Shani was getting dressed as well.

"You're not coming with me, are you?" he asked.

"No, I thought I'd hang around here in the buff until you got back." She twisted her hair back into a ponytail. "Relax. I'm going back to St. Luke's. It seems like the ghost gets riled up every time you people do something. Someone needs to be at the hospital to hold things together." She looked up at him as she fiddled with her hair. "Everyone has a place on a team, and I know where mine is."

He knew it wasn't meant to be a rebuke, but it felt like one. McCain gave her a fast kiss on the cheek, jammed his feet into a pair of boots, shoved his car keys into his pocket, and ran. He didn't bother with the elevator, just sprinted down the stairs to the parking garage. He dialed Jeane's number as he ran. Her voice was groggy when she answered.

"Good morning, starshine. Laurel's baby is missing from the hospital." He repeated what Shani had told him and read off the address of Will and Laurel's house. "I'm on my way there. Meet me."

"What about Ngan?"

McCain grimaced. "I guess we'd better." He crashed through a final door and into the cavern of the building's parking garage. "Did you tell him what we found out about the Steiner blood?"

Jeane hesitated for a moment then confessed, "No."

He cursed then sighed. "He's going to be pissed."

He turned off the alarm and unlocked the doors on his car as he ran toward it. There was no way around Ngan's anger. The guilt he'd ignored all evening came crushing in on him.

"Just get him and bring him to the Tavish's," he said. "We'll worry about his reaction then. Don't waste any time though—I'm going to go in if I'm there before you."

He didn't have to go in alone. After a dangerously fast trip through Chicago's nearly empty nighttime streets, McCain pulled up outside Will and Laurel's house only to have Jeane come up behind him almost immediately. Ngan hopped out of the passenger side of her car.

McCain blinked and said, "That was fast."

"He knocked on my door just as I was trying to call him," Jeane explained.

"I woke up with a premonition," said Ngan simply. Of the three of them, he looked the least like he had just rolled out of bed. "I was needed at Jeane's, so I went. I had Jeane call Ned as well. He's on his way."

McCain grabbed him and kissed him on the forehead. "Bless your wrinkly little head and all its premonitions!"

He looked up at Will and Laurel's house. It was a moderately large semidetached, two-story brick structure with a well-groomed little yard out front. No lights illuminated its windows. It didn't look as if anybody was home. McCain climbed the porch steps and tested the front door. It was locked, of course, and it seemed solid. It was going to be a bugger to break down. He took a few steps back, but before he could run at it Ngan caught his shoulder.

"May I?" he asked and produce a slim piece of metal. He stepped up to the door and deftly picked the lock. Jeane moved in behind him, an intimidatingly large pistol at the ready.

"Jesus, Jeane, where'd the elephant gun come from?" McCain gasped.

"Souvenir from the old job. Just stay behind me."

She nodded to Ngan, and he swung the door wide. Jeane paused, then stepped through and swept the room in two sharp, economical movements. She looked back to Ngan and him and motioned them inside silently. McCain slipped through and Ngan came after, closing the door behind them.

Streetlights outside cast big pale rectangles through the windows and onto the living room floor. Nothing was stirring. The room was nicely decorated but had a lived-in messiness to it. There were newspapers lying around and a dirty plate and glass sitting beside the couch. A pair of shoes and a basket of laundry sat on a flight of stairs, waiting to be taken up. McCain recognized the look of a man living on his own. Will had more to worry about right now than picking up after himself. Still, McCain remembered how he had spoken about the voice that whispered to him. If it had really been driving Will as hard as it sounded, McCain would have expected things to be at least a bit more run-down.

Jeane gestured for them to stay put while she stepped through an open doorway and into the kitchen. McCain watched her cover that room with the same precise move-ments. She advanced a little farther and peered around another corner under the stairs, then came back to them.

"The garbage needs to be taken out," she whispered, "but there's nothing else in there."

She gestured to the stairs and added, "The door to the basement is through the kitchen and under there. Do you want to look up or down?"

McCain realized that both of them looked to Ngan when she said it. The old man hesitated for a moment then pointed up. Jeane nodded and led them upstairs.

The bathroom at the head of the stairs was empty. So was the next room, neatly decorated and unused. McCain assumed it was a guest room. That left two rooms, both with their doors closed. Jeane chose one, and Ngan flipped the door open for her again. It was the master bedroom. The bed was unmade, and there were clothes on the floor, but everything else seemed normal.

"I haven't seen any preparations for a baby," Jeane mur-mured.

McCain bit his tongue. It was true. There was nothing. As if someone had swept through the house, erasing any evidence that Laurel Tavish had ever been expecting.

"The last room," Ngan suggested.

He led them back out of the bedroom swiftly. He didn't wait for Jeane to cover him but just flung the last door wide.

It was clear that the room had been intended as a nurs-ery. A changing table and a bassinet snuggled against a wall decorated with a border of clowns. A crib, still in its box, leaned against another wall. A cute little chest of drawers had clowns as well, and so did the curtains on the window. Along with all of that, though, were things that didn't belong in the nursery, all thrown in and jumbled together. A high chair. Dishes with playful bunnies. Baby bottles. Books on babies. A package of diapers had been ripped open and strewn around the room. The drawers in the chest had been pulled out and their contents emptied onto the floor. Beside the door, part of the clown border had been ripped away from the wall.

Jeane whistled and said, "This doesn't look good." She stepped back toward the stairs. "I'm going to check the basement."

"Make it quick. I don't think they're here at all." McCain stretched out a foot and nudged a box, flipping it over. An infant car seat. The box was empty. He looked up. "I didn't see a car in the driveway."

"Will's still out with the baby somewhere?"

"Not just somewhere. He's gone to Bachelor's Grove." He stood up and faced Ngan. "We've got something to tell you."

"Perhaps in the car?" Ngan was already leading the way back downstairs. "Jeane, forget the basement. I think Michael is right."

They left the front door unlocked. With a missing baby and pretty clear signs that something was wrong with Will, anyone conducting an official investigation would likely make the assumption that he had left the door unlocked himself. A strange car, abandoned on the street was less likely to go unnoticed, however. Ngan climbed into the back seat of McCain's car, and they followed Jeane as she drove over a couple of streets. When she had parked again, she trotted back to McCain's car and knocked on the driver's window.

"Move over," she said.

"What?"

"We drove three blocks, and you couldn't keep up with me. I'm driving."

McCain started to protest, but Ngan cleared his throat. "She's a better driver than you, Michael."

"Fine."

McCain shifted himself over into the passenger's seat as Jeane got in. He glanced at his watch. Bachelor's Grove was roughly a forty-minute drive from downtown. The door alarm at the hospital had gone off fifteen minutes before the nurse had called Shani. It had taken another fifteen minutes for them to converge on the Tavish's house and search it.

"If Will's not at the cemetery already," McCain said, "he'll be there soon."

Jeane bit her lip as she gunned the engine and headed for the expressway south. "It's going to take us about twenty minutes if we push it all the way and no cops stop us," she said. "And that'll be dicey."

"I can take care of that," Ngan said, reaching forward with his hand out. "Give me your telephone."

She fumbled the phone out of her pocket, passing it to him. He sat back again and began placing his call. Jeane glanced over at McCain very briefly.

"Maybe you should call your buddy Jessop in Midlothian. They should be able to get someone over to the cemetery fast."

McCain shook his head as he watched the scenery whip past. "No. I don't think we want to bring the police in. It could get messy," he said. "I want to keep Will out of trouble as much as I can. The cops aren't going to try to arrest a ghost, they're going to pin all this on the most likely *living* person. Will doesn't deserve that."

"Fitz, he's already kidnapped his baby from the hospital."

"Fine." He glowered at her. "Think of it as keeping the Institute from getting publicly involved, then. It's not like we can testify in court that we're movie location scouts who moonlight as air-conditioning repairmen."

Jeane frowned but didn't look at him again. She cut across the street abruptly, up a ramp, and onto the Dan Ryan Expressway. Even at this hour, there was traffic on the expressway. Jeane didn't let that stop her from pushing the gas pedal to the floor and picking up speed.

"I still think we need someone over at the cemetery sooner." She pulled out and passed a fast little sports car. McCain saw the driver's mouth go wide as they zipped past him. "Get on your phone and call Van."

"What?"

"He's in Midlothian and he already knows something is going on."

"It's too dangerous. . . ."

"Mucking about with ghosts is what he wanted, isn't it?" She leaned on her horn. "Just do it." She rattled off the number.

"Fine. Whatever." He dialed the number and waited while it rang. A sleepy voice answered.

"Hello?"

"Van, this is Fitz. We need you now." He outlined the situation swiftly. "Can you get over to Bachelor's Grove and keep an eye on things for us?"

Van sucked in his breath. "I could get in *so* much trouble for this!"

"More than you would have if your mother found out about the séance?" McCain sighed. "Look, Van, you don't have to do this. We found something out today. We know that the Madonna's rising had nothing to do with you. You don't owe us or Laurel anything, but we really need your help now. Can you help us?"

He didn't even hesitate. "Yeah. I can take my bike and be there in ten minutes."

"Great." McCain nodded to Jeane. She smiled. "Don't go into the cemetery. Just stay outside, watch and wait—and don't do anything stupid." You're still young, he added to himself, you'll get lots of chances to do stupid things. "We should be there in about twenty minutes." He hung up. "Van's going to watch for us."

"Excellent."

Ngan poked his head up and dropped Jeane's phone back onto the front seat. "I'm not sure that's wise," he said. "Things might happen tonight that a member of the general public—especially a teenager—would be better off not seeing."

McCain laughed. "Ngan, how many Institute agents started off by seeing something they would have been better off not seeing?"

"Except that Van is—"

Jeane's phone rang, cutting him off. McCain snatched it up and answered. "Where the hell are you people?" screamed Ned. "You drag me out of bed then when I come to meet you, you're not there!"

"Change of plans, Ned. We're heading to Bachelor's Grove. Meet us there." McCain held the phone away from his ear as Ned cursed him loudly. "Yes, Ned, I love you, too."

The psychic groaned into the phone, and McCain heard a car engine start in the background. "Just wait for me before you try going into the cemetery. Where are you now?"

"Heading south on the Dan Ryan, just coming up on 55. We'll switch to 57 when . . ." Flashing lights in the rearview mirror caught his attention. "God damn it!"

McCain twisted around to stare out the rear window. Two police cruisers were just coming down off the last on-ramp they'd passed and were catching up to them fast. Their lights were flickering like the sharp edges of knives.

"We're screwed, Ned," McCain said. "Just get to Bachelor's Grove as fast as you can."

He hung up. Jeane was staring at the approaching cruisers.

"Should I pull over?" she asked.

"Easy." Ngan was leaning back in his seat. "They're for us."

"What are you talking ab—"

Before he could even finish the cruisers had caught up to them and split, one coming up on either side. McCain caught a glimpse of the officers in the cruiser on the passenger side. For a moment, they looked back at him with the barely concealed curiosity of people obeying unexplained orders. Then they were past and taking up position just in front of them.

"Match their speed," Ngan told Jeane.

She glanced down at the speedometer and shook her head in disbelief. "Hot damn. Who did you just call?"

"The Institute has certain contacts it can call on in an emergency." Ngan sat back. "Michael, you were saying there was something you had to tell me?"

McCain swallowed and looked to Jeane, but she had her eyes fixed on the road. Convenient for her. He twisted around to face Ngan. He might as well keep it short and simple.

"We found out something today that we should have acted on right away. I persuaded Jeane—"

"You don't have to cover for me, Fitz."

He ignored her comment. "I persuaded Jeane that we didn't need to act on it right away, that everything would be all right. That was a mistake." He took a deep breath. "Will's ancestors aren't exactly who he thought they were. In fact, there's a pretty good chance that that family, the Steiners, is responsible for the hauntings in Bachelor's Grove, either raising the ghosts or . . . well, *being* them. Apparently, there's also more to the story of the Madonna, too. She inadvertently killed her own baby, and after that the Steiners wouldn't bring their children into the cemetery."

McCain looked at Ngan. The old man seemed remarkably calm, as imperturbable as he had looked before the move to Chicago. McCain crossed his fingers and hoped the mood would last.

"We think," McCain continued, "that it was actually

Laurel and Will's visit to the cemetery that roused the ghost. The baby was so close to being born that they were essentially bringing a Steiner child into the cemetery. Its presence woke the ghost, and it lashed out at Laurel."

"No," said Ngan.

McCain blinked and looked at him sharply. "What do you mean 'no?' "

Ngan avoided his eyes. "There's something I should have told you as well." He looked up again. "Did you know that Laurel and Will's child is a girl?"

"I didn't. Jeane?" She shook her head. McCain turned back to Ngan. "I guess nobody mentioned it. Does it matter?"

"Yes. What did Will tell you the voice whispered to him?"

"It wanted Laurel. It wanted him to bring her to it." Ngan shook his head and McCain frowned. "That's what he said. I'm sure of it."

"It may be what he said but it's not what the whispers said."

McCain tried to remember his conversation with Will and the exact words the man had used. *Whatever was in the mist, it wanted Laurel. It wanted her any way it could have her. Even dead.* He shook his head. No. That was Will's interpretation. It wasn't what the whispering voice had said. The whispers had said . . .

McCain's head snapped up. "Bring *her* to me. Oh my God, the Madonna was never attacking Laurel. It wanted the baby all along."

chapter

4TEEN

Ngan nodded slowly and watched McCain fall back in his seat, stunned. Jeane, he noticed, just set her jaw and drove a little faster. He admired her focus. The idea that the Madonna was after the baby, not Laurel, had stunned Ngan as well when it first came to him. He'd been back in his office, poring over the agents' various reports and trying to find the clue that would link everything together. The revelation of what—or who—the ghost was really after had eluded him until late at night. The solution seemed so obvious, yet they had been so focused on Laurel and Will that the baby, only just brought into the world, hadn't even seemed like a separate consideration. And it had been the link all along.

No, Ngan reminded himself, *she* had been the link. It was still hard to think of her in terms of a person, and maybe that's why it had been so easy to overlook her significance. The ghost had known though, and McCain and Jeane's discovery of the secret Steiner blood answered the "how?" of that knowledge. It answered Ned's mystery of how a ghost could manifest in three apparently diverse places, as well.

Steiner blood had drawn the Madonna from Bachelor's Grove to Will, and in the hospital she hadn't been manifesting around Laurel but around the Steiner baby inside her. Ngan had even seen the ghost leave Laurel and seek out the baby. He should have guessed then at the baby's importance.

He hadn't, though. He and McCain had been so busy fighting each other that he hadn't even thought of it. Worse, their enmity had put the child at grave risk. That shamed him more deeply than he could ever tell even Lily. It was a problem that needed to be fixed before it got any worse. He sat forward, leaning between the front seats so that the lights from their escort flashed in his eyes.

"You should have come to me, Michael," Ngan said.

It was the wrong way to begin, and he regretted it instantly. He had meant it as a consolation, that McCain could have told him anything, but as soon as the words were past his lips he knew they could be too easily misinterpreted.

McCain did just that, his face twisting into a scowl. "Twist the knife a little more, Ngan. I know what I should have done. I'm rather acutely aware of it at the moment."

McCain turned to glare at Ngan. Their faces were close enough that Ngan could smell the sourness of interrupted sleep on his breath.

"Of course," McCain continued, "you can do no wrong. You're the leader. We're your agents. You hold something back from us, that's a completely different story."

He wanted to explain himself to McCain and Jeane, tell them what he had told Lily, but all that fled his mind.

"Perhaps I wouldn't have held back if I knew you wouldn't dismiss anything I did or said as a personal insult to you."

"Did you ever stop to realize that your orders really were insulting?"

"Did you ever stop to think about why I gave them?"

"Stop it!" Jeane shouted.

Her right hand left the steering wheel, her arm tucked in and back, and her elbow whipped out, hitting McCain hard in the back of his head. The blow sent his skull cracking against Ngan's. They both fell back, blinking away the haze of sudden pain.

"Do either of you ever actually listen to the other?" Jeane snapped. She shot a harsh glance at both of them. "It comes down to Ngan's promotion. Both of you have been pissing vinegar since he got it. I don't think either of you likes it, but you'd better damn well suck it up because we've got bigger problems." The lines of her face were hard. "Have either of you thought about *why* the Madonna wants Laurel's baby?"

Ngan rubbed his head and fought to regain control over his emotions. His argument with McCain was over. He had told himself that this afternoon, and yet the young man still had the power to stir him to anger. He would not let him do it again.

"Our original theory of vengeance against the living still holds true, I think," Ngan said.

"It fits even better, now," McCain added. "The Madonna lost her child, and Steiner mothers avoided Bachelor's Grove because they knew she would strike out against theirs."

He glanced back and met Ngan's eyes. McCain was rubbing his head, too. He snatched his hand away and turned back around in his seat.

Jeane grunted. "It's nice to see you two can agree on something. Even if you're both wrong. We've all missed something crucial by focusing on vengeance. If the

Madonna just wanted to strike out against the baby, why not attack her at the hospital?"

Ngan frowned, trying to follow Jeane's logic. "It lacked the strength, perhaps? The only direct physical action it has ever taken was pushing Shani—and possibly opening the doors at the hospital tonight for Will."

"And what do you call being chased down a never-ending highway by a dead hit man's car?" demanded McCain. "Just a little nonviolent object lesson?"

"How do you know that . . ." Ngan's blood was rising again.

He took a deep breath. McCain would not drive him to anger. The problem was resolved—McCain just didn't know it yet. Ngan forced himself to answer calmly and without insult.

"You don't know that the phantom car had any physical form. What would have happened had it caught you? Perhaps nothing." He turned back to Jeane and said, "The involvement of the ghost car is another riddle answered by the link of the Steiner blood. If the same power gave rise to all of the ghosts in the cemetery, and the Madonna shares in that power, it may have a measure of control over the other ghosts of Bachelor's Grove."

Jeane nodded. "It certainly seems to be most powerful when it's manifesting in the cemetery. That still doesn't explain why it wants Will to bring the baby to it, though. If it has enough control over him to make him do that, it must have enough control to make him harm the baby directly. That's not what it wants."

She drummed her fingers against the rim of the steering wheel. Her lips twisted as if there was something she knew, but didn't want to say aloud.

After a moment, she said quietly, "Ghosts are often said to be looking for a way to finish something they couldn't finish in life."

McCain was the first to grasp the significance of what she had said. "Oh," he whispered. "Oh, hell."

He sat back in his seat. Ngan gave him a questioning look. McCain just shook his head. Not out of malice or obstinacy, but clearly out of shock. Ngan sat back himself. What could the Madonna be trying to finish? Perhaps they had its motivations wrong. Perhaps it wasn't trying to harm Laurel's baby but to somehow make amends for the death of its own child. But that didn't fit with its pattern of behavior. He tried to think in a broader sense, of things left undone. There were so many possibilities, though. They knew so little of the Madonna's life as a living woman, only that she had a child and a husband and that . . .

"Ah," Ngan said simply as the truth dawned on him.

What had the Madonna left unfinished? The resurrection of her beloved husband. The first unsuccessful attempt had taken the life of her child. What manner of magic did the Steiner blood carry? He couldn't guess. But how many tales of magic from around the world told of one person dying so that another might be reborn?

The death of a Steiner child for the life of a Steiner man. And that was why the Madonna needed Will and Laurel's daughter at Bachelor's Grove.

"How long until we reach the cemetery?" he asked.

McCain glanced at his watch. "Maybe another ten minutes. It's hard to guess." There was no argument in his voice now.

Time passed swiftly behind the wheel. Jeane kept her eyes on the lights of their police escort, not paying much attention to the other cars they passed or the urban landscape that blurred by in the night. It was hard to tell where they were. When they switched from the Dan Ryan and 94 to I-57, the change was barely noticeable. She was aware of the little things in the car, though. The way Ngan was absolutely still and silent in the back seat, gathering himself, she presumed, for what might lie ahead. The way McCain checked his watch with annoying frequency and rubbed his head where he'd smacked skulls with Ngan.

Jeane felt a certain perverse pleasure in bringing that particular skirmish to an end. After being caught between Ngan and McCain for the better part of a week, finally being in a position to do something about their interminable bickering was satisfying.

The shrill ring of her cell phone broke the long tension of silence. McCain picked it up off the seat and answered. "Hello? Yes." He paused, listening. "Yes. Yes. I see. Thank you very much." He hung up. "Time to slow down, Jeane. That was our escort." He gestured with the phone. "The exit to Midlothian is just ahead."

She nodded and moved her foot from the gas to the brake. The exit came up on them sooner than she expected, maybe because the police cruisers in front of them didn't signal a lane change. When the exit appeared, she was the only one to pull onto it. The cruisers sped away on down the interstate.

"They're not coming any farther?" Jeane asked.

"No," said Ngan from the shadows of the back seat. "That's as far as they could take us. We're on our own."

"By the way," McCain added, "the officer I was talking to asked me to pay his respects to you."

"That was kind of him." Jeane glanced into the rearview mirror to try to catch Ngan's face, but all she could see was a silhouette.

The exit ramp deposited them on the main road west through Midlothian. After travelling so fast for so long, driving at the speed limit felt like crawling. Any time they'd gained on the expressway would be wiped out if they were stopped for a ticket now, though, and Jeane held herself strictly to the limit. Midlothian crept by, sleeping in the night. Her foot itched with the need to slam the gas pedal down and speed to the cemetery.

Ngan reached up and touched her shoulder. "Easy," he murmured.

In fact it was less than five minutes before they pulled over on the shoulder of 143rd Street. There was another car there already, the kind of sporty sedan a young couple might drive until they had a family. Jeane jumped out of McCain's car immediately and ran up to the other car, laying a hand on its hood. The night was as cold as the wind outside Ellie's had promised, but the metal of the hood was still slightly warm.

"He can't have been here long," Jeane observed. "Assuming this is his car."

"It's a safe bet," McCain said. He had the big black flashlight from under his car seat. He shone it in through the car windows. "Baby seat. Parking pass from Presbyterian-St. Luke's."

"Ignore the car," Ngan said. "They will have gone straight to Bachelor's Grove."

He walked up to the end of the gravel path that led into the forest preserve. Away from the streetlights, it was pitch black. The sky was clear, and the stars shone like brittle bits of broken glass. Jeane had seen the moon riding high in the sky from the window of her apartment, but now it hovered at the western horizon. It had been entirely full tonight. The Madonna's moon. She and McCain joined Ngan, McCain swinging the flashlight along the edge of the woods. The beam caught something bright half-hidden just inside the line of trees—a bicycle.

"Van's here," McCain said.

Ngan frowned. "I fear for him."

McCain nodded and took the lead, the flashlight making

a pool ahead of him. Ngan hissed quietly and he switched the light off. It was the sensible thing to do, Jeane knew. They didn't need to alert Will—or the Madonna, though Jeane suspected that a little light wouldn't be what would give them away to a dead thing. But sensible or not, it left them creeping slowly through the moon-tinted dark, moving as fast as they dared. She couldn't help noticing that in spite of the friction that had kept them divided, they fell easily into the coordinated silence of a team.

Her eyes adjusted to the dark after a few minutes, and she found that she could see a little bit. It was quite a change from the night before—had it really been just a little over twenty-four hours since they had been out here? The moonlight then had turned the woods into a place at once beautiful and eerie. The long, deep shadows of the moon just made it a void. Anything could be out there, or nothing at all. Even the little sounds of nocturnal birds and animals fell silent with their passage. No, that wasn't right. She paused for a moment, holding her breath. Ngan paused, too, and the black shape of his head turned toward her.

"What is it?" he asked.

"It's still," she whispered.

It was. There were no animal or bird sounds, but neither were there sounds of tree branches moving in the wind or distant cars rushing by on the highway. The night was utterly still, just as it had been in the mist on the turnpike before the approach of the phantom car.

"Hey!" husked McCain urgently.

He was somewhere just a little ahead, but Jeane had lost him in the dark. She caught a muted, ruddy glow as he capped the flashlight with his fingers and flicked it on just long enough for her and Ngan to locate him. He was kneeling on the ground. Another shielded flash of his light revealed why. Van lay huddled at the edge of the path.

"Damn!" Jeane knelt as well, and took the flashlight

from him. "You two close your eyes. There's no sense in all of us losing our night vision."

She turned the flashlight on. The glare was momentarily blinding, but she forced her eyes open and bent over Van. His skin was a little pale and slightly cool. For a moment her heart skipped. She pressed her fingers against his neck and sighed with relief when she found a pulse.

"He's alive," she reported for the benefit of McCain and Ngan.

She turned Van's head and peeled back one of his eyelids. His pupil contracted immediately. He jerked, his other eyelid snapping up and his mouth opening as he sucked in air. Jeane slapped her hand over his mouth before he could scream.

"It's Jeane—it's okay." She fumbled the flashlight around so that it wasn't shining directly into his face. "It's okay."

His panicked breathing slowed, and she took her hand away.

"What happened?" she asked him.

He sat up and whispered, "Someone hit me from behind."

Jeane felt the back of his head. Van gasped as she touched the lump that was forming there, but she didn't feel any blood.

"There was already a car out on 143rd when I got here," Van said. "I grabbed the light off my bike and started in to the cemetery." He felt the back of his head himself and winced. "I heard a noise, but before I could turn around, I got clobbered."

"Will must have still been on the path and seen your light behind him," Ngan guessed. With his eyes screwed shut, he looked like some kind of blind seer. "He must have waited and ambushed you."

"I swear I didn't see anybody."

Ngan shook his head. "The shadows are deep—and Will may have supernatural help just now."

It seemed as if the Madonna had helped Will get the baby out of the hospital. What else might she do to help him? Jeane didn't want to think about it.

"How do you feel?" she asked Van.

"Like I got hit with a tree."

He started to stand up. Jeane caught him.

"You're staying here," she said. "This is dangerous."

Van gave her a look of disgust, the flashlight throwing dark angles of shadow across his face. "But it was okay to send me in to stand watch for you?"

He had a point, she realized guiltily. She looked over at McCain and Ngan still kneeling down with their eyes closed and asked, "What do you two think?"

"Bring him," McCain said. "He's earned it."

Ngan nodded his agreement, and Jeane helped Van to his feet. "You're in, but do everything we tell you and stay out of the way."

Van smiled and snapped her a cocky salute that only made his eagerness more obvious. We'll see how long that lasts, she thought. She snapped off the flashlight and the night closed in again. Someone—Ngan—took her hand in the dark, leading her as her night vision slowly returned.

At first she thought the luminous streaks of red among the trees were just her dazzled eyes playing tricks on her. They didn't go away when she blinked though. Red lights dancing in the darkness. "Ngan . . ."

"I see them."

"What are they?" whispered McCain.

Van answered him. "Ghostlights. A couple of stories describe lights in Bachelor's Grove. Blue in the cemetery itself, red along the path."

The young man's description sounded vaguely familiar, like something chased out of her head by the strain of the night. Maybe having him along would be good. They pressed on. The ghostlights stayed off in the woods, flickering among the trees, sometimes a little ahead of the team, sometimes marching beside them. They reminded Jeane uncomfortably of the flashing lights of the police cruisers she had spent so long following: an escort. Did the Madonna know they were here? Had she sent the li—

One of the lights darted in very close, swooping up beside the path. Old reflexes kicked in. Jeane had her gun in her hand and trained on the flickering patch of light before even bothering to wonder how much good the weapon would be against it. Likely very little. She held the gun steady anyway. The light came no closer, just hung there for a long moment—then vanished. Jeane lowered the gun slowly.

"Should we be worried about that?" she asked.

"Not about the ghostlights, I think," Ngan replied.

He took the flashlight from her other hand and turned it on, cupping his hand over the end as McCain had done. Even that weak glow was enough to show her what she had missed in her focused concentration on the ghostlight.

Mist streamed along the ground, swirling up to her ankles and climbing. It was getting thicker, too, and when Ngan turned off the flashlight, the gathering mist was still faintly visible, a pale luminescence in the night.

"How close are we to the cemetery?" Ngan asked.

"There's a bend in the path just ahead," Van said. "Bachelor's Grove is just around it."

For every step they took, though, the mist rose higher and grew denser. The red ghostlights faded into it. After only ten yards, the engulfing dark of night had been replaced by the radiance of the mist—light or dark, they were still effectively blind. The mist deadened even the careful, muffled sounds of their footfalls and breathing. The chase on the turnpike came back to Jeane, an unending race through the mist.

"Join hands," she ordered, sliding her gun back into the holster. She reached out and felt Van and Ngan connect with her. "Fitz? Ngan?"

"Here," said a voice from behind Van—McCain. "Shouldn't we be there by now? Have we missed the turn in the path?"

"No." Ngan's voice was confident. "I'm still standing on gravel. Which way does the path turn, Van?"

"Right. Bachelor's Grove is on the right, too."

They shuffled forward carefully, an eternity of tiny baby steps, until Ngan stopped suddenly.

"I'm off the path now," he said. "Turn—I'll follow the edge of the path."

More shuffling steps, Ngan making noise now as one foot trailed through fallen leaves and the other debris of autumn. Jeane searched the mist ahead for any sign of the cemetery gates. Or anything else. There was nothing except the starshine glow of the mist with occasional billows and wisps that made her want to snatch her hand away from Van and pull out her gun. She resisted the urge and just kept watching. For the gates. For the cemetery's chain-link fence. For a tree. For Will. Anything.

"The mist is getting lighter," hissed McCain abruptly.

It looked to Jeane as if the mist was as heavy as it had ever been.

"You're imagin—"

"No," McCain interrupted, "I can see my hand."

"Hard right turn," Ngan suggested. "Michael, lead us to where the mist is thinnest."

After two steps, Jeane could see Van's back in front of her. After three, she could make out McCain in front of him. And on the fourth step, she was out of the mist almost completely. The sagging, rusted gates of Bachelor's Grove hung only a few feet in front of them. The sky was perfectly clear overhead, stars shining down. All around the cemetery, the mist loomed like a wall but within the boundary of the fence it was little more than a thin ground cover. A gentle blue glow pervaded the cemetery. It struck a frosty sparkle on the scattered gravestones and the bare branches of the tree. It sent shadows reaching across the shifting surface of the mist.

And it illuminated two figures strolling slowly among the graves.

So peaceful. So calm. Will looked terrible—his face was haggard and hollow, his hair stood on end, and his clothes were in disarray—but he gazed with adoring serenity on the tiny, blanket-swathed bundle in his arms. Beside him paced a woman in a frontier-style dress, long and pale, its color washed away by the moonlight glow. She had long sandy brown hair only a little lighter than Will's. It lifted and stirred as if blowing in a breeze that affected nothing else. A breeze, Jeane realized, or a gentle current of water, as if it were still submerged. What had she expected the Madonna to look like? A gaunt spectre? A terrible hag, still dripping with water and wet leaves from her drowning in the lagoon? The ghost was a woman. She looked at the bundle she carried with exactly the same adoration as Will.

Or perhaps Will gazed with the same adoration as her. They matched each other pace for pace, walking with eerie synchronicity. Where the Madonna stepped, Will stepped, too. Where she turned, he turned. When she stroked a finger along her baby's face, Will touched his daughter and smiled the same joyful smile.

And while he played with the baby, the Madonna raised her eyes toward the gate, and blue light flashed in cold, empty eye sockets.

"She knows we're here," McCain said as he flung himself at the hole in the fence. "Will!" he yelled. "Stop!"

"Michael!" Ngan went after him almost immediately but he wasn't quite fast enough to keep McCain from slipping through the hole in the fence.

Jeane heard Ngan growl something incomprehensible, then he went through himself. She was right on their heels, drawing her gun as she moved, vaguely aware of Van coming after her. If Will heard or saw any of them he gave no indication of it. The Madonna turned away and he turned with her . . . toward the lagoon.

"No!" screamed McCain. "Will!"

He sprinted forward. Ngan glanced back at Jeane once, then ran forward as well. She ran, too, gun held low and alert for hazards that might be hidden by the mist. What good they were going to be against the Madonna, she didn't know, but Will was mortal enough to tackle, and he was the one they really had to stop.

The mist stretched up from the ground before they got anywhere near close to the pair. At first Jeane thought the pull at her feet was weeds tangled on the ground. The resistance grew stronger, pushing against her shins, her knees, her thighs—the mist was rising, and it was like trying to run through water. The faster she tried to move, the greater the resistance. McCain, out in front, was struggling even harder. Ngan had dropped to a walk and was forcing his way slowly forward. Jeane spared a glance back at Van. The young man had all but stopped, staring in horrified fascination at everything that was happening.

Behind him, back beyond the gates and outside of the cemetery, the mist was roiling like a storm front. Something was moving in it, approaching the cemetery with a slow, deliberate pace. Jeane froze. The Madonna had summoned up the ghost car on the turnpike when all they had done was investigate the cemetery. What could be in the mist now?

The tale of the two-headed monster that McCain had ridiculed leaped into her mind. Suddenly it didn't seem so funny anymore. Behind them was an unknown danger, in front of them, unreachable, the Madonna and Will. Of all the dangers in the cemetery, she knew there was one she could do something about. She brought her gun up to firing height and leveled it at Will, aiming low, aiming for his leg.

"Stop!"

Ngan's voice was like a whipcrack, impossible to ignore. McCain stopped and turned. Jeane's eyes leaped to Ngan, though her hand remained steady.

"We have to do something, Ngan," she said. "Look behind us."

She saw his eyes flicker, then come back to her. "Not Will," Ngan ordered. "You might hit the baby."

"I won't."

"You might." His eyes bore into her. A heartbeat passed. Damn. She spun around. "Down, Van!"

She barely waited for him to hit the ground before she fired three hard, fast shots into the swirling mist beyond the gate.

Something yelped—then shouted, "Jesus H. Christ! Hold your fire!"

Jeane's finger locked, just ready to squeeze down on the trigger a fourth time. "Ned?"

chapter

F 1 5 T E E N

McCain watched Ned Devromme emerge from the mist. It literally parted before the psychic, rolling away as though reluctant to touch him. There was a look of intense concentration on Ned's face.

"Don't you people wait when you're told to?" Ned snarled.

"You're just lucky you still have your head attached," Jeane spat back.

"Hey! Enough!" McCain shouted at both of them. "Ned, can you stop them?" He turned and pointed after the Madonna and Will.

They were still moving deliberately toward the lagoon—maybe even a little faster than they had before. The mist didn't hamper them at all, though it was still clinging to McCain, Jeane, and Ngan, dragging at their legs and holding them back. McCain didn't know exactly how Ned was keeping the mist back, but he wasn't about to second guess him at a time like this. Maybe Ned could do what they hadn't been able to do.

The psychic didn't need any further instruction. He glanced after the retreating pair. The set of his face shifted subtly for a moment, and he grunted.

"Two can play at that game," he murmured and concentration settled back over his features.

Will jerked to a sudden halt, his arms wrapping protectively around the baby. For the first time, he looked up and around, as if only now truly aware of where he was.

"*Will!*" McCain shouted again. He forced all the air in his lungs into that cry, as if the extra effort might somehow bring Will back to them. It made him twist around at least.

Will's eyes went wide. "Rob? What—?"

The Madonna reached out and drew one finger down Will's cheek. His head followed her motion, dropping until he was looking at the baby in his arms once more. A happy smile bloomed on his face.

"Will, *no!*" McCain started to shout.

He barely got the sound past his lips when the Madonna whirled to glare at them. At Ned. Contentment was gone from her face, and only hate burned there. She opened her mouth and screamed.

At least it looked like a scream. There was no sound that McCain could hear, but every inch of his skin crinkled tight. The mist lying along the ground before the Madonna rose up in waves and billows sweeping toward them. McCain cursed and threw himself aside. His hands touched the ground for just a moment as he tumbled, and he could feel the earth trembling like a train was passing by.

He scrambled to his feet just in time to see the others diving for cover as well—all except Ned. The psychic stood his ground. He frowned, and the waves of mist parted around him, though the force of their passage made him stagger.

"Go!" Ned yelled.

The Madonna's silent scream had cleared the mist away. Ngan and Jeane were already up and moving. Van had fallen back to stand closer to Ned.

"Hail Mary," McCain muttered and sprinted forward, running straight for Will. He was still the closest. He still had the best chance to grab Will.

But the ghost's cold blue eyes darted toward him, and suddenly a new drift of mist coalesced out of the night between McCain and Will. It wasn't just a cloud or a wisp this time, but a strangely cohesive arm as thick as the trunk of a tree.

McCain dodged toward the end of it. The mist slid over itself, more of it boiling out of thin air to block him. Nice try. He dropped to roll under it.

The mist expanded that way, too, growing down as quick as a thought. Hitting it was like hitting a packed snow bank: solid and as cold as winter itself. Colder. McCain's left shoulder and arm went instantly numb. McCain gasped in shock and wrenched himself away. Hands helped him to his feet. Jeane and Ngan.

"Don't touch it!" he spat.

"Double team," Jeane suggested shortly.

She went for one end of the mist. McCain moved for the other. Good plan. It might not be able to stop all of them.

If all of them worked together.

Ngan hadn't moved. McCain felt a hot flash of anger. Fine! Let the old man stand and do nothing. McCain jumped at his end of the mist, faking left, then right as he might have on a basketball court. The mist kept up with him, then lashed out abruptly with a whiplike tongue of mist. McCain fell back—and kept falling back as the mist pressed in toward him. Jeane wasn't faring much better.

"Ngan!" McCain snapped. "Help us . . ."

"Patience," was all the old man said. His voice was tight and McCain realized that every muscle in his body was tight as well. He stared fiercely at the Madonna and Will. Poised. Waiting.

On the other side of the icy mist, the Madonna turned back to Will. She shifted her baby—for the first time, McCain saw that it was shriveled and grey, not a baby at all but a tiny corpse—and held it in one arm while she reached the other toward Will. With that action, something changed about her. She had always looked real, but suddenly the air of otherworldliness that had clung to her seemed to vanish. McCain didn't know how, but he knew that, just for a moment, she was as solid as anything else in Bachelor's Grove. She could touch things. She could hold a baby.

Will looked up at the Madonna and started to hand her his daughter.

"No!" shouted Ned. "It mustn't take the baby!"

The ghost turned her head toward Ned sharply. Instead of screaming this time, she hissed. The sound was silent again, but the action was unmistakable. The mist trembled as if a sword had sliced through it, and the crinkling across McCain's skin turned to a sharp, almost unbearable prickle, like standing naked in a storm of sleet. Ned cried out in agony and dropped to his knees, clutching at his head.

And in that moment, Ngan leaped. His muscles uncoiled, pushing him up into the air, up to somersault entirely over the bank of mist that had held them back, even over Will and the ghost herself. He landed in a soft crouch, knees absorbing the shock, hands barely brushing the ground before he sprang up. He reached out and snatched the baby from Will's arms.

The Madonna threw her head back in a soundless wail and vanished.

The icy mist that had been holding him and Jeane back

began to sink and McCain rushed forward. He caught Will just as the other man sagged and started to collapse.

McCain shot a hard glare at Ngan and said, "You could have warned us. What if that stunt had failed?"

"It seems to me I've heard similar words before," Ngan replied calmly. "Except that they referred to a certain young agent."

Ngan cradled the baby gently. Her eyes were open, staring at everything in silent wonder.

McCain flushed and turned back to Will. He was shaking and crying, and like his daughter, he was staring. McCain had the distinct impression, however, that Will wasn't really registering anything he was staring at.

"Will?" he asked softly.

"Rob? Oh God, Rob, what have I done?" Will struggled to sit up. "Johanna? Where's Johanna?"

McCain glanced at Jeane and frowned. "Your grandmother?"

"No," Ngan answered for him. He stepped forward and held the baby where Will could see her. "She's safe, Will."

A sharp whistle cut the night. Ned was hobbling toward them, leaning on Van for support.

"Get your asses in gear!" the psychic shouted. "We need to get out of here!"

"But . . ." McCain blinked and looked around. Everything seemed peaceful. "The Madonna's gone, isn't she?"

Ned stamped his foot, sending little drifts of mist gusting up. "We're not *that* good. She's just waiting. I can still feel . . ."

His voice trailed off as he looked at the ground. McCain followed his gaze. The drift of mist his foot had disturbed was still moving. All of the mist that lingered in the cemetery was moving, streaming slowly over the ground, pouring in the direction of the lagoon. More mist was rising up from the water.

"Move!" Ned yelled. "Move!"

He let go of Van and shoved the wide-eyed young man in the direction of the gate, then went after him. Ngan followed, the baby held tight. Jeane bent down and helped McCain haul Will to his feet.

"Leave me!" the battered man moaned.

"Not a chance," muttered McCain.

They half-supported, half-carried Will after the others. The mist was whipping past their feet faster now, and McCain could feel a stiff breeze pressing against his face and pulling at his back. It tugged at his hair and jacket, growing stronger with every second.

The blue light that had suffused Bachelor's Grove was changing as well. It was becoming harsher and shifting so that it came from behind them. Stark shadows jumped out in front of them, flickering as the mist rippled beneath. Up ahead, Ned turned to look back. The light made his face pale, and McCain saw it grow even paler. He reached out and grabbed Van, dragging him back and into the shelter of two large gravestones that stood close together.

"Everyone behind here—fast!" Ned commanded. There was a tinge of fear in his voice that sounded strange coming from the big man.

As they hustled Will over to the gravestones, McCain risked a glance over his shoulder.

Back over the lagoon, the mist was whirling around, squeezing together into a blue spark that grew as he watched. The breeze—now a wind—wasn't just blowing toward the lagoon. It was air rushing into an unnatural void, sucking leaves and loose clumps of dry grass into a swirl of mist and blue light.

The last few steps that got McCain, Jeane, and Will behind the shelter of the gravestone were a fight against a howling gale. Heavier debris, twigs and thin branches, was being plucked from the ground now. McCain spared a last glance for the light over the lagoon as he dropped. There was a gaunt figure forming there.

"She's coming back," he shouted over the wind, "and she isn't happy."

"I can sense her anger," Ned confirmed. "I get the feeling that all of you know something I don't know about her. Anyone want to share?"

Ngan quickly outlined what they had guessed about the Steiners, the Madonna, and her desire for Will's baby. It left Will staring at them with his mouth agape. McCain took his hand.

"I'm sorry you had to find out this way, Will."

Will shook his head slowly as if trying to clear it. "I don't . . ." He sighed. "You don't really work for a ventilation company, do you?"

McCain shook his head. He could sympathize with Will. Finding out so much, so suddenly—so drastically. He gave Will's hand a squeeze.

Will looked up at him and said, "At least I know I wasn't going crazy. In a strange way, everything makes sense now."

"No, it doesn't." Ned was frowning. "I mean, it all makes *magical* sense—except for the part about actually raising her husband. I can see trying to finish the unfinished task, but it's impossible. How can she hope that one ghost can bring another back to life?"

Will drew a deep breath. "She doesn't," he said, tapping his head. "I know it all. She told it to me. If she manages to bring him back, she knows that he'll only die right away. That's what she wants. Her failure the first time left him trapped between life and death, but if he dies cleanly he'll go on to the other side, and that will release her, too. They'll be together again."

"But *how*?" insisted Ned.

"By teaching me the rite and having me perform it." He

shook his head again. "Ever since I took Johanna, that's all she's been talking about. She kept saying that only Steiner blood could complete the magic." There were tears in his eyes. "Oh, God. I'm so sorry this is happening. She told me all I had to do was bring Johanna here and everything would be fine. Then she wouldn't let me go. She started telling me about what I would have to do . . . what *she* had done!" He looked to Jeane. "That first day we were here, she tried to make me kill Laurel and perform the rite before Johanna was even born. But she wasn't strong enough. Since then she's been waiting for the full moon and keeping Laurel in a coma until Johanna was born—like Laurel was some kind of incubator."

He tried to sit forward. Jeane helped him with her free hand. She looked to Ned and asked, "Do you think we can make it out of the cemetery before the Madonna forms again?"

"Against this wind? Not bloody likely."

Ned uprooted a handful of long grass with a heavy clump of dirt still attached at its roots. He tossed it up into the air. The vortex of wind seized it and swept it away before it even completed its arc. "I might be able to hold her off, but not for long and certainly not long enough for you to get all of the way out of the woods. The Madonna is strong. The best thing to do—"

The wind stopped, leaving behind an overpowering silence and the oppressive stillness that was starting to become too familiar. McCain twisted around to peer over the gravestone. Harsh blue light still radiated from over the lagoon, so bright it hurt to look directly at it. The Madonna was fully formed and drifting across the surface of the water, heading straight toward them. Her hair was whipping and streaming as though the wind still blew. Her arms and legs were monstrously long and thin, and her fingers seemed like talons. Her dress hung in tatters. New mist was forming, too, a wispy tide sweeping across the ground. It wasn't white anymore, though, but an angry storm grey.

McCain dropped back down. "Trouble has come looking for us," he reported. "Ned, how about that best thing to do?"

The big man reached into his coat pocket and produced a very long, rusted nail. "We have to pin her. Or rather Will has to pin her. If the Steiner blood can make ghosts in this place, it can trap them."

He put the nail in Will's hand. Will just stared at it.

"What am I supposed to do with this?" he asked Ned.

"Drive it through her and into the ground. Or through her shadow, though the other way is more effective. It's an old Roman trick for dealing with ghosts."

Will looked at the nail dubiously. "It'll stop her?"

"For now."

"For now?" barked Jeane. "What do you mean, 'For now?' "

"I mean for now! It's a temporary solution. If someone pulls out the nail, she's free." Ned looked to Will. "It's going to buy us the time we need to get away. But until that ghost is laid, she's going to keep coming after you. If she could reach you in Chicago, there's no place she won't find you given time. Your heritage gives her a connection."

"What about an . . . an exorcist?" Will asked. "Are they real?"

"Real but rare and not always effective. The ghost's connection to you might be too strong. If the Steiner blood is what she needs to put her at rest, she's always going to come after it." Ned risked a peek over the top of the stone. "Make your decision fast, Will."

McCain saw Will's eyes flick from the nail to his daughter, still strangely silent, and back again. A deep love blazed suddenly in those eyes, and McCain felt a knot twist his guts.

No, he thought.

"I've decided," Will said quietly.

He dropped the nail and grabbed Johanna away from Ngan, leaping to his feet to hold her high. He shouted something McCain couldn't understand and stepped swiftly away from them all.

"Will!" yelled Jeane. "What are you doing?"

She reached out after him, trying to stop him. McCain stopped her instead, holding up his hand to stop Ned and Van as well. Jeane was still struggling.

"Let me go!" she raged.

"Will's up to something," McCain said urgently.

He pushed Jeane away. How could Will have looked at his daughter with such love then just give her up? He turned to watch Will—and caught Ngan's eye as he did. The old man, he realized, had been the only one who hadn't moved. Ngan nodded to him and McCain knew he hadn't been the only one to see Will's eyes.

Will was walking purposefully toward the Madonna— and she retreated before him, moving back to the lagoon. About twenty feet away from the edge of the water, he stopped. For the first time, the baby he held was starting to squirm, and Will was forced to lower his arms and cradle her against his chest. He looked down at her once, then glared up at the Madonna and began to chant.

The language he spoke was resonant and deep, and it rolled flawlessly from his tongue. A few words sounded halfway familiar.

"It's German," supplied Van. "I've been taking it in school."

"Can you catch any of it?" McCain asked.

Van concentrated. "Some of it. It's a weird accent." He ran a tongue around his lips as he listened. "He's repeating himself. Something about the blood of the stone calls the dead from the earth. Come up out of your . . . something.

Graves?" He went pale. "It's the Madonna's magic. He's performing the rite."

"Keep translating," McCain ordered.

Something was happening down by the lagoon. The water was stirring, and another figure was forming. Unlike the Madonna, this one emerged into the world gently. A warm flicker lifted from the surface of the water, slowly filling out as Will chanted.

Van's translation played counterpoint to the chant. The blood of the stone calls the dead from the earth. Rise out of your graves. Smell the wind, drink the water, feel the warmth of fire. You should walk on the earth, not dwell within it. You know it should be that way. From the earliest days, the dead of the earth have come to the call of the stone. Come back to the earth and take up your life again. I prepare the way, I open the door, I am the price that balance demands. The blood of the stone calls the dead from the earth. Rise out . . .

Ned stared at Will with awe and said, "He's naming himself, not the baby."

Jeane looked at him, puzzled, and Ned shook his head without looking away from Will.

"Listen to those words," Ned told her. "This is an old, old magic, but that key phrase about the way, the door, and the price, that's common in many forms of magic. Magic, even whitest magic, always demands a sacrifice or a holy vow of some kind. But usually the phrase would be more like 'I prepare the way, I open the door . . .' "

" 'I *pay* the price,' " Ngan supplied. He was watching Will as well. "Balance demands a death for life reborn and Will's blood has the same power as Johanna's."

"So Will . . ." Jeane's eyes went wide.

"Maybe not," said McCain. "Look."

Will was slowly stepping back away from the lagoon. The figure over the lagoon was fully formed now, a man wrapped in the windings of a shroud. The Madonna smiled happily and began to walk toward him. Her harsh blue light dimmed as she walked, and her figure began to shed its angry shape. Her dress rewove itself. Her limbs took on natural proportions. For the first time since they'd seen her, her hair fell and did not move of its own accord. Will glanced over his shoulder and gestured them forward.

McCain stepped out from behind the gravestone without hesitation and sprinted over to where Will stood. He sucked in his breath as he approached. Will was pale and trembling. Dark-bruised circles had formed under his eyes. His shoulders were slumped, and the struggling weight of the newborn child he cradled bent him like a bow. He held her out to McCain and sighed gratefully when McCain took her.

"Is it safe to go?" McCain asked him in a whisper.

Will nodded. He put his hand on McCain's shoulder and they turned away from the lagoon. The others still waited behind the gravestones, watching them with urgent eyes. McCain took a careful step, slow so that Will could keep up with him.

It wasn't slow enough. Will stumbled. Swiftly, McCain shifted the squirming baby to one arm and grabbed Will with the other, steadying him. It kept him from going down, but the jarring near-fall sent Will's teeth clacking together. The chant faltered. For a heartbeat, silence fell again in the cemetery.

The Madonna shrieked. It was a real sound this time, and if her silent cries were bad, this was even worse. It was high and thin, as if someone in the distance had cut glass and was grinding the fresh edges together, trying to rejoin them.

McCain cringed. Will choked and doubled over, and the baby began to wail in terror. The blue light flared in time with the Madonna's shriek, and the mist stirred and began to rise. McCain shot a fast glance back to the lagoon. The shrouded figure of the Madonna's husband was drifting apart.

"Will," McCain shouted. "Chant!"

"Leave me . . ."

"No," McCain said, trying to drag Will to his feet, but Will managed to slip out of his grasp, sliding down to find a seat on a fallen gravestone.

"I'll be fine. Get Johanna out. I'll be right behind you." He looked up. "For the love of God, would you just do it?"

The Madonna let out another horrid keen. Will gasped again, then took up the chant once more without waiting for an answer. His voice was forceful and strong, and he gave McCain a hard, hard look.

There was nothing left to do. McCain took Will's hand and gave it one last squeeze, then he turned his back.

"Go!" McCain screamed at the others. "*Go!*"

Van didn't need any encouragement. He was off like a racehorse. Ned and Jeane hesitated only a moment, then followed. Ngan stayed the longest, but after a moment he turned and ran as well.

McCain followed them all, moving as fast he dared through knee-high mist, hugging Johanna close to his body. Behind him, the Madonna was still crying, and Will was trying to shout her down with the chant. Was it working? He didn't dare look. He picked up his pace, running faster and faster. The cemetery gates drew closer.

Will's chanting was right beside him then, and an arm reached out urgently, signaling for him to slow down. McCain caught sight of Will's face. The other man's eyes were desperate. He pointed down at the ground ahead.

Laurel had been running for the gates when she fell.

McCain stopped and reached out with his foot. He barely had to extend his leg at all before his toes connected solidly with a big chunk of rock. He swallowed hard and nodded to Will.

Together, they walked cautiously out of the cemetery, Will chanting the whole way. The others were waiting just beyond the gates. Will led McCain past them and back down the path. Some of the Madonna's radiance seemed to cling to him, pulsing as his voice rose and fell in the chant, and he moved easily through the darkness. All McCain had to do was follow him. McCain was aware of the others following them now, but he didn't want to take the chance that he might trip on some unseen obstacle if he looked back. He kept his eyes on Will and the ground until Will paused after a few minutes and fell quiet.

Silence surrounded them. Not the unnatural silence of the Madonna but the entirely normal silence of the woods at night.

No, he realized, of the woods in the grey of pre-dawn. The sun would rise soon. McCain turned back to look at the cemetery—and found the others staring at him.

"What?" he asked.

"Why'd you stop now?" asked Jeane.

"Because Will stopped."

He turned around again, but Will had moved on, leaving the path and cutting through the trees toward an old farmhouse. Light spilled through an open door and across the porch. Will started to climb the steps. McCain moved to follow him, but Ngan put a hand on his shoulder. McCain glanced back. Ngan's face was serious. McCain looked after Will again. The house was gone. Will was gone.

"But . . ." McCain started.

Ngan looked at Ned, and the psychic's face grew distant for a moment. "What I felt from the Madonna is gone completely, but I can feel something new. That way." His hand came up, pointing into the trees in the direction where the farmhouse had been. "It's weak. Fading." He blinked. "It's gone."

McCain looked at them all. "Will never left the cemetery, did he?"

Ngan shook his head.

Steiner blood had laid the Madonna to rest.

The sun was peering over the horizon when Ned and Ngan stepped out of the woods and climbed up onto the Midlothian turnpike a little distance west of Bachelor's Grove. McCain and Jeane were both there waiting for them, Jeane with McCain's car pulled over onto the shoulder of the highway, McCain with Ned's. Jeane had been very particular about that as they made their final plans in the aftermath of the night. She refused to climb into Ned's car. That had led to the inevitable round of insults between them until Ngan had put his foot down firmly. They had decisions to make, and they would make them. Unfortunately, of course, that had prompted a sour look from McCain. Ngan had studiously ignored it. There would be time for that later.

Ned was the first one up the bank. He glanced over his car, then nodded approvingly to McCain and said, "You know, from what Ngan told me about

Jeane's driving, you should be lucky your car is still in one piece."

"From what I've seen of the rust on your car," Jeane shot back at Ned, "you should be lucky *it's* still in one piece."

He winked at her, climbed into his car, and drove off.

Jeane glared after him. McCain let out a little chuckle, and Jeane punched him in the shoulder hard enough to make him stagger. She stalked around the car and got into the passenger side. McCain slid behind the wheel, and Ngan got into the back seat.

"The police came right on time," Ngan reported. "I imagine the heavier one was your friend Jessop."

"Probably." McCain started the car and pulled out onto the road. "You got away without them seeing you?"

Ngan nodded.

"You might want to look out the window then," McCain said. "Bachelor's Grove is coming up just over there."

Ngan turned and peered through the glass. Beyond the thin screen of trees and across the still waters of the lagoon, three men in blue uniforms stood over a body sprawled on the ground, the mortal remains of Will Tavish.

There had been a fourth police officer, but before Ned and Ngan had left their hiding place near the cemetery, they had made sure she'd picked up the baby left just outside the cemetery gates. She took the child back down the path to meet the ambulance that would be arriving shortly.

Watching over Johanna Tavish had been their part in the careful cover-up of what had taken place in Bachelor's Grove. The circumstances of Johanna's abduction and Will's death had to look as natural as possible—with no hint, of course, that the Hoffmann Institute had ever been involved at all.

After some discussion, Ngan and Ned had taken Johanna back to the cemetery. Or at least as far as the gates. While Ned insisted that the Madonna had truly been laid to rest,

Ngan didn't want the baby going back into Bachelor's Grove just in case. Outside the gates, they had kept her warm and safe until the police arrived to find her.

Meanwhile, McCain had called Shani Doyle with instructions that she was to wait ten minutes, then approach the police at the hospital and mention that Will had developed an obsession with the cemetery where his wife had been injured. Ngan had been confident that the police would snap at that well-baited hook. They hadn't disappointed him. Call made, McCain had driven Ned's car to the rendezvous at the side of the turnpike.

Jeane's role, before going to the rendezvous as well, had been to spirit Van and his bike home before his absence there was discovered. Van had been flushed with excitement after his adventure. Unfortunately, Jeane also had to swear him to strict secrecy. Ngan knew that would be hard for a young man who had experienced the most fantastic event of his short life, but he also had a sense that Van would stick to it. Jeane had described him once as perceptive, and Ngan guessed that Van would quickly grasp the importance of keeping the Institute's work a secret.

"Van did make it home safely?" Ngan asked Jeane.

"I saw him walk into his house without setting off any explosions. Whether his mother was waiting for him or not, I don't know. Everything looked quiet, though. There were no lights on." She twisted around to look at him. "I think Van might make the Institute a good agent some day."

Ngan nodded. "As do I. As does Ned. While we were waiting with Johanna, he told me he had sensed something special about Van, that he might have the potential to develop psionic skills—that's why he thought there was a chance Van's amateur séance might have aroused the Madonna."

"Wow." Jeane turned around again, but then twisted back. "You know, Van would like to go to college but he can't afford it. Do you think the Institute could . . . ?"

"A scholarship?" Ngan smiled. "I will see what I can do."

"Shani had news, too," McCain said. He met Ngan's eyes in the rearview mirror. "Laurel woke up last night."

"When?"

"Sometime while we were fighting the Madonna. If Will was right and the Madonna was responsible for her being in a coma, maybe the fight with us took so much of her attention there was nothing left for Laurel. Shani says she looks to be in pretty good shape considering she's been in a coma for three weeks." He hesitated, then added. "Laurel wants to see Will and the baby. They haven't told her exactly what happened yet."

Jeane's face twisted. "That's not going to be easy."

"No, it won't." Ngan shook his head slowly and folded his hands in his lap. "Especially because we can't tell her the truth. What happened here must be concealed. We will be the only ones who know the truth of Will's sacrifice. The rest of the world must see only the death of a madman who kidnapped his own daughter."

McCain made a face as well. "So everyone is going to think Will was a psycho? Can't we at least tell Laurel?"

"No," Ngan said flatly, not at all happy. "The Institute will keep an eye on Johanna as she grows up and perhaps investigate the Steiner line, but that's all."

"That sucks," McCain commented. His eyes in the rearview mirror were challenging.

Ngan sighed. It was time to bring this problem to a resolution as well. "You have a problem with my leadership of this team, Michael."

Jeane groaned with frustration, but Ngan put a hand on her shoulder. He leaned forward so that he was inside McCain's field of vision.

"Don't you?" Ngan pressed.

"I thought it was pretty clear," McCain spat back harshly. "I do."

"So do I." Ngan sat back. "That's why I resigned my promotion yesterday."

McCain twisted his head around so sharply that Ngan wondered if he might have done himself an injury. "You what?"

"I resigned my promotion, and Field Director Adler accepted. As of yesterday afternoon, I returned to the rank of agent, with only the additional responsibility of acting as the team's liaison with our superiors in the Institute." He smiled. "I think tonight proved that we work far better as equals than as leader and subordinates."

McCain looked doubtful. "You still found time to issue a few orders tonight."

"Which, I noticed, you obeyed without question."

McCain opened his mouth, but Jeane jabbed an elbow into his side before he could say anything. "You might not have management experience, Ngan," Jeane said, "but you've got field experience."

"And it's good to be back in the field," Ngan commented. "Office work does not agree with me."

He knew it was the truth. He had felt more relaxed the moment he left Lily's office yesterday, had felt his old habits and rhythms returning through the night.

"Speaking of office work," McCain said, "I don't suppose this means you'll be giving up your luxury, agent-in-charge office?"

"In fact, that office was one of the things I hated most about the promotion. It was too big. I am giving it up—in a way." Ngan sat forward again, looking at both Jeane and McCain. "I think it would be good for the team to share an office. Don't you?"

[eNd of 2]

DARK·MATTER™

an excerpt

IN FLUID SILENCE

G. W. TIRPA

March 2001

Fenton was what Jeane liked to think of as a Post Industrial Gentleman. He was courteous and polite, refined in a gruff, American way. He moved quickly, but in a determined fashion. He was comfortable in his own home, but barely. He moved from room to room like a teenager moved through a mall—knowing full well where everything was, but aware that it was all put there by someone else.

His decorator might have used the term Post Industrial Gentleman as well. The place was too full of furniture that was too heavy for Jeane's more contemporary tastes. The furniture was all wood, varnished to a high gloss. Some of the pieces looked like antiques, but were more likely new pieces designed to look like antiques.

The apartment was clean—professionally clean—and there was none of the mundane evidence of the place being really lived in. There was no clutter.

There were no magazines or mail laying around. There were no television remotes balanced on the arms of chairs, no half-finished projects or empty glasses. When Jeane followed him into the surprisingly enormous living room, she saw that their shoes made footprints in the bone-white carpet as if it had been vacuumed every time someone walked across it.

There was no TV or stereo in the living room, no computer or any other sign of technology. There was a cabinet that might have been made two hundred years ago in Virginia but was more likely only a couple years old. Jeane guessed the TV was hidden in there. The penthouse was big enough that Fenton likely had an office there, so that's where the computer would be, a fax machine maybe, certainly a telephone.

One wall was dominated by French windows and double French doors that opened onto a narrow terrace. Beyond was the darkness of Lake Michigan at night.

Jeane kept her hand on the little purse and managed to remember to walk in what she hoped was an alluring fashion. The rug was thick, though, and the heels made her footing treacherous at best. She compensated by standing in one place.

Fenton stopped, realizing she wasn't following anymore. "We'll need to get some business out of the way, then," he said with a smirk.

It took Jeane a second to process what he was talking about, then she smiled and said, "That's okay. You have an account at the service and they told me you understood the, uh . . . pay structure."

Fenton laughed. He had a pleasant laugh. He came closer to her, and she fought back the impulse to shrink away. He was handsome and obviously successful, smart and educated, but Jeane couldn't imagine having to sleep with the man. She knew too much about him already, and the sight of him left a bad taste in her mouth.

"Then we should start with a drink," he said.

He looked at her, waiting for her to say something. She could smell alcohol—not a lot, but it was there—on his breath. He hadn't had enough to dull his eyes or his senses. Maybe just one or two after a long day at work.

"Wine?" she said quickly, knowing she could fake her way through a glass of wine without getting drunk.

Fenton smiled and turned, crossing the room casually— he was at home after all—to a small bar set with sparkling clean glasses and an array of crystal decanters. "Red or white?" he asked along the way.

"White," she said, though she preferred red.

For some reason she felt that if she'd asked for red it would have revealed too much of herself to him. She was in character, and her character drank white.

She scanned the living room, taking in details quickly: the three other exits, the white furniture, all leather, the coffee table with nothing on it, and the wall of bookshelves full of books both old and new.

"I have a reasonable Chardonnay," he said, and she noticed just the trace of an accent that might have been New York or Philadelphia, but a long time ago. "If that's all right."

"That's fine," she said, still not moving. "Thank you."

Fenton walked behind the little bar and bent to retrieve the bottle. He placed it gingerly on the top of the bar and reached down again. He was looking somewhere under the bar when he said, "It's not chilled, I'm afraid."

Jeane shrugged, not realizing that he couldn't see the gesture. He looked up, and she had to shrug again. She smiled and knew it looked sincere because in a way it was. She couldn't help being amused that he seemed genuinely worried that a hooker enjoy her wine.

He returned her smile and said, amiably enough, "You can come in. I don't bite. I'm sure they told you about me at the service."

They had. They'd told her that his tastes tended toward the mundane. He insisted on white women with certain features. He liked large-breasted women with athletic bodies. He liked certain facial features, blue eyes mostly but he was flexible on that. None of the girls who'd gone with him reported anything violent or kinky. It was all very ordinary.

Jeane nodded and said, "The girls all said you were a gentleman."

This made him smile. He found what he was looking for under the bar—a corkscrew—and started to peel the lead off the bottle of wine. "The girls," he said quietly.

He started to uncork the wine, and Jeane ventured a few steps into the room. She stopped next to a long white leather sofa.

Fenton nodded at the sofa and said, "Sit, please."

She sat, crossing her legs and making a point of not smoothing down her skirt. She figured she should show him some thigh to keep the illusion intact.

The cork came out of the wine bottle, and Fenton poured three fingers into a gleaming crystal glass.

"You look like someone," he said, putting down the bottle of wine and taking up a cocktail glass. He opened a leather-covered ice bucket and broke up some ice with polished silver tongs. "Marilyn Monroe, I think."

Jeane smiled. She'd heard that before but had always ignored it. Most of the men who'd said that had been the type who talked to her breasts, not her face. She assumed, and still did, that the comparison stopped there.

Fenton poured a good three shots of a caramel-colored liquor into the glass, then dropped a few ice cubes into it. A few seconds later, Jeane could smell the whiskey in the air. He put one hand on the bar and leaned on it heavily. He took up his drink in his other hand and took a long sip, looking at her with eyes that were coldly appraising. Jeane had seen men look at cars that way.

"You've never had anyone notice the resemblance?" he asked.

She shrugged. "Men see what they want to see," she said, trying to make it sound chatty and succeeding well enough. "I've been told I look like Cheryl Ladd."

Fenton's brow wrinkled and he said, "No, no, definitely Marilyn."

He set his drink down and came out from behind the bar, going to the bookcases. He went right for the book he was looking for and pulled off a tan, oversized hardcover. From where she was sitting she couldn't see what was written on the spine.

Fenton flipped through the book, looking for something in it, as he came across the room to her. He sat down in a chair across from her, and Jeane suppressed a sigh of relief that he hadn't sat next to her. He found the page he was looking for and nodded. He set the book down on the polished coffee table and turned it around so she could see the photograph there.

On the left-hand page were two columns of text. On the right-hand page was a full color photograph of Marilyn Monroe. Jeane had never seen this picture. She wasn't too interested in movie stars.

"Her hair is different, of course," Fenton said, "but there's a—Jesus, I forgot your wine." He stood up and went quickly to the bar as Jeane looked at the photograph.

Marilyn Monroe was standing on a beach, wrapped in a green towel. She might have been naked underneath. She was holding the towel closed with her left hand and holding a glass of wine—white wine—to her lips with her right hand. She was smiling, and Jeane had to admit her own smile was similar. She had the same inward slope to her teeth she always thought she should have had fixed as a kid. Marilyn's nose was pointed in a way similar to Jeane's as well. It was obviously windy the day the photograph was taken, and

5

Marilyn's bleached blonde hair was disheveled and dirty. Her skin, like Jeane's, was freckled, but not too badly.

"I saw a movie," Fenton said, placing the wineglass on the table next to the book, "where there's a group of call girls who've all had plastic surgery to make them look like movie stars."

Jeane flushed, and didn't want to look up at him. She looked back at the photograph in the book and noticed the simple caption: just the year, 1962.

"Don't get me wrong, of course," Fenton said. "I'm sure that's not the case—you don't look that much like her, but . . . anyway, I meant it as a compliment."

"You don't have to—"

"I know," he said, cutting her off.

She looked up at him, and he took another long sip, pursing his lips. The look in his eyes changed, and Jeane all of a sudden really felt like a whore.

He smiled, and Jeane couldn't help thinking he knew he'd demeaned her in a very real, though very subtle, way, and he was enjoying it.

"Have you been doing this for a long time?" he asked. "You aren't young—don't get me wrong, you're lovely, and I enjoy mature, sophisticated, experienced women, but . . ."

"Six years," she said, making this part up as she went along, "give or take. I was a—" she almost said cop "—hairdresser for a while, but I got a divorce. He got everything, and there wasn't much, so after a while I got sick of living paycheck to paycheck."

Fenton nodded, obviously only pretending to understand, and drank some more.

"What about you?" she asked, leaning back, letting her dress ride another half an inch up her thigh. "What do you do?"

"That makeup you're wearing," he said. "What is it?"

Jeane knew to say, "Natura."

Fenton nodded and said, "I'm the chief operating officer of Natura Industries."

Jeane feigned being impressed. "That seems like kind of an oxymoron," she said.

Fenton's brow wrinkled again, and he was just about to say something when he swallowed the rest of the whiskey in one gulp.

Jeane felt uncomfortable in the silence. She knew she had to keep him talking. "I mean," she said, "Natura makes you think 'natural,' but 'industries,' well . . ."

He smiled and nodded. "You won't want to know what that really is that you're putting on your face," he told her with a wink.

He put his empty glass on the coffee table, and she reached for it, brushing the rough skin of his fingers with hers. She picked up the glass and stood. Her dress clung to her legs a little, and again she made no move to fix it.

"Can I get you another one?" she asked, letting her eyes settle on his.

"Thank you," he said.

She went to the bar walking carefully on her tall heels. She knew he was watching her walk. She pulled the stopper from the decanter of whiskey and poured a little more than he had poured for himself over the melting ice.

"Six years," he said. "That must be a lot of men."

She didn't turn around. Jeane put the stopper back in the whiskey decanter and took the top off the ice bucket.

"If you don't want to talk about it . . ." he said. "The other girls probably told you I would bring it up. I like to hear about . . . it's part of . . . what I want."

She dropped two ice cubes into the nearly full glass of whiskey and turned, a smile fixed on her face.

"It's okay," she said softly, not moving.

"You've been with all sorts of men," he said, looking at her body. "Men like me?"

"Sometimes."

"Rich men?"

"Sometimes."

"You don't know, though," he said, finally looking at her face, "before you get to their houses or hotel rooms, what they look like?"

She crossed to the chair and held the drink out to him. He didn't take it at first.

"Lean over and hand it to me," he said, his voice suddenly husky and threatening.

Jeane was sure she was smiling as she leaned forward at the waist. She handed the glass to Fenton and he took a long, unashamed look down the neck of her dress at her black lace bra. "No," she said, "It's not up to me."

He looked at her eyes and she stood up. "You've had sex with niggers," he said.

Jeane had expected to hear something like that. Both Ngan and the woman at the service had prepared her for it, but still she could feel her face turn red.

"Not if I can help it," she said, knowing it was what he'd want to hear.

Michael McCain awoke with something licking his face.

The name Sparky leaped to his dull, half-asleep mind. That was his dog's name, wasn't it? But Sparky died fifteen years ago.

McCain opened his eyes, and bright light seared them, so he clamped them shut. The dog stopped licking him for a moment, startled probably, then started up again. He was licking McCain's bare chest now, moving down toward his stomach. He could feel a thick, warm, viscous liquid covering most of his body.

He tried to push the dog away but couldn't lift his arm.

He'd never felt so tired. His head spun, but was starting to clear at the same time. He opened his eyes again and the light wasn't so bad now, he'd just been in complete darkness for a long time.

Walls came into focus, sheet metal over thick wooden cross beams. The sheet metal was fairly new, and the treated wood still had a greenish cast to it. He looked down at the dog and his body convulsed all at once—not from any physical cause but from the shock of what he saw.

It wasn't a dog.

He was being licked by what looked at first like a little child, but within the first second or so McCain could see that this was no child. It was barely human, if it was human at all.

It looked like a little man, old, wrinkled, skin turning brown streaked with grey. A wide flat nose dominated its face, and its cheeks were pinched and drawn back. Its wide eyes were closed. It had no hair.

Its tongue was as wide and as long as a big dog's and it was busily licking a thick, honeylike liquid off of McCain's quivering, naked body. When McCain flinched away, the thing looked up and opened its eyes, revealing black pits that seemed to absorb light. McCain opened his mouth to scream, but no sound came out.

The thing reacted to the non-scream by fluffing wings McCain had mistaken for a grey leather coat. The wings were like the wings of a bat.

McCain brought one hand up, his arm responding now, if weakly, and the little man scurried backward. It bumped into a steel barrel and tipped it over. A loud clang echoed in the big, mostly empty space, loud enough that the little man covered its ears with hands that were tipped by brown, prunelike fingers. The golden liquid dripped from its twisted, bloated lower lip.

"Is this . . ." McCain managed to almost bark, ". . . hell? Am I in hell?"

9

The little man, who must have been no more than a foot and a half tall, folded its wings and said, "*Ich ausführen nicht verstehen Sie.*"

McCain knew what he said, not realizing that he wasn't supposed to be able to understand German. He never studied the language in school, never spent any time in Germany, or around Germans. But the little man had said: I don't understand you.

McCain wanted to know where he was, so he said, "*Wo bin ich?*" though he still didn't remember ever learning to speak German.

The little man tipped his head at McCain, as if the question made no sense. McCain went over the words in his head and was sure he'd said it right.

He propped himself up on one hand and felt rough concrete under him. He was suddenly cold and drew his arms and legs into him. The strange liquid spread over him like thick oil.

"Who are you?" McCain asked the little man. "*Wer bist Sie?*"

"*Nichts,*" the little man said, his voice surprisingly deep.

"Nothing?" McCain asked. "*Sie haben null angebracht?* You have no name?"

The little man took one small step closer to McCain, who shied away, scraping his rear on the concrete before he came to rest against a low stone wall behind him. The stone was as rough as the cement floor. McCain's body started to tremble, shivering violently.

"*Ich heiße Nichts,*" the little man said.

"Your name . . ." McCain translated through chattering teeth, "is Nichts."

The little man smiled, and McCain screamed, then screamed again, only this time louder.

DARK MATTER ™

(Four)
Of Aged Angels
Monte Cook

"They've been here for fifty some years, but they were here before, too. Long ago, down the bottomless throat of time, they came to the world, and they walked as gods through the forests. The people of that time had no name for these ancient angels, but they saw their effects. The caress of these gods put ripples in the world like a child's light touch on the surface of a pool."

For a moment—just for a moment—McCain was caught up in his poetry. For that moment, he believed that this really was Jim Morrison.

"But then they left, for there was war in heaven," Morrison said, looking at the ceiling. "Dark were the skies, heavy with the conflict of birds as seen by a snake. When they fled back through the doors, they left behind something cherished among them—and among us since then, at least those few who knew that it truly existed."

"What was it?" McCain asked, his voice barely a whisper amid the darkness and stone.

Without a pause, Morrison told him, "The Holy Grail."

July 2001

DARK•MATTER

(Five)
By Dust Consumed
Don Bassingthwaite

Ned looked over at Jeane and asked, "Are you sure you're ready for this?"

She snorted. "I was trained as an ATF investigator. I have been shot at, burned, dropped, beaten, and damn near blown up several times. I have been to crime scenes that would make most people vomit. I have seen . . . things . . . that would make *you* wet yourself, Ned." She took a deep breath and produced the key that Hollister had left for her. "No, I'm not ready."

The safe deposit box was larger than she had expected. The top clicked open when she turned the key in the lock. She took another deep breath before lifting it any further. Inside, two envelopes rested atop a plain beige file folder. A yellowed newspaper clipping had slipped partway out of the folder, exposing the date: August 6, 1962. Just slightly less than a month before her birth, the trained investigator in her noted. The rest of her, though, was focused on the smaller of the two envelopes and the words that were written on it in a light, open hand forty years ago:

For Jeane.

December 2001

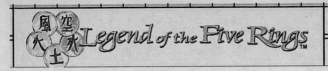

The Phoenix
Stephen D. Sullivan

The five Elemental Masters—
the greatest magic-wielders of
Rokugan—seek to turn back the
demons of the Shadowlands.
To do so, they must harness the
power of the Black Scrolls, and
perhaps become demons
themselves.

March 2001

The Dragon
Ree Soesbee

The most mysterious of all the clans of
Rokugan, the Dragon had long stayed
elusive in their mountain stronghold.
When at last they emerge into the Clan
War, they unleash a power that could
well save the empire . . . or doom it.

September 2001

The Crab
Stan Brown

For a thousand years, the Crab have
guarded the Emerald Empire against
demon hordes—but when the
greatest threat comes from within, the
Crab must ally with their fiendish foes
and march to take the
capital city.

June 2001

The Lion
Stephen D. Sullivan

Since the Scorpion Coup, the Clans of
Rokugan have made war upon each
other. Now, in the face of Fu Leng
and his endless armies of demons,
the Seven Thunders must band
together to battle their immortal
foe...or die!

November 2001

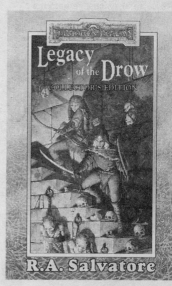